THE OGRE'S WIFE:

Fairy Tales for Grownups

By Richard Parks

© 2002, 2011, 2020 Richard Parks

Cover Art: SelfPubBookCovers.com/LadyLight

Table of Contents

Things That Go Bump in the Heart: An Introduction vii

THE OGRE'S WIFE 1

How Konti Scrounged the World 16

Doing Time in the Wild Hunt 39

My Lord Teaser 46

Doppels 64

Wrecks 77

The God of Children 91

A Respectful Silence 107

The Trickster's Wife 120

A Place to Begin 126

Take a Long Step 140

Judgment Day 147

Borrowed Lives 153

Golden Bell, Seven, and the Marquis of Zeng 161

About the Author 178

Acknowledgments

For Carol, Who Makes All Things Possible

First Print Edition Obscura Press 2002

Introduction

© 2002 Parke Godwin

The Ogre's Wife

SF Age, September 1995, © Sovereign Media

How Konti Scrounged the World

Realms of Fantasy, February 2000, © 2000 Sovereign Media

The Beauty of Things Unseen

Quantum SF, August 1999, © 1999 Obscura Press

Doing Time in the Wild Hunt

© 2002 Richard Parks. First Publication.

My Lord Teaser

ELF MAGIC, DAW Books, © 1997 Tekno Books

Doppels

NOT OF WOMAN BORN, Roc Books, © 1999 Constance Ash

Wrecks

Odyssey SF, #2 © 1998 Partizan Press

The God of Children

Asimov's SF, December 2000, © 2000 Penny Press

A Respectful Silence

Realms of Fantasy, December 2001, © 2001 Sovereign Media

The Trickster's Wife

Realms of Fantasy, February 2001, © 2001 Sovereign Media

A Place to Begin

Weird Tales 323, Spring 2001, © 2001 Terminus Publishing

Take a Long Step

Realms of Fantasy, April 1999, © 1999 Sovereign Media

Judgment Day

Realms of Fantasy, October 2000, © 2000 Sovereign Media

Borrowed Lives

PROM NIGHT, DAW Books, © 1999 Tekno Books and Nancy Springer

Golden Bell, Seven, and the Marquis of Zeng

Black Gate Vol.1 No. 1, Spring 2001, © 2001 New Epoch Publishing

The Ogre's Wife: Ghost, Gods, a Dragon, Assorted Legends, And Things That Go Bump in the Heart: An Introduction

When Richard Parks asked me to introduce his first collection of fiction, I jumped at the chance. When I read through the manuscripts, some of which I'd admired in their original magazine appearance, I knew I held in my hands one of the best SF/fantasy collections I've read in years, and perhaps the hardest work to describe since Jonathan Carroll's *The Land of Laughs* and *Voice of Our Shadow*.

Like any fine writer Parks doesn't label easily, which makes him hell for lazy-minded pigeonholers, but his themes are consistent and clear. He uses fantasy to underscore reality: the nature of our humanity and the inescapability of what we are, the choices we make and the price we pay for each, right or wrong. In the present collection, whether fantasy, science fiction, or verging on mainstream, he can step imperceptibly from deadpan funny to deeply affecting truth with an utterly transparent style that has the reader racing down the page. He has the rare ability to say profound things simply, as in "Borrowed Lives": "The price of losing the pain is losing everything else."

I first heard from Rick back in 1978 when he wrote praising a story of mine in Fantastic. Very gratifying because back then no one had heard much of me yet and nothing of the taciturn kid from Mississippi who mumbled diffidently over the phone, looked like a good ol' boy fullback from Dogpatch, and wrote like a prophet. Back then Rick was being published in semi-pro zines at a quarter of a cent a word, but he was already good -- not there yet, not fully formed, but coming up fast.

That was twenty-odd years ago. Now he's there, and the harvest is yours in THE OGRE'S WIFE.

Richard Parks is, thank God, no overnight success. So many of them are forgotten by morning. There were "star" names in fantasy/SF twenty years ago, wunderkinder that I can recall now only with difficulty, but trust me on this: Mr. Parks has been and will be around when the cows come home.

Whatever his setting in these stories, he's completely at home, as you'll be, though you'll find his furnishings unusual. Of the three ghost stories, none could be called horror. "The God of Children" is Japanese, done with a wistful oriental subtlety. "Wrecks" has a yearning heart, a story of the need to believe or disbelieve, freeing a tormented spirit and perhaps one's own soul in the process. "A Place to Begin" and my favorite, "A Respectful Silence" deal with choices taken or not, regrets, mistakes and the aftermath of so much humanity during a lifetime -- Parks' pervasive theme.

In "Doppels," a star actor is replicated by Corporate decision. With no say in the decision himself, the star's career situation is "serious as a tiger with a toothache." As the doppel becomes more real than the original in his holo-roles and life, including the relationship with his girl friend, the actor sees how his whole existence has been little more than image to begin with -- but how to find his real self again under the years of glitz?

There are the cosmic themes of "Take a Long Step," a deceptively transparent allegory of those entities we call God and Satan, and which one gets to go up on the cross next time around. Katzanzakis, author of THE LAST TEMPTATION OF CHRIST, would have salivated over this one as I did. Or "Judgment Day," a monologue by God himself as he flashes back and forth along the human time stream from Creation to the future, trying to answer the question endlessly put to Him: "Why is there suffering?" -- and at the end, clueless Himself, being given the unexpected answer.

Parks' side trips into myth and legend are equally delightful. "The Trickster's Wife" drops in on the twilight of the Norse gods with a vindictive hint of wifely payback. "The Ogre's Wife," done with understated deadpan humor, defines the difference between what we call human and inhuman. In "The Beauty of Things Unseen" and "My Lord Teaser" the magic of Fairyland always resonates with a sense of very real life and sets off the magic of our world against the glamor and monotony of immortality.

Hey, did I mention this collection gives a whole new meaning to "eclectic"? It does that, but heed this volume's subtitle: Fairy Tales for Grownups. It's meant. Watch how you tread as you pass through these pages, and keep a weather eye to Parks' skies wherever you find them. They can turn as dark as a summer thunderhead without warning or lighten as quickly. Thus warned-- enjoy!

THE OGRE'S WIFE

On the day after her seventeenth birthday, Marybeth's father gave her in marriage to an ogre. Her father had his reasons.

"The Council agreed it was the only way," he said.

Marybeth felt her heart sink in regret. She considered herself no great beauty; her complexion was darker than most due to her mother's Southron blood, which also gave her brown eyes and a slightly hawkish nose. Still, her skin was clear, she had all her teeth, and her hair was thick and black and fell in long sinuous waves to her shoulders. She'd hoped to do better.

"The only way to do what?" asked Marybeth's mother. "Cheat us of the Bride Price?" She loved her daughter dearly, make no mistake, but she was a practical woman and knew this day would have come sooner or later, with or without an ogre attached to it.

"The only way to get rid of the ogre," Marybeth's father said wearily. "Those men with eligible daughters drew lots. I lost. It was fairly done."

The village of Tumby had known the ravages of the beast for nearly three years. At first the losses were confined to sheep and the occasional ox, but within the past month three outlying farmhouses had been raided and their furnishings ransacked and pilfered. One farmer who went off alone to seek revenge had not been seen since. The village mustered what men and weapons it could and sought the beast on several occasions, and on all those occasions the villagers had come home hungry and tired without even catching a glimpse of their quarry.

"What of the Earl?" asked Marybeth's mother. "Are we not entitled to protection?" It sounded more complaint than hope.

Marybeth's father had a look of exaggerated patience. "The Earl is away on the King's service, and most of his men with him. Those that remain are guarding his own holdings. We'll get no help from him."

"How do you know that?"

"The ogre told us. I tend to believe him, Wife."

After a bit more prodding the whole story came out: the ogre had appeared, pretty as you please and almost as polite, at the monthly meeting of the Tumby Council.

"By now you know you cannot catch me," the ogre had said, pausing to swat a foolhardy youth who approached him with a kitchen knife. "If I did allow you to find me, I swear you'd regret it. So I have an alternative: give me a pleasing maiden from among you to be wife to me and I will spare your village. Deny me and the weeds will grow over your bones."

"What did he look like?" asked Marybeth, not very hopefully.

Marybeth's father obviously considered the question foolish. "Like an ogre," he said. "Over two ells tall, tusks like a boar, bristly hair. Well-spoken, for all that."

"Perhaps he's enchanted," said Marybeth's mother, though she didn't sound convinced or convincing.

Her father shrugged. "There's some magic about him, right enough. He's an ogre. But I'll not send my daughter to her new husband bearing unreasonable expectations. That's no way to start a marriage."

Marybeth's father gave his wife a meaningful look, and she merely lowered her eyes and said nothing. So it was decided. Marybeth went to pack her belongings while her parents once more did not speak their minds to each other.

•

The ogre's directions hadn't been very specific. Marybeth was to walk out on the main road until she reached the Burling River, then turn left at the bridge. She came to the bridge after walking for an hour or so, her clothes in a bundle on her back, her orange and black calico kitten Lissie riding on her shoulder. Marybeth walked into the forest bordering the river on the left. She walked until the farmland near the road was behind her and there was nothing but trees surrounding her and the first few peaks of the hill country in the distance. The forest was quiet except for the crunch of leaves under her feet and the occasional birdsong.

"I suppose," Marybeth said to Lissie, "that he'll find me when he's ready."

"You suppose correctly," the ogre said just before he ate her kitten.

Marybeth had no warning. One moment he was not there, the next moment he was. The opposite was true for poor Lissie. Marybeth's mouth moved up and down as if she was trying to speak, but no sound came out for a long time. She finally managed to scream.

"Lissie!"

The ogre frowned. He was every bit as ugly as her father had described, and the frown didn't help. Marybeth wanted to be terrified, knew she damn well *should* be terrified, but she could only manage one emotion at a time, and right now anger would not share the stage with anything.

"You monster!" Marybeth beat her fists against the ogre's barn door sized chest, tears of rage welling in her eyes.

"Yes," he said. "I'm an ogre. Did your father not explain that to you?"

"You ate Lissie!"

"The furling? I assumed it was a present for your new husband, and very thoughtful at that since I was feeling peckish. Was I in error?"

Marybeth blinked through her tears. He certainly looked like an ogre, and acted like an ogre, but he didn't sound like one, or at least what she'd expected. "She was my dear Lissie...you ate her!"

The ogre put his hands on his hips and stepped close, plainly irritated. Marybeth had to look almost straight up at him. "Don't go on about it, girl! I could have eaten *you*," he pointed out. "And I might yet. I trust I won't have to remind you of this in future. Follow me, Wife."

It didn't sound like a request. Marybeth fought her tears and followed her husband. It wasn't as if she had a choice. "I am Marybeth," she said, sullen. "What shall I call you...er, ogre?"

"'Husband' will do. Or 'ogre.' Both are what I am, though perhaps ogre is closer to the mark."

Marybeth needed no reminding, but there it was. Her husband wasn't an enchanted prince or enchanted anything—he was what he was.

"Ogre it is," she said.

Marybeth was a country girl and not very sheltered. She knew what normally passed between a Husband and Wife. But she was married to an ogre, and from the time she'd understood that fact she'd wondered what an ogre would want with a human girl, other than a meal. When they reached his lair in rocky cave near the river, Marybeth finally thought she understood.

"You want me to clean this?" she said, staring in disbelief.

The ogre's home was more like the den of an animal, only not so tidy. It wasn't a true cave, Marybeth realized. More likely it had been carved out of living rock by the ogre himself. There was an ogre-sized chair and bed, and a hearth, and cupboards, but there were also pieces of trees and broken stone lying about, and bones piled in the corner in heaps. The smell wasn't too bad, more like old earth with a hint of compost than real decay, but the rest was almost beyond belief.

"Why, what's wrong with it?" he asked. "It's comfortable."

"It's filthy. I can't live like this," Marybeth said.

"Then I suppose you'll have to clean it, unless you want me to eat you instead? I'm still hungry."

"I'll clean it," she said. "So if I am to live you'll have to eat something else."

"I'd best catch it then. I wouldn't try to leave, if I were you. Even if you could." He stepped out through the entranceway and locked the huge door behind him. Marybeth heard his massive footfalls fading in the distance. She looked around, sighed gustily, and got to work.

Marybeth was a little surprised to find a working broom. It was very old, but serviceable. She rearranged the bones and swept out the hearth, arranging the dust in a mound by the bones since she had no way to sweep it out. Soon she had a sizeable fire going that burned off a little of the dampness. She paused long enough to make herself a cup of tea with some of the brownbush leaves her mother had given her in parting, then went back to work. She was trying to straighten out one of the shelves in a huge alcove when memories of Lissie suddenly returned and overwhelmed her.

"My poor dear kitty..."

"Mew?"

The sound was muffled but close by. Marybeth traced it to a lower shelf and a small earthen crock. She lifted the lid with trembling fingers and peered inside. An orange and black kitten sat blinking in the weak light. It was Lissie. There wasn't a doubt in Marybeth's mind, even before she noticed the scarred right ear where one of her father's hounds had snapped at the kitten just a week before.

"Mew!"

Marybeth held her up and looked into the kitten's too-familiar face. "I saw the ogre eat you, Lissie."

The kitten was not impressed, though she was clearly glad to be out of the jar. But why was she alive, and how did she get in the jar in the first place? The ogre hadn't been out of her sight before he left the den. Yet here Lissie was, good as new. At that point Marybeth didn't care. She hugged the kitten close and cried for joy.

"I'm back," the ogre announced.

Marybeth wasn't sure how many hours had passed. The ogre had a young ox draped across his shoulders. Its throat had been torn out and the carcass had apparently bled dry; at least it wasn't dripping where she'd swept.

The ogre looked about with mild interest. "Somewhat different. Not greatly so."

"I couldn't lift the stones or the tree-trunks," Marybeth said. "or sweep out properly with the door shut. I did the best I could." She held Lissie close in her arms.

The ogre glanced at the kitten. "I thought I felt my stomach twitch. You must have found Dara's Cauldron."

"I found Lissie in a crockery jar," Marybeth said. "How-how did she get there?"

"You put her there," he said, dropping the ox on the floor. "The cauldron tries to give you what you desire most. That's its nature. I gather you wanted this little fleabag back."

"Yes," she said.

"It's a good thing you didn't wish for your freedom, then," he said. "Freedom cannot be contained in a crockery jar. That's *its* nature. Though the poor cauldron might have split itself trying. Here, you must be hungry too." He tore off a haunch and handed it to Marybeth.

"I can't eat this," she said. "It's raw."

"Then I guess you'd better cook it," the ogre said, in a tone that made it clear it was all the same to him.

Marybeth went to work at the hearth. She was annoyed but she couldn't say why. What he'd said was simple sense, if a little callous. Still, after Lissie's unfortunate first meeting, Marybeth didn't suppose the ogre normally bothered to cook his meat. She glanced back at him but got no hint. The ox lay where he'd dropped it, and he'd settled into his great chair, watching her. At least he hadn't set his attention on Lissie again. Marybeth found a knife and skinned the haunch, then prepared the meat as best she could with what few herbs she could find and roasted it.

The ogre broke the silence first. "How is it?"

Marybeth was startled. The ogre had sat unmoving during her preparations and the time it had taken to cook the meat. She had cleared herself a place on a bench and taken a few bites when he'd finally spoken; she'd almost forgotten he was there.

"Well enough," she said, and her manners pressed her to continue, "Would you like to try it?"

"It always seemed a strange practice to me, but I'll admit to some curiosity. Yes, I will try it."

He took the bone she offered, which had far more meat left on it than she'd be able to eat in several days, and sucked it in like a child eating a cherry. In a moment the pit of a bone went sailing across the room to land in Marybeth's now almost-clean corner.

"Interesting," he said, looking thoughtful. "I don't suppose you could prepare the rest of it like that?"

"Not quickly," Marybeth said, eyeing the mass of flesh. "And not without help."

That didn't work out too well. For all the strength required in properly butchering an ox, there was also a great deal of precision needed, and the ogre wasn't very good at precision when he wasn't eating kittens. Marybeth, for her part, didn't fare too well moving a fifty stone carcass on her own.

The ogre seemed to consider. "I have something that may help," he said. He went into the alcove and returned with a small stoppered bottle. "Drink this," he said, then continued, apparently noticing the look she gave him, "It's not poison. If I wished you ill, there would be no subtlety about it. Do as I say."

Marybeth shrugged and drank the potion. It was bitter and smelled faintly of garlic. She felt a slight tingling all over her skin, as if she were covered with thousands of ants running in all different directions at once. She shivered, but the feeling passed quickly.

"Now tend to the ox," her husband said.

Marybeth shrugged again and took hold of a foreleg. She tugged once and the carcass was suddenly three feet closer to the hearth. She hadn't felt the least bit of effort. It was like moving a leaf.

"I think you'll find that strength is a useful virtue in an ogre's wife," he said.

Much later, when the bones were clean stripped and piled in the corner, the ogre lay down in his massive bed and went to sleep. He didn't snore much, and for that

Marybeth was grateful. He hadn't touched her, and Marybeth was even more grateful for that. It wasn't just that he was repulsive—though he was certainly that—but she'd gotten a glimpse of his naked body when he'd stripped for bed, and the only thing she could think was that, if the ogre ever came to her as a man to a woman, she would die. And there were certainly less painful ways to end a life.

Maybe I'll have Dara's Crock make me some poison. Just in case.

For now, she and Lissie found an unused corner of the bed and curled up to sleep.

The ogre's den might have been made to order, but it connected to natural caves in the back closer to the Burling. They were lit with a faint glow from the walls, but Marybeth was reluctant to enter them until Lissie, exploring every almost-cranny and near-nook of her new home found them and scampered off into the twilight.

"Lissie, come back here!"

Lissie of course did no such thing, and finally Marybeth followed down to retrieve the wayward kitten. The descent was steep at first, but then the incline relented, and Marybeth found herself in a great open cavern. She could hear the flow of the river beyond the far wall, but here it seeped partway into the cavern, forming a quiet pool. It was a lovely place but large and echoing, and it reminded Marybeth too much of being alone.

She picked up the kitten. "I wish I had someone besides you to talk to, Lissie. But I can't imagine who would fit in that silly little jar—"

"Hello."

The sound didn't come from the cauldron this time. A beautiful woman appeared in the center of the pool, just her head and neck showing above the water. She had hair even blacker than Marybeth's, and large, dark eyes. "You're the ogre's wife," the woman said. "We heard he'd married a human, and we were curious."

"I'm Marybeth."

The woman bowed her head slightly in greeting. "We are Merrow. Our folk are of the sea, but a few of us live in the river now."

Marybeth had heard stories of the river maidens, but she'd never seen one. Though the rumor was that you *didn't* see one and live to tell of it. Marybeth's new-found strength was a comfort then, but she kept her distance. "'We'? Is your name not Merrow?"

The woman shrugged her shoulders, sending ripples across the pool. "We are *all* Merrow, my sisters and I. It is our nature."

"My husband just calls himself ogre. That's his nature, I guess."

The woman smiled. "Of course." She eyed Marybeth critically. "You are pretty but not overly well-favored."

"Are all Merrow so rude?" Marybeth asked in astonishment.

The woman showed mild surprise. "Is it rude to tell the truth? I'm sorry, but the ways of humans are strange to us."

"This is all strange to me as well, but I see you meant no offense. So let me ask you—is it so odd for an ogre to marry a human, especially a plain one?"

Merrow shrugged. "Plain or lovely, it's all the same to an ogre, by comparison. And no, it happens all the time."

"Why?" It was a question Marybeth had been asking herself for some time now. The ogre seemed to like her cooking well enough, but it didn't seem overly important to him. Nor did her housekeeping. Nothing about her seemed to matter much to her husband. His seeming indifference was beginning to annoy her, and she didn't know the 'why' of that either.

"Perhaps you should ask him," Merrow said.

The thought had occurred to her but Marybeth decided not to act on it just yet. Her annoyance still had a way to go before it overtook her fear, and the answer she got from her husband might not be one she could live with—for long. For the moment, it was nice to have someone to talk to. Marybeth decided to take a different sort of chance.

"Merrow, would you like a cup of tea?"

The woman smiled. "Yes. That would be lovely."

There was a brief roil of water around Merrow, and for an instant Marybeth was certain she saw the edge of a fin at the surface. But, when she came out of the pool with a white muslim gown clinging wet to her body, Merrow walked on two human legs.

Later, with the tea brewing and the conversation going by turns fascinating and frightening, Marybeth dared ask another question. "How did you change to human form? I'm sure you don't go on two legs in the water."

Merrow smiled. "One advantage of knowing your true nature is that it's easy to change your appearance and form. It doesn't change what you are, and your true self is never fooled. It's nothing. All those Not Born of Eve have the trick. Humans only develop the knack with great difficulty."

"Why is that?"

"Because your own true nature is a mystery to you. You cloud it with myths and stories and you make up lies about what it means to be human. You want to be so many things that you are never sure what it is you *are*. A body so filled with uncertainty cannot change itself for fear of never finding it's own form again."

"You're a myth," Marybeth said. "Or legend, or story, to some people."

"To some people, but never to ourselves. I am a Merrow. Your husband is an Ogre. I and all my sisters know what that means, and so does he. When you say 'I am human,' what does it really mean to you?"

Marybeth poured the tea. "I don't know," she said. "I'd like to."

Merrow held up one of the golden cups Marybeth had managed to scrounge from the former debris of the den. "My own service is of mother-of-pearl and silver. Let me show it to you some day."

It took a week or more to gather her courage, but Marybeth finally did ask the ogre why he had sought a human wife. "Because it was time," he said, and that was all he would say on the matter, though Marybeth did prod him as much as she dared. She finally gave up.

The days and weeks that followed fell into a predictable pattern. The ogre would rise in the morning and go out and about an ogre's business, locking the great door behind him. Marybeth, more out of something to do than any real desire, kept house. With her new strength Marybeth had no trouble turning the den into something approaching a home. The shelves were set to rights and dusted, the floors swept clean. Even with all this to occupy her Marybeth found herself alone and idle for much of the day. Lissie's company made it easier to bear, and Merrow would come now and again for tea and conversation, but even these good visits weren't enough.

One day Marybeth confronted the ogre husband with this. "I'll go mad cooped up here," she finished. "My housekeeping skills would suffer."

The ogre looked around at his now orderly den. "I will admit I've stubbed my toes far less often since you've arrived, and I've gotten used to having you and your furling underfoot. But this is where I live and this what I am and there's no changing either. What would you suggest?"

"At least let me go into the woods to gather herbs and berries. It'll be a change for me and no burden to you. I might even find some wild mushrooms to go with your beef. I'll not run away."

"Very well, then, but see that you don't," he said. "Or your entire village will suffer for it. You being wife to me may be a whim but it is *my* whim and I will satisfy it."

Her husband was as good as his word. The next morning the ogre left the door unlocked when he set out from the den. The massive door still took effort to move, even with Marybeth's new-found strength, though the ogre had opened it with ease. That understanding banished any thoughts Marybeth may have had of using her new fortitude to overpower him. She settled for taking a reed basket from its hook and stepping back out, for a while, into the world.

The world was not the same.

Marybeth stood for some time, blinking in the morning sunlight and trying to decide what the difference was. Lissie, still kittenish but growing fast, stalked imaginary mice in the weeds by the doorway.

"Did you notice it, Lissie?"

Lissie glanced at her, yawned hugely, and went back to the phantom mice. Marybeth looked back at the forest, trying to turn her certainty into words. Nothing really looked different: the trees, the river, the sky all looked as she remembered. She was glad to see them all, after her time in the den, but it wasn't simple gratitude. The forest and the river and even the sky seemed to have a glow about it, as if anything could happen there. As if what up until now had seemed so changeless was suddenly full of possibility.

That was before I met the ogre. And Merrow. There is so much more to the world than I thought there was.

Before the ogre came, her life lay out before her like a story she'd heard too many times before. Familiar, even pleasant, but not such a great or wondrous thing. Instead, here she was, barely seventeen and married to an actual ogre rather than a man who might just have the manners of one. Marybeth thought of what being an ogre's wife had meant so far: she had a decent home that she even thought of as hers now that her work had made it so. It was carved into a hill but not so very different from the masonry and thatch houses of Tumby. The ogre provided well, and Marybeth was not mistreated. She didn't even lack for company. Marybeth wondered how very different her life would be with a human husband. She only knew of one thing for certain, and at this point in Marybeth's life that particular subject had more to do with idle dreaming and fancy than anything real. Not so much a regret as a matter of curiosity, of myth-making and what-if.

Say what you will, girl. Merrow spoke the truth of that.

By the time Lissie tired of hunting and curled up to nap in the sun, Marybeth had found some wild onions growing in the clearing by the hill; she pulled a few and rinsed the shoots clean in the river before walking deeper into the woods. She traveled some distance in her search for mushrooms but she always kept the crest of the hill by the river in sight. Marybeth had just finished harvesting a particularly large patch of plump mushrooms near the edge of a clearing when she heard voices. Well aware of the sort of people she might meet in the forest, Marybeth decided to hide herself behind a bramble bush. She took her basket and crouched down, out of sight.

My heavens...

At some point music was added to the murmur, music so ethereally beautiful that Marybeth's eyes grew misty at the sound. Then, two by two, the most splendid folk Marybeth had ever seen emerged from one side of the clearing and neatly progressed to the other. They were dressed in all the colors of the rainbow in gowns of gossamer and tunics of linen fine as spider web. Their faces had a lean angularity about them that was at once inhuman and strikingly beautiful. They walked in pairs, each Lord to his Lady, while invisible minstrels played the pavanne. Marybeth watched them pass, each couple strengthening an odd sensation Marybeth felt in the pit of her stomach, a feeling that she could not put a name to, like a pain and a longing all mixed up together. She watched until the last couple passed her by, unable to speak even if she'd wished to.

The last to emerge from the woods came out alone. He was dressed like the others, he even looked like them. He was tall, well-formed, and handsome, with long fair hair and sky blue eyes. But there was a difference. There had been something missing from the others, despite their beauty. A coldness in the eyes, a hauteur in their bearing that spoke of time and distance and separation from all that Marybeth was or ever would be. There was none of that in the man walking slowly across the clearing now, no hauteur, no ice. There was a smile on his lips and a merry gleam in his eye, and there was something about him that seemed almost familiar, though Marybeth could not name it. Just before he vanished into the trees with the others, the man turned and looked directly at the bush where Marybeth hid.

"A lovely game of Hide and Seek, Maiden. Thank you. But will you find me as easily?"

Then he was gone.

"They were the Lords and Ladies of the Sidhe, of course," Merrow said from the pool. She had answered as she usually did when Marybeth rapped on the stalagmite that spired out of the edge of the pool, but this time she would not stay. There was Merrow business afoot that evening, it seemed. "I don't know of the Lord you mentioned; I've not seen him before. Why do you ask?"

"He saw me," Marybeth said. "He spoke to me. I wondered if there was cause for concern."

Merrow looked grim. "There is always cause for concern when the Sidhe are near. Be careful, Marybeth. You live among the Not Born of Eve under your husband's protection, but there are powers in the wood much greater than his."

That was worth knowing. Marybeth thanked Merrow for her advice and watched her slip away under the water. Up above, the great door had opened and the ogre was calling for her.

"Coming, Husband," she said, and hurried up to the den. The ogre had brought home venison this time, a good change. Marybeth prepared the food and they ate together. The ogre spoke little even for him, which she didn't mind now. Marybeth didn't feel much like talking. Her mind kept going back to the handsome Lord with the sky-blue eyes. Later, when the ogre and Lissie were both asleep, she sought out Dara's Cauldron.

Its appearance hadn't changed, but, with practice, Marybeth had learned to see the magic in it, even peer beyond the surface to get a glimpse of its true form, just as she recognized the aura of power surrounding several other innocuous-seeming items on the ogre's shelves. He'd managed to accumulate much that was both strange and wonderful during his predations, but now it was Dara's Cauldron she sought.

    It had been some time since Marybeth had asked the cauldron to make something for her. She'd tried for poison, soon after her arrival, but all the cauldron would do was produce something like stinkberry jam. Marybeth had finally decided that she didn't really want poison after all. But now there was something she did want, and the cauldron created it immediately—a shiny new mirror. There was even a comb to match, and a red ribbon and pins for her hair. Marybeth hadn't thought to ask for those, but the cauldron made them for her just the same.

It seemed inordinately pleased with itself.

Finding the Sidhe Lord turned out to be easier than Marybeth had expected. She didn't even think of herself as looking for him, but the next day, at about the same time, she found herself on the edge of the same clearing, standing by a fairy ring of toadstools. These she did not pick, of course. She knew better. When the voices and the music came again she ducked back behind the same bramble bush and waited for the fairy pavanne to pass by her. Again the single Lord of the Sidhe followed the dancers, and again he paused for her.

"Have you found me, Fair One?"

Marybeth stood up, though her knees were trembling just the slightest bit. "So it would appear."

"I am called Blackbone," he said. "and I love you."

Marybeth didn't know what she had meant to say, or meant to do. Her emotions were not clear where the Sidhe Lord was concerned. But hearing his name made a difference. It was like a slap of cold water after a long sleep. After a moment she even knew why. She smiled at him, but she kept her distance.

"I am Marybeth," she said. "The ogre's wife."

Blackbone frowned. To Marybeth it looked like a gathering storm, splendid and terrifying. "What is that to me?" he asked. "Or to you? The ogre is taciturn and brooding. He has no understanding or appreciation of what he has in you, no skills to tend either your heart or your sweet flesh's garden. He is no fit mate for a human girl; I am no mortal, but I could be much more to you than he. Speak your heart and it will be given thee, if it is myself to be given."

"I am honored," Marybeth said, "but I am still myself pondering what it means to be the ogre's wife, and I do not yet know my heart. May I have leave to think on what you offer me?"

"Very well, but do not dally, Marybeth. My flesh is eternal but my patience is not. That is my nature, and I fear there is no changing it."

"Whatever I would ask, I would not ask that."

Marybeth was no Lady of the Court, but she managed a passable curtsey. In a moment she was alone again in the woods.

That evening when the ogre returned he asked her how her gathering had gone because, Marybeth was certain, the onions and mushrooms she'd used to flavor the venison had been to his liking. Marybeth took the pair of rams he'd offered and made their supper as best she could without being able to alter the seasoning.

Perhaps in the spring I'll try a garden. There's room enough by the river, and many herbs would do well near the shadow of the hill.

She kept having thoughts for the future, plans and notions all during supper and the grunts and nods that normally passed for conversation with her husband. When the meal was done. He sat by the fire for a while, motionless as stone. Marybeth could not even sit down. Her mind was in a whirl.

It's a dirty trick you're thinking about, Marybeth.

But what did it mean, and what would be the consequences? Marybeth didn't know. She thought, perhaps, a little certainty was due her just now. She even had an idea of how to get it.

Marybeth left the ogre sitting beside the fire and crept off to the alcove shelf where they kept Dara's Cauldron, among the other wonders.

"You know my heart's desire," she whispered to the little crockery jar. "Can you help me?"

There was a soft hum, then a clink! of metal from within the jar. Marybeth reached into the crock and pulled out a small golden ring. She looked at it carefully, and finally decided that it was no more than it seemed—just a plain gold ring, with no magic or special virtue about it.

She smiled. It was perfect.

Marybeth returned to her husband, now snoring with a sound like a small earthquake by the hearth. While he slept, Marybeth quickly put the cauldron's gift to use.

The next morning she again stood alone with the Sidhe Lord in the clearing.

"My answer is yes," she said, matching Blackbone gaze for gaze. "If you want me, then I am yours."

"What of your husband?" he asked, a gleam of mischief in his eyes.

Marybeth smiled at him. "You and I are all that matter now."

"This is as it should be, Lady. You will see."

I am a girl from Tumby Town and no Lady, Marybeth thought, *but we most certainly will see.*

Blackbone kissed her then. His mouth was warm and sweet against hers and she returned the kiss, hesitantly at first but then with more confidence. He was not the first she'd ever kissed, but what was to come after would be new indeed. Blackbone gathered her up in his arms. She felt his confident strength as he carried her somewhere, at first she could not tell to where. Then he lay her down on something soft and yielding. It was the bed in the ogre's den; Marybeth recognized the smell of the fresh washed bedding, changed just that morning.

Blackbone apparently saw the question in Marybeth's eyes. "Do not worry. He will not trouble us."

Marybeth reached for him in answer. "I *am* afraid of the ogre," she said, "but not the way you think."

"How, then?"

She kissed him again, briefly. "When the time comes, I think you'll understand."

Blackbone smiled. "A hint of mystery. It's important to human women, I am told. I'll not deny you so little."

Marybeth held her hand over his lips for a moment, silencing him. "Right now," she said, "You'll deny me nothing."

It felt a little like drowning.

Or rather, how Marybeth imagined drowning to be. First a struggle, long or short, or rather a *striving* for what seemed impossibly far and yet so close and so within reach. Then the waves, one after the other rising higher and higher until she went under. Then memories of the struggle, then surrender and calm floating back to the surface again. Even a little bit of death, in the darkness of that very last tide.

Drowning would not be so pleasant, except perhaps with Merrow's help... Marybeth smiled at Blackbone, lying silent beside her. He was not sleeping. His eyes were open wide, and he was not smiling. Marybeth sighed. It seemed that the time of reckoning had come. Now she would see if there had been any worth to any of this, beyond the moment.

Blackbone finally sat up. He did smile now, and it looked like a smile of triumph, not joy. Marybeth watched him closely but she did not move.

There was a new rumble in his voice from the first word he spoke. "And now—"

It was like the dance of two vipers, but Marybeth struck first. "And now, *Husband*, you will explain why you tried to play such a dirty trick on your wife!"

Blackbone's smile was crushed under the weight of pure astonishment, along with the face and form of the Lord of the Sidhe. In a moment Blackbone was gone. The ogre lay in his place in the bed beside Marybeth his wife, almost shrinking under the glare of her eyes.

"You knew? *How* did you know?" he asked.

"Just as an ogre is an ogre, or a merrow is a merrow, it seemed to me that a Lord of the Sidhe would be a *Sidhe*. Yet you gave yourself a name to court me. I heard that name, and I all I could think of was a mask. It did not seem right."

"That is a suspicion, Wife. That is not a certainty."

Marybeth reached up toward his head and the ogre almost flinched. Marybeth grasped a strand of his long coarse hair and held it up for him to see. Neatly tied near the end of the lock was a plain band of gold. "The nature of gold is that it is unchanging. It remains. I knew that, whatever form you took, by this sign I would know you. I've answered your question, Husband. Answer mine."

The ogre shrugged. Marybeth would have sworn he even looked a little guilty, if not contrite. "This is the way it is always done. I certainly could not come to you in my true form," he said.

Marybeth knew the truth of that, but still: "Why come to me at all? Why not have a proper ogress for your wife?"

He smiled a little sadly. "Perhaps there was such a thing as an ogress, once. No one has seen aught for a thousand generations. My race was doomed, unless another way could be found."

"Humans?"

The ogre nodded. "If an ogre breeds with a river maid, she *bears* a river maid. The same for the *Sidhe*. They know their nature, and there's no other road to take. Yet there's not a human maid born so sure of her own nature that she could impose it on her child, even if she wished. The child might be human. It might be an ogre. That happens sometimes even without an ogre's seed at root of it all."

There was truth again. But it wasn't the whole truth, and Marybeth wanted it all.

"If I had not seen through your trick, what then?"

"What else? I would have roared and gnashed and threatened. Most of all I would have had your own guilt to weigh against you, to shame you and protect my child."

Marybeth nodded. Now it made perfect sense. It would have been easy enough for the ogre to take a fair form and cozen any number of village maids, but then the ogre child would have had its brains dashed out the moment it was born. Now Marybeth understood why the ogre needed a human wife. That just left one question to answer.

"An ogre needs a human wife. Why does a human girl need an ogre husband?"

He blinked like a sleeper trying to waken. "I don't understand."

"My life is still in your hands, Husband. I know that. But your child's life will be in mine. Do you honestly think there is nothing I can do, no subtleties and midnight herbs and omissions, tricks that reveal nothing and yet harm your seed in a thousand ways? If fear was enough, you wouldn't need this trap of guilt you laid for me."

"You would not harm my son...." There was fear at work now. It nestled in the ogre's eyes and made its home there. Before now Marybeth had resisted the urge to strike him. Now she resisted the urge to hug him and pat his hand in comfort. She did not relent.

"No, I very well might harm your son. But I certainly would not harm *our* son."

Marybeth thought the ogre looked surprised before. It was nothing compared to now. "Wife, you astonish me."

"It is my nature, Husband—you said as much yourself. A merrow can only be a merrow, an ogre an ogre, a sidhe a sidhe. But a human maid can tell lies and try on any nature that suits her. She can also tell herself the truth now and then. She can choose, the one thing the Not Born of Eve can never do. Strange as it does seem, if she finds the company congenial and the life full of wonders, she might even choose to be an ogre's wife. With a little persuasion, perhaps."

The ogre just stared at her a long time, as if his flesh were made stone under Marybeth's gorgon-gaze. Finally he shook his head wearily. "Your life is in my hands, but I think my future is as much in yours. So, then. A gift for a gift, fair exchange all around. How may an ogre court his lady?"

"Well," Marybeth said. "You may be an ogre and a beast, but you could adopt the human custom of hiding it now and then. I know you won't be able to pretend for long at a time, but it'll do you no harm and will please me. More, I think you'll find that any contentment you give me will belong to us both in time. Will you try?"

In a blink, Blackbone had returned, bearing a smile like summer. He reached for her hand and kissed it tenderly. "I *am* an ogre and a beast and always will be," he agreed. "But I am not a fool."

There *were* fools about in the land, though. And heroes and questing farm lads. When they appeared, as they eventually did, to beard the ogre in his lair and steal this bit or that of his treasure, Marybeth would pretend to take pity and help them carry away some trinket or other that her husband didn't really miss. The ogre in turn would roar and gnash but still allow the reckless brave ones to escape by the narrowest of margins to tell the stories to their grandchildren, over and over. It was one game of many the ogre and Marybeth learned to play, as husband and wife, while they watched their own family grow and prosper.

Every now and then over the years Marybeth would stop and wonder how her life could be so full and happy. After all, she *was* married to an ogre. Then she would smile and remember that, in the ancient scheme of man, woman, husband, and wife, it was nothing really new.

How Konti Scrounged the World

It is said, and it is so, that the First Gods were very busy in that time of the first Creation. All were bearing worlds from their loins, creating them fully grown from nothing, or rolling them up from the Sacred Dung of the Heavens or whatever vile substances the priests could later imagine—and they could imagine things surpassingly vile indeed, truth be told.

None of this mattered to Konti. He was brown and very small, the weakest deity in the heavens. Hardly a god at all, to tell the truth twice in the same tale. He had his place among them and, if no one had questioned that, it was only because to be in the heavens at all probably meant you must have had a place there, somewhere. Then again, perhaps it just meant that the First Gods were too busy creating to watch the gate. Either way, Konti watched the stronger gods doing all the things he could not do, and he was not happy. Konti was a clear-minded sort, god or no; he already knew his limitations. Now he wanted to discover his potential. So he thought about this, for that was all he could do about it, as he watched the mighty sky god Pondadin work at creation, shaping clouds with wind and lightning.

"I want my own world," Konti said.

"Then you must make it. That is the Law of Heaven," Pondadin said to him, for despite his bluster he was a kindly god, and as close to a friend as Konti had.

"'The Law of Heaven'? Who made such a thing that even the gods must bow to it?"

Pondadin frowned, and thunder rumbled. "I don't know," he said. "I only know that it is." His tone clearly said that he'd exhausted both knowledge and interest in the subject. "So. What power will you use to create a world?"

"I have none that I know of," Konti said, looking melancholy. "All I have is this sack that I found." He held it up for Pondadin to see, and it was a pitiful looking thing of shadow and wish, and probably not so much lost as discarded as useless by some better-equipped deity.

"For a god that is a problem indeed." Pondadin rested in his labors for a moment, scratching a spot on his curling beard with a fork of lightning. "I'd help you, but it will be all I can do to finish the work I have already begun. Still. . .." Pondadin scratched another acre of beard, pondering. "My own world is full of clouds and sky, and to my mind no proper world is without them. I will not miss a bit of either. Do you want them?"

Konti lost a bit of his melancholy at Pondadin's kind offer. "It's a start. Thank you." He held up his sack and Pondadin pushed the cloud and a bit of blue sky inside with a gust of wind. To Konti's relief they all fit in his sack very well indeed, even the gust of wind that was more afterthought than gift. He bid Pondadin a good creation and strode off with the sack of cloud, sky, and wind on his back.

Konti walked for some time, then stopped to rest on a bare patch of heaven.

Those were getting rarer, as more and more of the firmament was given over to various new Creations. He looked at a few of them, from his vantage point on the firmament, and soon thought of another reason for wanting his own world: he couldn't imagine living in any of the others at all. He tried. He admired Pondadin's majestic skyworld of billowing clouds and brooding storms, but it was wet a good bit of the time and there just wasn't a good place to sit down anywhere. Another world was all bare mountains and plains of dark earth. Nice for sitting, and dry, but certainly nothing to look at. Konti considered all the fledgling worlds he could see and found serious fault with every single one.

"Why should all the worlds be so limited?"

There was no answer, of course. There was no one to ask, so far as Konti knew. There were rumors of a being called the Transcendent One whose plane of existence was beyond even that of the gods, but none in the Heavens actually claimed to have seen such a one. Perhaps that was the one who made the Laws of Heaven. Perhaps it didn't matter. Konti had to deal with the Heavens as they were, and how they got that way was of lesser concern than his current predicament.

"Limited or not, at this rate the created worlds will fill up the firmament soon and there won't be room for another world. Even a small one. I can't dally here."

Konti looked around, and considered for a while. "I know from Pondadin's skyworld that a creation with no place to sit and rest simply won't do. What's needed is earth, and since I can't make it . . ."

"Steal it."

Konti looked around again, saw nothing among the swirling chaos of new creation. "Who said that?"

"You did." The voice came again, closer. It was a voice close to laughter, Konti thought, but not so pleasant as it should have been, for all that.

"No, I did not say such a thing. I would remember. Show yourself!"

"Well then, doubtless you were thinking it. I can never remember which."

A figure appeared out of the Haze of Creation. He was tall and handsome, except when he was short and handsome and excepting further when he was tall and beautiful and short and beautiful and probably not a "he" at all.

"What are you? You keep changing."

"I am Asakan. And thank you."

Konti blinked. "Did I compliment you? I didn't intend to. Nor to insult you, for that matter. I don't know you."

"I am Asakan. It's true I do keep changing, and I took your observation as a compliment, of course. How dull to be the same thing all the time!"

"Very well, then. What do you want from me?"

"I want to help you. Why else should I give you such good advice?"

Konti put his sack over his shoulder. "I don't know. There may be other reasons." He started to walk away, but there was Asakan beside him.

"What haste, friend Konti?"

"I am not your friend; we just met. And I am in haste because Creation is proceeding without me."

Asakan, looking more male than anything else at the moment, shook his head. "Run all you like. It won't help. You need earth underfoot, since the Firmament cannot be part of any world. To get earth, you must get it from the goddess Susaka, for only she can make it. Why would she give her precious earth to a pitiful little godlet like you?"

"I don't know, but there must be another way." Konti didn't know of one, but Asakan's idea made him wince, as if he'd stepped in something unpleasant.

"Why 'must' there be?" Asakan asked. "And even if there is, what makes you think you can find it?" The god vanished, leaving Konti alone to ponder that question for some time.

•

Stealing a bit of Susaka's earth would be easy enough, Konti decided. There were so many places to walk and hide in Susaka's creation. It's true her earth was dry and cracked, and the sky was nothing to remark upon, nor was there much in the way of shade or refreshment. Still, there was a stark beauty to it that Konti admired as he wandered past bare mountains and sandy valleys, trying to decide what to do.

"What if Asakan is right?" he asked himself, and he feared to learn the answer. Feeling more than a little ashamed of himself, Konti pulled the bag from over his shoulder and bent down to scoop up some of the precious earth.

Boom!

Konti immediately crouched behind a rock, afraid and ashamed that Susaka had found him out. After a few moments and nothing else had happened, Konti peered out of his hiding place.

BOOM!

The same sound, as loud as Pondadin's majestic thunder but without the same roll and crash at the end. His curiosity quite overwhelming his need, Konti dropped the bit of dry earth he'd taken, put his sack back over his shoulder, and went to find the source of the noise.

Susaka was creating a mountain. She stood with her feet planted widely apart, her strong arms lifted in a gesture that was at once command and enticement. The earth before her responded, breaking its crust with the booming sounds Konti had heard earlier. The mountain spired ever higher, till Konti had to tilt his head far back to see the top of it.

"Marvelous," he said aloud, "but it looks like a great deal of work."

Susaka lowered her arms and turned to look at him. It was the first time Konti had seen her face. He thought it rather pleasant, though why it was pleasing to him was something he could not have put into words. She was solidly built as befit the nature of her dominion, with broad strong hips and wide shoulders; her hair was like a spray of melted copper.

"Konti," she said, looking him up and down, "I've seen you before. Why are you here?"

"I came looking for some dirt," he said, since honesty was his first impulse usually.

"Then you've found it. Admire it quietly and be on your way. I'm busy." Her voice had the same dry quality as her Creation.

That seemed to be the limit of her generosity, though Konti wondered if perhaps Susaka's ill humor might have had more significance. "I am sorry to disturb you, but you seem tired. And something more than tired. Is something missing?"

Susaka had turned back to her birthing mountain, but Konti's words made her look at him again. "Are you saying there is a flaw in my creation, little god?"

Konti hardly thought that last bit fair, since she was, if anything, a little shorter than he was. "I'm saying there's something missing. Something your world does not give you. Water, for one."

She looked puzzled, and when she spoke again there was a softness to her voice that had been missing before. "My throat is dry and my lips burn me, if that is what you mean. Will this 'water' ease that pain? What is it?"

"Something I found in Pondadin's Creation. A wonderful place, though of course he has nothing like your mountains. Still I found the water that falls from his clouds quite refreshing when my own throat felt dry."

She shook her head. "Perhaps you're telling the truth, but I have no time to seek Pondadin out nor could I give him any reason to spare part of his creation."

"I have the makings of Pondadin's clouds with me," Konti said, patting the sack over his shoulder. "And you certainly have something I would want in return."

"My precious earth?"

"Only a little, as I have only a bit of Pondadin's clouds and cannot give them all to you. If you honestly think the water is not what I have said, then I will ask nothing."

Susaka admitted that this sounded fair enough. Konti very carefully opened his sack, taking care not to let the wind out at all, and set loose a bit of cloud. It boiled and grew overhead just as Konti had seen the clouds do for Pondadin, and in a few moments the cloud went black and then rain fell on Susaka's dry Creation. Susaka caught the rain in her cupped hands and drank. She shivered as cold rivulets caressed her body and puddled at her feet. Even more marvelous than the rain itself was the effect it had on Susaka's earth, forming soft mud that squished between her toes. Konti saw her smile at the feel of it. All too soon, though, the rain ended and the spent cloud boiled away into nothing.

"Well?" Konti asked.

"That was very pleasant," Susaka admitted. "Different. I don't think I would like it all the time, but for a bit... Well, enough. You may have some of my earth in exchange."

Konti quickly took as much as he thought prudent and tucked it away in his sack between the wind and the rest of Pondadin's clouds. He was careful, too, to include a bit of the mud created by the rain cloud. It felt malleable in his hands, full of possibilities. Susaka apparently felt so, too. When Konti left her she was taking the mud into her hands, and seeing what shapes she could make there, the mountain all but forgotten.

Asakan was waiting for him outside of Susaka's Creation. He glanced at Konti's filling sack. "You got it, didn't you? You are more clever than I thought."

Konti frowned. "You're a god. Why are you following me instead of working on your own Creation?"

Asakan grinned. "Why do you think I am not?" he asked, and then vanished again without waiting for an answer.

Konti sighed. Asakan was a strange sort, but Konti didn't have time for riddles. He took stock of the pieces he had collected, and considered. There was earth to sit on and clouds and rain for thirst, and that was very promising. Yet Konti remembered how hot and dry it had been in Susaka's world, and how damp and cold in Pondadin's. It was closer to balance now, but still he knew something was missing.

"Some shade from the sun or shelter from the wind would be a good thing, and I'm not sure a hole in the dirt would be enough. What else might serve?" Konti hoisted his sack again and set out amongst the growing Creations to try and find out.

Konti found what he was looking for in a Creation being formed by an obscure fertility god named Verdku. Such was Verdku's power that he brought forth green growing things from the air itself, taking space in the firmament but not really of it. Konti watched, fascinated.

"That is a marvelous talent."

Verdku frowned. His speech and thoughts were as slow as the roots that grew out of his trees, and just as single minded. "They grow," he said, "and then they die."

That part was true enough. Verdku brought forth a great tangle of trees and twisting vines with little more than his desire to create them. They hung, green and alive and splendid for several hours over Verdku's Creation, then they slowly withered, shed leaves, and died. Verdku banished them with a thought and then created them all over again. And again. "They grow," he repeated, "and then they die."

Konti nodded in sympathy. "It must be a great pain to you, to lose all your work over and over again. Perhaps I have something that can help you."

Verdku frowned again, his face as dark and furrowed as the bark of one of his great oaks. "Help. Me? How?"

"A time or two now I've come across problems with various Creations, and in all cases the thing needed is a thing missing, something found in another Creation altogether. I happen to have a few pieces of various Creations with me and with your consent I'll try them."

Verdku nodded, and Konti opened his pack. "Let's see. I've still a bit of cloud and sky from Pondadin. Let me try a little of that." Konti released a piece of cloud into Verdku's creation. In no time at all he had small storm raining on Verdku's trees, and for a moment Konti thought he had the answer: browning leaves turned to green again and withering blossoms opened anew. That lasted longer than before, but still not for so long as one might wish. Soon all was dead and brown once more.

Konti considered. "That was good, but not enough. Perhaps the water goes away too quickly." Konti brought another cloud forth, but this time he was careful to fix some of Susaka's earth to the various roots to hold the water in, and this time the green remained for a good long time. Verdku was impressed.

"Might. I?" he asked.

"Certainly," Konti said. "But I've not so much than I can spare more than a little. In return I would like a few of your marvelous growing things."

"They grow," Verdku said. He looked at the remaining bits of green, so much in contrast with the rest of his Creation, then he looked at Konti. "They live. Done."

Konti took a few grasses and flowers and one small tree, careful to fix these into Susaka's earth kissed with a little water from Pondadin's clouds. There wasn't so much left of either as there had been, but it would have to do. Konti put the bag over his shoulder again and left Verdku admiring the green spots in his Creation.

Again, outside on the firmament, Asakan was waiting. "You're quite clever," he said, "for such an insignificant godling."

Konti shrugged. "Since I cannot be great among the gods it remains that I must be content with what I am," Konti said. "Now please go away. I have a world to create."

Asakan nodded quite affably. "I'll leave you to it, then." True to his word, he vanished.

A strange sort, Konti thought again, but that was all the thought he could spare for the subject. There was no time to ponder. There was no time for hardly anything. Konti quickly found the last unclaimed patch of the firmament, a spot only a few times wider than Konti was tall. There he emptied his sack and began to assemble his pieces of borrowed creation like a puzzle box. From his experiences in the other Creations he had a pretty decent idea of how the pieces needed to relate, but there was still room for choices and changes. He started with water one time but that made the earth wash away, and not all the green things floated as well as he thought. He started over with Susaka's earth for a base and that worked much better. Earth below, sky above.

It was a start, and that's all Konti needed. In almost no time at all he was done, and as the last piece of Heaven's firmament became his, so did all of creation come to a halt. The gods stepped outside into whatever places they could find and admired their handiwork.

"Majestic," said Pondadin.

"Massive," said Susaka.

"Green. For a while," said Verdku.

Of all the gods, they were the only ones even slightly pleased. The rest just stared at their Creations with a sort of resigned disappointment, for what they had created was no more or less than they had to create, as dictated by their natures. And yet...

Lealys, a goddess of love and procreation was left with a Creation of nothing but sighs and longing. Golgondan, a god of competition and strife, got pretty much the same result as Lealys, even if he approached the whole concept from another direction entirely.

"What good is love," Lealys said, if there is no one to love?"

"What use is strife," grumbled Golgondan, "if there is nothing to oppose?"

Various other deities chimed in their disappointment until the din of whining in Heaven threatened fair to overwhelm even Pondadin's majestic rolling thunder. Asakan strolled through the crowd of complaining, bickering gods. He was whistling. One by one the other gods stopped their complaining long enough to look at Asakan and wonder what he had to be so happy about. After all, he had no Creation at all. Golgondan said as much.

"I have no need of one," said Asakan. "I'll just live on Konti's. It's better than any of yours."

This was of course followed by even more noise. Nonsense! Absurd! How could that flea of a godling make anything to compare with our grand creations? Asakan just smiled.

"Come and see," he said.

Still bickering and complaining, the gods fell into line behind Asakan and he led them to the small patch of the firmament where Konti stood gazing at his creation and smiling a smile of pure content.

The gods fell silent.

Konti's world was not majestic, or loud, or massive, or full of either strife or longing, but none of that seemed to matter just then. All the gods looked at Konti's jewel of a creation. Susaka's earth was divided by rivers and blue oceans, and clothed in Verdku's green. Above all, Pondadin's swirling clouds flowed by.

Susaka spoke first. "Even though my earth is mostly covered, I must admit the effect is rather lovely."

"But it's so small," Golgondan said.

Konti shrugged. "I worked with what I had. I am satisfied."

The other gods looked at each other, then away, then at nothing. The swollen Creations, the Firmament, or what was left of it, anything but Konti's perfect Creation. Borrowed, yes, but no less perfect. None of them not one could say what Konti had just said, and know it for truth.

"But it's so small," Golgondan repeated, for it was his nature to find fault. "What could you do with it?"

"I shall live on it, of course," Konti said. "As I am a small creature, it is quite large enough for me."

Pondadin, silent until now, spoke up. "I want to live there, too."

Konti nodded. "You're quite welcome, friend Pondadin, though it will be cramped."

"If Pondadin is coming, so am I," Golgondan announced, and several more of the gods chimed in.

"Oh dear," Konti said, "You cannot. There's not enough room— "

"What friend Konti meant to say," Asakan interrupted quickly, "is that you're all welcome to come, and bring your Creations with you."

"That's not..." Konti never finished. One by one the other gods hurried away and returned bearing the entirety of their Creations with them and, though, Konti had not thought it possible, his own Creation grew to receive them. First earth, then green growing things, then clouds and water. Golgondan and Lealys were last, bringing desires and longing into what was now a very large Creation indeed. Konti and Asakan followed when all was done.

Konti looked around. "Where are the others?"

Asakan smiled. "All around us, friend Konti. Don't you see them?"

Konti looked at the earth beneath his feet, and the sky above, and all the trees and grass and flowers, and had to admit that he did, everywhere he looked.

"It's fine to have them near, but now I think that perhaps something is missing after all."

"Longing has entered Creation, Konti. How can it be otherwise now?"

Konti looked around. "I don't understand, Asakan. I forgive you for the trick you played on me, since this world is very grand, but now I just see the others reflected by their natures, all around me. Yet I am not changed, nor are you. Are we not gods?"

"I am here because I am always here."

"I don't understand," Konti said.

"I know. As for you, if you are a god, tell me why you were able to create what none of the others, with their powerful yet limited natures, could? Perhaps you are something else, something with even more potential. Sort it out. You have time."

"Perhaps, but where should I start?"

Asakan looked thoughtful. "Susaka found a very interesting property in that 'mud' substance you made for her. Her handiwork is down by that river. You might start there. Until then..." Asakan leaned forward and kissed Konti full on the mouth.

Konti blinked. "What was that?"

Asakan smiled. "A gift."

Konti considered this. "What shall I do with it?"

"When the time comes, you'll know."

Konti watched Asakan walk away. He looked different, somehow. For a moment, it seemed, Konti could have sworn that Asakan looked like every god Konti had ever met in the heavens, all at the same time, all their aspects taken into one. It was a silly notion, and Konti had to smile.

Konti waited until Asakan disappeared and then he walked down to the river, and there he found something very interesting indeed. Susaka had shaped wet clay into a likeness very much like herself. Konti thought the likeness very beautiful and, remembering Asakan's gift and moved by the longing now filling Creation, he leaned forward and kissed the image's cold lips. Immediately his breath was taken into the clay and in a moment it changed. It moved. And it was not clay at all.

"Hello," she said.

I'll sort this out too, Konti thought, though he had the feeling it would take a very long time indeed.

The Beauty of Things Unseen

The mists of evening were gathering in the glade, as were hundreds of the Seelie Court. Lord Mordhu looked out on a host of glowing red eyes and took his stand.

"It's *my* turn to die." The elderly pooka asserted his rights firmly and quickly. The chance at a fairy funeral made even the most level headed members of the Court get a bit grabby, and Mordhu was taking no chances. The fay population of Durien Wood wasn't what it once had been but, even so, to miss his chance now might mean another century or two of waiting. Such injustice was not to be borne. Especially not now.

There was some grumbling among the Host assembled, but no one disputed the claim. At least not directly. Mordhu saw Bramble stand up to speak and couldn't suppress a groan. The prospect of one of Bramble's speeches had been known to make fully grown ogres flee in terror, and the wisest sages agree to any point he cared to make just to shut him up. Fortunately, the Queen spoke first.

"Lord Bramble, it is Mordhu's turn as we all well know. Therefore, I rule both debate and discussion out of order." With a wave of her crystalline scepter Her Glory then declared the Moot adjourned and swept out of the glade followed by her closest retainers.

Now the muttering was replaced by deep sighs of relief all around as Bramble, looking petulant, slowly sat down. Bramble lived for debate but even he wasn't foolish enough to argue with the Fairie Queen. So it was settled. The Host broke apart and then regrouped according to their assigned tasks. A Fairy Funeral was a somber and significant occasion and required due preparation. Every fay, from dwarfish hob to the most ethereal will-o-wisp, knew his or her or its area of responsibility. Mordhu, now officially The Honored Dead, had little to do but watch and dream.

Or so he thought. One of the Fairie Queen's retainers remained behind, the radiant Lady Foxglove. To his great surprise and greater delight she sidled up to him.

"Lord Mordhu, wait a few moments and then follow where I have gone." That was all she said. Mordhu tried to be as nonchalant as possible as he noted the patch of forest into which she disappeared.

It's not what you think, he told himself firmly. There had been a time, not so very long ago, when perhaps it might have been exactly what he thought. But then the time had come for Lady Foxglove's own funeral and that had changed everything. Lady Foxglove had forgotten what they had meant to each other; it was the way of things. Still, he didn't have to like it. And what good was immortality without hope?

And just how long was a few moments to the Timeless anyway? Mordhu made the best estimate he could and then followed lightly on the trail of Lady Foxglove.

After a bit Mordhu came to a stream that flowed into quiet pools and there his step turned heavy again. There was still a little light in the sky, though the day was darkening fast. Mordhu made the mistake of glancing into one of the pools. It was the first time he'd seen himself in a while. He was, frankly, revolted.

Has it really gone as far as this?

His skin was dark as stone, the nails of his hands long and jagged, his hair a wild halo around the wrinkled face. His nose was the shape of a hawk's bill and probably, he thought, as sharp. He didn't look at all as he remembered from...when? Long ago. So long he no longer remembered what he had been, or how that face had shown itself to him then. He only knew that he was very old, wizened, and ugly, and more so of all three than he had previously imagined. Lady Foxglove had been equally ancient and weary for her own funeral, but she had not looked like this. Not to him. Yet he was sure that Lady Foxglove saw him now exactly the way that cold, merciless stream did.

"No hope at all," he said softly.

Female laughter. "You haven't even heard my request yet."

Mordhu looked up. It wasn't Lady Foxglove smiling a bemused smile down on him, though she stood a few feet away with the other Ladies in-Waiting. The Fairie Queen stood across the pool. Mordhu scrambled to his feet before remembering his manners and dropping to his knees again, which only made the Queen's smile go wider even though, it was plain to see, there was a shadow across her brow.

"Stand, Lord Mordhu. What I have to say may take a moment and I'll get a stiff neck looking down so far."

Mordhu stood, though he didn't think it really helped much. With his best posture he barely came to the Queen's waist.

"Lady Foxglove summoned me, Your Majesty. I am at your service," was all he said, though his glance in Lady Foxglove's direction was wistful. After a few moments of silence Mordhu turned his attention fully on the Fairie Queen. She had not spoken, and there was something in her manner that the pooka had never seen before. She was hesitant. Almost...afraid.

"Your Majesty, whatever is the matter?"

She sighed. "We have an enemy in the wood, Lord Mordhu. Something is interfering with the Glamour that keeps our haven safe, and many fays have sensed its presence. You have perhaps been distracted by your upcoming funeral, or you would surely have noticed this yourself."

It was true that Mordhu had curtailed his trickster activities lately, partly for lack of appropriate travelers to practice upon, but as much because any such activity was almost too much like work to him now; there was no joy in it. Another reason he had been looking forward to his funeral. "Does this enemy have a name?"

She looked wistful. "Almost certainly, but I don't know what it is. I have other

Powers searching and have for some time, but your peculiar talents may serve better. I want you to find our enemy, Lord Mordhu. Partly for the sake of all the Wood, but as much for yourself."

"I will of course do as you command, but why me particularly?"

"Because, until the Wood is safe again, the Funeral your funeral can not proceed. A funeral is a delicate matter, easily disrupted. You may be willing to accept the risk but I am not and will not. I'm sorry, Lord Mordhu, but I have spoken."

•

No wonder she cut Bramble off at the knees, Mordhu thought sourly. *It was a last kindness before she did the same to me.*

That wasn't particularly fair and he knew it, but Mordhu wasn't in a charitable mood. Already he saw his Blessed Interrment slipping from his grasp. For what? He had seen no sign of any enemy, nor even heard rumor of such. Granted, he hadn't spoken to many of the Folk for some time; all he wanted to do lately was sleep. He still wanted to sleep. It would have suited him very well to sleep until the funeral, but that wasn't possible now. He had been given a task. All that remained now was to decide how to begin. The beginning? Certainly, but where was that?

He smiled. Where else?

I must go talk to Stone.

•

It wasn't that simple. Mordhu went to the stream by the hillside where Stone had been lingering for the past few centuries. Stone wasn't there. Mordhu found a spot totally devoid of moss that looked like where Mordhu had seen Stone last, but that was all.

Stone...moved?

Mordhu sat on a rock as the enormity of the notion sank down on him. Stone never moved. That's why he was Stone. And yet...

Mordhu examined the spot more closely, found a dried smear on a rock that might have been a footstep against the moss. A little further on he found another. They disappeared on a bare stretch of rock, but by then Mordhu had worked out their direction. He followed along the stream as the hill rose about him and the water in the stream became swift and noisy. He stopped at a place where the stream emptied out of a crevice in the rocks to pour down several feet into a shallow basin, then out down the hillside. He found Stone sitting in the splash of the waterfall, looking almost as lifeless as his namesake.

"Stone?" There was no response at first. "Stone!"

One eye opened, in what would be a face if a stone had a face. Water poured off the immobile fay; spray glistened on his dark skin. His hair was like water weeds flowing over a rock. "Mordhu," he said from a crevice of a mouth. "Noisy."

Mordhu put his hands on his hips. "I've spoken to you exactly twice in the past century," he said. "I hardly call that noisy, even by your standards."

"Not you," Stone said wearily. "It. Him. That."

"I don't understand," Mordhu said. "I came to ask you about the trouble that our Queen speaks of. No one knows the state of our land better than you." Which was the plain and simple fact, since Stone was closer to rock and earth than any other fay. Practically kin, if the truth be told.

Stone nodded with his whole body, causing a flare of spray that drenched Mordhu's feet. "Noisy," he repeated. "Always talking. Talk talk talk. It fills the earth. It filled me, while I let it. No more."

"What's always talking?" Mordhu asked.

Mordhu got the feeling Stone would have shrugged then, if he'd had anything remotely like shoulders. "A voice. Whose? I do not know. It does not speak of that."

"What does it speak of?"

"Gods devils world guilt faith betrayal life death tragedy comedy why why why why." Stone shook his head again. "Hurts me still."

"Is that why you moved here?"

Stone nodded again. "The water is noisy, but always the same. After a time it fades, and the Voice stays muffled. I do not think I will leave here for a while."

In Stone's view, "a while" was close enough to forever as to make finer distinctions pointless. Mordhu saw him yawn; his mouth opened and closed with a sound like a baby earthquake. Mordhu doubted Stone had spoken so much in a millennia.

"One more thing, then I'll let you sleep, Stone. Do you know where the voice comes from?"

Stone yawned hugely. "From the earth. From the dead thing. Seek the White Ladies, if you must know further."

Mordhu felt an emotion so strange that it took him a moment or two to remember the name of it: Fear. Pure, chattering fear. "The White Ladies? Why?"

"They killed it."

•

As a pooka, Mordhu traveled quickly and quietly, even by the standards of the Seelie Court. So it came as something of a surprise to him to realize he was being followed. Mordhu flitted up to an oak branch and settled back to wait, invisible as only a pooka who doesn't wish to be seen can be. After a few moments his sharp eyes picked out a familiar shape sliding through the shadows.

"Bramble, explain yourself. In less than an epic, if you please."

Bramble look startled, then annoyed, then sheepish and defiant in rapid succession. "I just happened to overhear that you were going to see the White Ladies and, out of concern for your safety, I thought I'd better follow."

Mordhu smiled grimly. "That's one Lie. You have two more. Do you want them both?"

Bramble managed to look even pricklier than his namesake. "How dare you accuse me! And what's this nonsense about 'two more?'"

"'This Nonsense' is the Queen's Rule of Three, which I hereby invoke."

"You don't have the authority..." Bramble's voice trailed off as the situation became a little clearer to him. Mordhu's smile grew even wider.

"Yes, I do, as you just realized. I'm on the Queen's Business, and as such '...may invoke Her Majesty's Power in matters directly relating to the aid of or against any obstructions to same.' At my discretion, Lord Bramble. Shall we start with the incident at the Ball of the Full Moon? Or how about the disappearance of three scrolls on rhetoric from Master Bog's library? I'm sure there are several matters that you could clear up."

It was no idle threat. Under the Queen's Rule of Three Lord Bramble was entitled to tell the Queen's Representative three lies. After the third he would be compelled to tell the absolute truth about any matter Mordhu cared to raise until the Queen's Business was concluded. As the rule had already been invoked, it was in force. Argument was useless; even for Bramble. And there was no point at all trying to hide from a pooka.

Lord Bramble went white as new snow. "No need for that, Lord Mordhu. I was following you because I wanted to be the one to remove this...whatever it is, from the land."

The words sounded like truth in Mordhu's ears, but he knew there had to be more to it. "For glory, Lord Bramble? That really isn't like you. And please remember there are only two lies left."

"If I solved the problem instead of you, the Queen would be grateful. She would grant me a boon."

"More than likely. What is it you want of her?"

Bramble grinned a thorny grin. "What else? Your funeral."

•

"Lord Bramble, I must say you've surprised me."

They sat on the rocky shore of a deep pool far downstream from Stone's hillside. Evening was coming on fast; the mist had already risen above the water. Mordhu and Bramble both kept a sharp eye out. Evening was the time for the White Ladies; if one had to see them, it was best to see them before they saw you.

"Why? All fays get tired of themselves sooner or later. Aren't you?"

"More than you know, yet I wouldn't have suspected the same in you. If you'll pardon my saying, I've always thought you the most smugly self satisfied creature in my entire experience."

Bramble cocked his head at Mordhu. "And why not? Even Master Bog doesn't dare dispute a point of law or logic with me now. I am the best."

Mordhu considered that more in the realm of obstinance and stamina than natural ability, but there was nothing in the Queen's Rule of Three that confined him to the truth, or compelled him to tell it. An argument with Bramble was the last thing he wanted now. It was pretty much the last thing anyone wanted at any time.

"My point. Why do you want to die now?"

Bramble sighed. "As I said: Even Master Bog doesn't dare dispute a point of law or logic with me. Nay, or anyone else about anything at all. I can hardly get 'good morning' out of the lot of them these days for fear of me. There's no one to talk to, nothing to do. I am bored, Mordhu! Bored past existence and unhappy in the extreme. I want this current existence ended."

"You've never been buried, have you?"

Bramble shrugged. "I am quite the infant as fays go. Barely five hundred and twenty...next October."

"Then how do you know it's what you want?"

"I don't know. But any chance of happiness is better than none. Which is where I stand now."

Lord Mordhu watched the swirling mists take shape out over the pool, as the sun faded and the water grew darker and colder looking by the moment.

"Lord Bramble, I would give you a heartfelt speech about the need to change yourself rather than being changed from the outside, that true happiness is within, and many other things that are probably true. There are two reasons I will not. One: You wouldn't listen. Two: The White Ladies will be here any moment."

Bramble smiled again. "Then I propose we table our competition until after our meeting with the White Ladies is done, with the understanding that you cannot legally use Queen's Power to prevent me from attempting your quest."

"And why not?"

"Because my attempt increases the overall chance of success. Hindering me is not in Her Majesty's interest."

Partly because Bramble was right, and partly because there was no time to argue, Mordhu nodded. "Agreed. Assuming, of course, that we survive this charming encounter."

Bramble didn't say anything. There was nothing more to say. Mordhu allowed himself a moment to enjoy the new fear in Bramble's eyes even as he tried to master his own. Together they looked out over the water at the gathering manifestations of Death. They were lovely past all understanding.

•

The White Ladies hovered over the pool, robed in mist. Their hooded forms seemed almost like a row of Gothic arches against the darkness of the trees on the other side. Only one of the White Ladies spoke, in a voice at once cold as ice and warm and inviting as summer.

"You are very curious things," she said.

Mordhu and Bramble stood together on the shores of that deep dark pool, almost but not quite too close to the edge. Bramble had started to say something but the effort died aborning. Bramble's interest in funerals didn't quite extend to embracing the abyss, apparently.

"In what way?" Mordhu asked, as politely as he knew how.

"Travelers come our way often enough, but none who understand what coming here means. Yet you two are of the Seelie Court and you know where you are. We find that curious. Perhaps we will wonder about it for a time after we kill you."

"Your graciousness precedes you," Mordhu said, trying to keep the quaver out of his voice. He almost managed. The White Lady smiled at him and he almost fainted.

"You are an amusing little hob. Yet I do not think that will save you. Nor, it seems, do you. What will save you, then?"

"I am on a mission of the Queen of Fairie," said Mordhu.

"A point of information that changes nothing," she said.

Mordhu glanced at Bramble, but there was no help there. The famed wit and debater merely stood there, staring, his eyes as wide and open as they could possibly be.

The one time a word or two from Bramble might be appreciated, and he's mute as a gagged post.

Mordhu was on his own, but he had expected that. Mordhu noted a change in the White Ladies. They were getting closer. He would have turned and run then, forgetting the mission, forgetting everything except saving himself, only he knew that would be a very bad mistake. The only worse mistake he could think of would be to take one more step closer to the pool. And, oddly enough, that was exactly what he wanted to do. He wanted to reach for death and embrace it gladly; such was the power and attraction of the beautiful White Ladies.

"Q-queen's Power..."

So Bramble wasn't entirely mute. Their misty forms swirled in cold breeze as the White Ladies turned their attention on Bramble for the moment. It was as if someone had thrown cold water in Mordhu's face; suddenly the attraction of death wasn't quite so great. It was for Bramble, though. He actually managed to take a step before Mordhu grabbed his shoulder, restraining him.

"It's nothing to them," Mordhu said in a harsh whisper. "They are not of the Court."

No one really knew what the White Ladies were. Some said the spirits of drowned girls, hungry for the life that had been taken from them too soon. Others said that they were an idea, born of romantic notions and fed on human and fay fancies of the serene beauty of death. Mordhu didn't pretend to know the truth. Perhaps they were some of both. In neither case was he going to embrace them if he could help it.

We've piqued their curiosity for the moment or we'd already be dealing with their full power. I need to use that while there's time.

"I was told you know of the voice that troubles this wood."

"We trouble this wood, you wretched little hob."

Mordhu bowed. "Your pardon, gracious lady. I meant 'annoys.' That's certainly a better term, yes? For that which will not be silent?"

The apparition actually hesitated in its slow, subtle glide toward the shore, and there was a deepening frown on her perfect white face. "Oh. That."

"I gather you and your sisters have felt it as well?"

"Of course, fool. We killed it. And it still refuses to be quiet!"

•

Mordhu and Bramble walked carefully in the White Ladies' domain. It seemed as if they walked through a shadowed valley, but a glance upward revealed a rippling ceiling of water where there should be sky.

Bramble looked around him. "This is interesting."

Mordhu was concentrating more on following the sound that seemed to grow louder with every step. Still, he couldn't let Bramble's remark pass unnoticed. "You sound surprised. Or did you really believe your experience of the world was exhausted? That there was nothing else to learn or be?"

Bramble scowled. "I might have been mistaken. So why do you want a funeral?"

"Because it's mine," Mordhu said simply. "And it is time."

"Time? What are you talking about?"

"About time. And my vast wealth of it, or rather, burden. Did you never wonder why I use my chosen name rather than that of some green, growing thing like the rest of you? I could explain it," Mordhu said. "but you'd have to be as old as I am to understand."

"False appeal to authority," Bramble said, looking smug. "Oldest trick in the book."

"It would be, if this were a debate," Mordhu said. "It's not. This is the Queen's Business. And to be about it, I suggest we split up. We can search twice as quickly that way."

"I'm younger and faster than you, old sprite. I'll find it first."

Mordhu smiled. "We will see."

•

Bramble had told the truth again. He was younger. He was faster. Neither of which Mordhu begrudged him, except that together they added up to one very unpleasant fact Bramble was winning. No matter where Mordhu went, or how quickly, or how far, there was always that faint crash in the undergrowth, the shadow through the forest, or a circle of spreading ripples on quiet water telling Mordhu that Bramble had been there before him. Mordhu knew he could catch Bramble if he had to, but there was no way on earth or under it to get ahead of him. Mordhu held a pace behind Bramble because he didn't know what else to do.

Mordhu didn't know if Bramble would be able to handle their adversary if he found it. He didn't know if he could do so himself, having no idea yet what the enemy was. Yet one thing was sure enough: at this rate Bramble would find it first. Mordhu wasn't quite selfish enough to hope that the enemy was beyond Bramble's power; if the danger was as great as the Fairie Queen said that could have meant the doom of the entire court. And yet...

I'll lose my turn for a funeral. Maybe forever.

Mordhu forced himself to consider the prospect, but it was painfully hard to imagine it, terrifying and terrible to try.

No new life without death. It's the way of the universe, even for the Not Born of Eve.

Not even fairie magic could change that law but there was a loophole. Death was necessary but Death, as the immortals had found, had more than one form it could take, with the right persuasion. Thus the Funeral. Fays lived forever, with or without it. Yet without it there was no new life. No renewal. Mordhu had only to face his reflection in any quiet pool to know where that road led. He would continue to diminish and, when his turn finally came again, there might not be anything of him left to care. Not dead, exactly, just...diminished. Forever.

Without Lady Foxglove; that was the worst part. Oh, for a while along the way he might be reduced to the size and appearance of a louse or flea, but even that would be temporary and Lady Foxglove not likely to welcome his company in any case.

"I'll be damned if I'll let Bramble do this to me," he said aloud.

Not that fays could be damned, as Bramble would have gleefully pointed out had he heard—fays have no souls. Mordhu didn't care. He'd find a way then, if he didn't find a way now. Yet he couldn't give up, not yet. There had to be a way, there had to be—

There was.

Mordhu smiled a wicked smile. Bramble was younger, faster, stronger, all the things that should have guaranteed him victory. Yet, Mordhu realized, there was one thing Bramble could not do, try as he might.

Bramble could not listen.

Mordhu stopped. He listened as intently as he knew how. He heard the young sprite mumbling to himself for many long minutes after they separated, but once they were far enough apart for Bramble's mutterings to fade the other voice was as clear as a trail. A blind hob could follow it, provided he was not deaf as well. Mordhu set off with new hope, and moved very swiftly indeed.

That trail led Mordhu back under the water, into the White Ladies domain. He hoped their indulgence still held, but this was no time to hesitate. He walked along the river bottom again, the banks rising like canyon walls to either side. He came to a place where the canyon narrowed, and there, where the rippling roof overhead turned swift and clashing, one last quiet deep pool formed in the embrace of stone. Mordhu came to a place of bones.

The stream washes such debris here.

There were sunken logs, and a flooring of fine pebbles that had been carried by swifter water to fall there; to Mordhu, still carrying the favor of sorts of the White Ladies, it looked almost like a quiet room with large log benches for comfort. Even the bones seemed to fit the idea; they all seemed to be at rest, victims of the White Ladies over time, certainly, but done with life for whatever reason. Quiet, contemplative, or merely inanimate, they lay in communal piles and scatters across the floor, long bones arranged to show the path of invisible currents, empty eyes staring at everything and nothing. Companions in the Company of the White Ladies.

All save one little pile.

These bones kept apart. They lay in a tumble against the curved rock wall, some tangled in scraps of brown cloth, others half-buried in the stony bottom as if attempting to dig their way free. The skull lay perched on a flat stone, rocking gently in a current Mordhu did not feel.

"It's you, isn't it? You're the one."

The skull rocked more violently, and now the eyesockets were turned directly at him.

WHO ARE YOU?

"I am Mordhu. Pooka, sprite, and a Lord of the Seelie Court, at least by age and courtesy. Who are you?"

The response was a low moan that grew louder and longer until the bones across the pool rattled, though whether in sympathy or answer Mordhu wasn't sure. He did know that a racket this loud would even draw Bramble's attention, sooner or later. "Whoever you are, I'm guessing that you're unhappy."

I AM DEAD.

"You were mortal. You died. It shouldn't have been such a shock."

More groans. Mordhu considered. He wasn't getting anywhere this way, and he wasn't sure how long he had before Bramble found him and upset whatever course Mordhu planned to follow, assuming he found one.

"If your bones can speak, they can make sense. Perhaps with a little more orientation?"

Mordhu sighed. What he was about to try might be a huge mistake, but he didn't see that he had either time or choice. The paradox is that I might have to make it stronger in order to defeat it.

"I summon The Queen's Power: Glamour."

It was so. The ragged pile of bones stirred as if caught in a vortex, rising, arranging, filling out and standing straight. The skull was the last to return to the heap, a pale white face to a body that was no more than bones and a few scraps of cloth, but now seeing itself in a mirror of Mordhu's devising.

One thing that Mordhu was old enough to understand about the Fairie Glamour was simply this: it worked both ways. Now the dead mortal wore the seeming that it expected, or remembered. A severe-looking little man with a tonsure and heavy brown robes stood before him, blinking as if he had just returned to full light after a long time in darkness.

"Now then," Mordhu said, "I ask again: who are you?"

"Theodius, former Brother of the Order of St. Francis."

"And now?"

His smile was ghastly. "Damned soul for all eternity."

Mordhu sighed. Whether he had it to spare or not, this was clearly going to take some time.

•

They sat on opposite logs. Mordhu was trying to get his fay mind around what Brother Theodius was telling him, but so far he wasn't having much success.

"So why were you making so much noise? It's quite distracting."

"I'm in torment. Shouldn't I scream my agony for all to hear? Sometimes, I understand, the Cries of the Damned reach the living in their dreams, and steer them away from the same path. Even now, shouldn't I serve as I can? Shouldn't I atone?"

"For what? Dying?"

"For succumbing to temptation."

Mordhu nodded. "Ah. The White Ladies."

"Demons," Brother Theodius corrected. "Devils. They tempted me..."

"They *compelled* you. It is their gift, and their power. Those that escape are few and lucky."

Brother Theodius shook his head. "You don't understand: if my Faith had been strong enough I could have resisted. They were so beautiful...I moved to embrace them. Me, who had foresworn such things long ago. I wasn't strong enough to resist."

"And so you are damned. One mistake, and damned. And this is Hell."

"I died in sin, unrepentant and unshriven "

"You mean you died quickly."

"It's the same thing!"

Brother Theodius was clearly warming to the discussion, and, for his part, Mordhu finally noticed something that seemed important: the voice. That is, he heard Brother Theodius as a man speaking now, not as a vast wail of pain and anguish that filled the wood, but just a voice speaking, as anyone's, mortal or fay, might do. Something Mordhu was doing was helping the poor spirit, and it wasn't simply the glamour that let Theodius pretend to be a man again.

He says he knows what's happened to him, and why, but I really think he's still working it out. And I think this is something he enjoys a great deal.

That is to say, debating. And when you have no one to argue with, do you argue with yourself? For, perhaps, eternity? That wouldn't do at all, but Mordhu didn't have to think too long to come up with an alternative. He spoke a name then, with the full power of the Queen behind it, a name that was also a summons.

"Bramble!"

Brother Theodius frowned. "What was that?"

Mordhu grinned. "Just calling someone I think you really must meet."

Bramble arrived in short order and Mordhu made the introductions. It was less than half an hour later when he quietly slipped away and left the two together in close conversation. He doubted if either Brother Theodius or Bramble even noticed.

•

"So the creature is finally at peace?" the Queen asked.

"Heavenly peace, Your Majesty. Or at least the closest to it he knew on earth. As for Lord Bramble, I think his condition could fairly be called the same."

"He's doing the Wood a great service," the Queen said.

Lord Mordhu bowed. "Indeed. I know Your Majesty will want to suitably reward him...when he returns. I fear that may not be for some time. Centuries, possibly."

The queen sighed. "That is really unfortunate. As it is, Lord Bramble is certain to miss your Funeral."

Lord Mordhu sighed as well. "Duty first, Your Majesty. I'm afraid that it simply can not be helped."

•

Lord Mordhu looked at blue sky and pillowy white clouds through a veil of cobweb and gossamer. Six elfin knights in full regalia carried his bier; ahead walked three score elfin maidens robed in white, weeping. Trailing all came the rest of the Seelie Court, with the glorious Fairie Queen at the center, surrounded by her Ladies in Waiting. All faces were somber so far as Mordhu could see, befitting the occasion. They processed for some time throughout the wood, until the proper spot presented itself, and there a detail of brawny hobs dug Mordhu's grave and lowered him in.

Lovely.

The first clump of earth fell on his feet. It felt warm, almost like someone had spread a blanket over his feet and wrapped them up snugly. As the rest of the earth fell Mordhu felt no panic, no need to fight for air and light; he had no need for either now. He snuggled into the earth like a child to the breast of its mother. Earth covered him over in warm safety. And there, for a time, he slept.

When he woke it was not as one creature but as many. Mordhu felt himself in a dozen places, a dozen forms. He was a beetle grub, awaiting its time in a cozy burrow. He was a tadpole, newly broken from its egg and exploring, briefly, the world. He was a minnow, a leaf on a tree about to fall, and later one newly budded. He was a rose, a bramble, a thistle, a twig, an oak seedling, a seed carried on the wind by a bit of downy thread. He was all these things and more besides, marveling at the world and the beauty of things unseen.

He paid for each new form with a bit of age and experience surrendered to the earth at each turn of the wheel. Mordhu gave them back to the source after holding them so long in trust, gladly shedding the burden of them until he had no more coin to pay. Then he was not all those things any more but one thing only, the part of him that always remained when all the debts were paid and all borrowed things returned.

The name was the very last to go.

Soon there came a time when he found himself struggling upward, the need for air and sun returning to him like a great hunger. He broke the surface of the earth in a place unknown yet very familiar, and wondrous folk were there waiting for him. They greeted him with expressions of joy. They bathed him carefully and dressed him in fine clothes, and one resplendent lady extended her hand in greeting.

She, too, seemed somehow familiar but he could not remember any more than that, try as he might. "Do I know you?" he asked politely.

"I am Lady Foxglove, chosen by the Fairie Queen and my own will to be your guide for a time. Please come with me."

She took him to a pool at a quiet stream, and there she bade him look at his reflection. A tall, handsome youth looked back at him from the water. He stared at the rippling reflection for several long moments, trying very hard to remember.

"Who are you?" asked Lady Foxglove.

"I do not know," he said, defeated.

The Lady Foxglove seemed oddly relieved. "Then you'll have to learn again, won't you? That's why I'm here." She looked him up and down and then considered. "You seem strong, and patient. I think I'll call you Oak for now."

"Do you...do you like that name?" he asked.

Lady Foxglove smiled the sweetest smile he could ever imagine seeing. "I do," she said. "Very much."

Doing Time in the Wild Hunt

*I*t's a goat.

That was the first answer Ray Wolver got when he turned the data over to the pattern recognition constructs in his brain: Four legs, large ears, white hide. His first answer was wrong, of course. Ray was used to being wrong, at this point in his life. He expected it. The best he could hope for was another chance. He pulled off to the side of the frontage road that led to the industrial park after glancing at his watch to be sure he had time for curiosity. He sat very quietly for a moment, then looked again at the wooded ridge that ran parallel to the road. The creature was still there. Not a goat, though. A doe.

A white doe.

"Holy..."

That was as far as he got. Somewhere off in the distance he heard the baying of a pack of hounds. The deer heard it, too. Her large ears switched to attention and then she was gone, vanished among the trees in a ghostly flash.

•

"I saw a white deer today," Ray said.

Susan didn't even glance up from her sewing. "My Uncle Syl claimed to have seen one, once. He drank a lot."

Ray put the evening paper aside. All the news was the same, anyway. Paste in new names and a new date and all the rest was boilerplate. "I admit it would be a rare thing, but albinism is nothing new."

"Then why are you going on about it?"

Ray started to ask why her Uncle's drinking had anything to do with seeing a white deer, but her question startled him into attention. Why was he going on about it? It was just a deer, and the paper company lands bordering the industrial park were full of them. White was rare, but not impossible.

Just a deer.

Ray looked about him. Susan's glasses were pushed forward on her nose as she worked the sampler. There was a streak of gray in her dark hair, but otherwise she was as she'd been when they'd first met. They were comfortable together after fifteen years, and he supposed that was something else to be grateful for; so many of their friends' marriages hadn't lasted half so long. They owned a decent home, in a decent neighborhood. Ray had a decent job. No reason to complain.

I just wish life was more interesting.

It wasn't the first time that thought had come, unbidden. It was, however, the first time it frightened him.

•

Ray saw the deer again. He hadn't expected that. He looked up at the ridge as he always did, as he passed it on the route to work. Not in anticipation, or expectation, or anything of the sort. As a reminder. He focused himself for that instant of time as he passed the ridge every morning, at the same time almost to the minute, pictured the elegant white doe with all the clarity he could muster. Only this morning, one week later, he didn't have to remember. The deer was there.

After a moment looking at her it occurred to him that he should have run into something by then. A tree, the embankment, another car. Something. He looked ahead and realized he'd pulled the car off to the shoulder of the frontage road, and stopped. All the time aware of nothing but the white doe. He looked back at the ridge and found her still there. She was looking at him, he was certain. Almost... well, waiting was the only thing that came to mind. Then she turned and disappeared again. Again Ray heard a distant sound, mournful.

The baying of hounds.

She's being hunted, he thought, and then remembered. *Again.*

•

Ray dreamed of the white doe. She bounded through the dark woods, seemingly without effort but Ray was not fooled. He followed hard behind her, not aware of how he could possibly keep pace with the deer as she leaped hedges and slipped through brambles, quick and elusive as summer lightning. Not caring. He followed and he knew her weariness.

I'm getting closer.

He felt as if he'd crossed an invisible line. Now Ray was aware of something besides the doe; he was aware of himself. Ray dreamed and knew he dreamed, but it changed nothing—he followed the deer as a white hound with red tipped ears and sharp white teeth, hungry for blood, hungry for the kill, and if there was any wrong in feeling that way Ray as hound knew none of it. Ray heard the pack on his heels and it was very good.

Closer.

It wasn't as if he could do something else, be something else. He had no choice. It was his nature. Almost on her flank, almost able to rend and tear...

Closer!

The doe cleared one last bramble hedge, the hound nipping at her heels. He leaped directly into the glare of the new-risen sun, hidden before by the hedgerow, waiting to blind him to the dream and tear the veil away from the waking world.

•

"Morning."

Ray held his coffee cup, unable for a moment to remember filling it. Susan glanced up at him from the table, then went back to her coffee and toast. Her eyes looked red and her face seemed wooden, without expression.

She looks tired.

Ray thought he should say something about that. Ray couldn't think what to say, and he let it go. One more time. It was easy now, almost beyond habit. Just let it go. He tried to decide if he was hungry, could not. He finally just sat down at the small table, across from Susan. She wasn't looking at the paper in front of her. She wasn't looking at anything. Especially not him.

"Can I have the sports?"

She slid the whole paper across the table, saying nothing. Ray didn't take it.

When did I start thinking this was comfort?

There was no comfort between them; there was only distance.

"Susan?"

She did look at him then, and all he could think for a moment was that her eyes looked familiar. He'd known her for nearly twenty years, but suddenly her eyes were familiar, or rather the things he saw there. Weariness. Distance. Something that might have been pain, only he couldn't see why that should be there. There was nothing wrong. At least, nothing he knew of.

"Is there something you want to talk about?" he asked.

"Like what?"

"I don't know. I just had the feeling you wanted to ask me something."

She glanced at the kitchen clock, and when she turned back she wasn't looking at him any more. "You'll be late for work."

Ray shook his head. *My imagination.* He leaned over, and she turned her cheek for his good bye kiss, and that was all.

•

There.

No surprise this time when the white doe appeared seven days later. She was right on time, and so was he. There was no conscious decision on his part, and no hesitation. Ray stopped the car, got out and hop stepped over the culvert and onto the embankment. The doe paused very briefly and then walked off at an unhurried pace into the trees. Ray didn't hesitate. He followed her. When he reached the top of the ridge, he glanced back at the road, at his own white Celica perched by the side of the road. Both car and frontage road seemed different, and smaller, and farther away than the few yards up into the tree line could account for. He looked back, found his attention drawn by a flash of white.

Follow.

The forest closed in behind him. Ray was on the trail now and he did not care when the open light from the roadway was swallowed into shadow. He followed a path that wore through the roots of trees and scarred rocks like the rain of centuries. It led deeper into the trees, and always just ahead he saw the white doe, not hurrying, not waiting. She kept her own pace, seemingly oblivious to the clumsy man following her.

She knows I'm here.

"She knows." The voice was all agreement.

Ray looked around. He saw no one. The white doe was not so distinct now. Ray hurried to make up the distance lost in his moment of hesitation.

"Who are you?" he asked aloud.

"One who belongs here. Can you say the same?"

Ray did not take his eyes off the doe. He didn't dare, for fear of losing her. It was only out of the corner of his eye, in spears of motion that the dim shape dogging his trail resolved itself.

"It's just a wood."

"As you say. No roads, no offices, no central air. Nothing yours that you didn't bring with you, nothing that doesn't serve its own purpose. What's here of interest to you?"

Ray didn't break stride. "She is."

"Why?"

Ray almost stopped again. He risked a quick look at his shadower, as quickly turned away. Nothing registered. There was a substance, perhaps, to the fall of shadow on a bramble, a darkening on the ground where no shadow should be. An odd arrangement of leaves and twigs that might have been a face, except it looked just like Ray and there was nothing served admitting that.

"Are you the Green Man?"

"Your mother read you fairy tales." It sounded like an accusation. "Bad influence, those. They feed the imagination with all sorts of nonsense. They make you do strange things."

"Like?"

"Like leave everything you know to chase everything you do not. Or is there some other reason you're here?"

Ray stepped over a bramble vine. "I don't know."

"I suggest you find out. You don't have much time, Mortal. The hunt has already begun."

Ray heard the hounds. They called to one another in the distance. "I've heard them before. They haven't caught her."

"Perhaps today will be different. Perhaps today something has made her hesitate, slow a half step or so. It wouldn't take much more, in the balance of things."

The pack was getting closer. Ray glanced back and saw what looked like red fireflies, floating up and down in perfectly matched pairs in the distant gloom.

Those aren't fireflies.

"They're my hounds."

Now Ray did stop. He looked around, but he knew he was alone now. But not for long. The red eyes were getting closer with every bound. Ray could make out the individual calls of the lead dogs. He turned away from the sight, looked back down the trail.

The doe was waiting for him. She had not moved since the last time he saw her. He ran forward, waving his arms.

"They'll catch you!"

The doe didn't move. Ray found himself narrowing the distance between them. Now he could see the deer's eyes. They were large and dark, but they were not like an animal's eyes at all. In fact, they were familiar.

Susan?

Susan was in the kitchen at home. He knew just what she was doing now; what she always did—clean away the breakfast dishes, load the dishwasher and then have a second cup of coffee. Stare at nothing. The few times he had remained at home on a holiday, or a sick day, the routine had not varied. Susan was not a deer, not being chased by a pack of red-eyed spectral hounds.

Why am I here?

The doe turned and trotted off down the well-worn trail. Ray followed, unable to answer his own question, unable to do anything but follow, faster and faster as the hounds closed in and the doe resumed speed.

Must catch her...

No questions now. And no matter how fast she moved, Ray kept pace. Ray felt himself change, shorten, bones contract, others expand and extend. Scent assaulted him next, high, heady smells of everything around him—the leaves and twigs rotting on the ground, the delicious musky spoor of the fleeing doe. He could almost scent her blood, trapped in warm flesh and eager for release. His jaws slavered, ready and eager for the taste of her blood. Ray coursed low to the ground, turned his muzzle to the leaf blocked sky and sounded the hunt. He heard the answer from his brothers following close after and it was good.

"Welcome to the pack, Ray."

The voice didn't matter. He knew what he had to do. The pack behind him could not catch her, but he could. For him she would hesitate, for him she would not run so very fast.

Ray heard the low moan of the hunter's horn and answered in kind. The pack behind him fell silent, yielding place. They followed; Ray could not see them but he could hear them slashing through the undergrowth behind him. They would share in the kill but he would make it.

Kill?

He was almost on her now. Just another few feet, one leap and bear her down...

"No!" It came out like a bay, like a growl. Ray skidded to a stop, a hound in all things except the sudden confusion in his brain, the words he tried to force out of a tongue and muzzle unsuited for anything like human speech.

Ray glanced ahead. The doe had stopped again, but the pack did not rush past him. They, too, every last one of them stopped as if they'd reached the end of one long invisible leash.

Ray saw the hunter. He stood some distance behind the hounds, standing upright like a man but with the antlers of a stag, a man in the face and a beast in the eyes. Not one and not the other, and it looked beyond him to the white doe with an expression that was at once blood lust and every other kind. Ray recognized the face. It was his own.

"Why did you follow the doe, Ray?" It repeated. "Wasn't it for the hunt?"

"I think," Ray answered, "it was to save my soul."

"You're just a man. It's just a deer," said the Stagman.

Ray smiled. "I am. But she isn't. And if she's not my soul she'll do till I find my own again."

"She belongs to me," the hunter said. "Stand aside."

Ray shook his head, now human again. "No, she does not. I understand, now. You are a half thing, undecided. You can't become what she needs and you can't let her go. How long have you worn those horns, now? How long to build the pack? How long has the hunt gone on?"

"When nothing changes, Time doesn't matter."

"When everything changes," Ray said, "it matters a great deal."

The huntsman raised his horn again, Ray felt himself change once more. He was certain he could stop it this time, he was also certain he didn't want to. His legs lengthened, slimmed, hardened. Twin spikes sprouted from his brow and branched and grew like young trees. His muzzle lengthened and his answering trumpet made the leaves quiver. The hounds leaped forward. Ray hooked the first one and spun it like a wet rag. It crashed hard against a tree trunk and exploded into mist, then reformed into a hound and took up the attack again. Ray lowered his antlers and took out two more, then wheeled sharply and fled down the trail. He saw the ghostly blur of the white doe ahead of him.

They won't catch her now—

Ray felt a burning bite at his left flank, kicked blindly. The hound gave out a very satisfying yelp but another took its place. Another leaped for his throat and only a sudden turn of Ray's head spoiled its aim. He was running full out now, but they were gaining on him. Ray kept his eyes on the doe, followed her toward a place where the shadows were weakening.

"Fool! You can't escape!" The hunter was very close.

Ray grinned fiercely. "I'm not the one who's trapped!"

The hunter shrieked in rage and urged the pack on. A hound leaped at Ray's hindquarters and tangled in his legs. Ray kicked free, staggered, almost went down. Not quite. He leaped the last bramble and was clear into the sunlight. It blinded him and he fell, dizzy, rolling. He put up his arm to ward off the hounds, but there were no hounds. And it was an arm.

Ray sat up, feeling the signals from his own human limbs as something strange. He was on the right of way by the frontage road, the edge of the woods was a good ten yards distant. The sound of the hunt was already fading as Ray's breath slowed to something like normal. He glanced at his watch. Five minutes elapsed time. That was all.

Close enough to forever...

Ray brushed a twig out of his hair and loose grass from his pants, then walked back to his car. He made a U turn and drove back the way he had come.

•

"Ray?"

Susan met him at the door, looking puzzled. He held out the white roses he had bought on the way home to her and she looked even more puzzled.

"You should be at work," was all she managed to say at first.

Ray nodded. He hadn't expected it to be that easy. There was a lot to make up for, and a long fight ahead. The flowers were weapons in that fight. A bit old-fashioned and primitive, perhaps, but he was a beginner and had to start somewhere. "I'm taking a few days off. I'm due. Maybe past it."

Susan looked at him as if he were someone she once knew, and couldn't quite place. "Come in," she said finally. As if he were a guest, and it didn't sound like a very strange thing for her to say.

"Thank you," Ray said, accepting the open door for the gift it was.

My Lord Teaser

Every man deals with pain in his own way. Some groan, some swear, some opt for stoic silence even when a little tactical complaint might bring relief. John of Devonleigh, called "Running Jack" by friends and foe alike, tended to philosophize. After a night in a bed that had nothing to do with sleep, and carrying a head that felt two stone too heavy—not to mention the size of a ripe melon—he had ample reason.

The only trouble with "the night before" is the morning after.

It was a minor paradox as such went, but this was as much mystery as Jack could handle just then. He came to a clear running stream just inside a grove near the forest of Dunby and there he didn't so much dismount as slide off his horse like a sack of loose grain. Reynard, the big dun gelding, drank gratefully from the stream without dwelling too much on the imponderables. Jack splashed his face with the cool sweet water and did little else.

Jack found a quiet pool where a boulder diverted the faster water to the side, and there he studied his reflection. It had been a while since Jack had taken notice of himself; time being the slippery thief it was, he was a little relieved to note that he was still a relatively young man. The black of his hair was untouched by gray as yet, and his dark eyes were still clear and bright. There were fine lines near his eyes and mouth that spoke of diminishing time, but not loudly. Not yet.

Still time to make a life for myself.

The question was: did it really matter now? Jack considered this, and came to the answer he always reached, because it was the only one there was.

"Reynard, they're going to catch me sooner or later."

Reynard cropped grass near the bank. If the horse thought of it at all unlikely he wouldn't have needed to ask who "they" were. They were legion: the brother of Jack's former knight and Reynard's former master, now deceased, too many inn and tavern keepers to count, the fathers and brothers of a dozen or more village girls and, for purposes varying from matrimony to mayhem, the village girls.

Jack never meant to complicate his life so much; indeed, he was working hard to avoid complications before the disaster at Charcross. Now he was forced to live life moment by moment, because the moment was all he could count on. Jack didn't like to think about it. He decided to soak his aching head instead; it seemed a more profitable way to spend the time. When he finally emerged from the water again he heard a horse whinny.

"Reynard...?"

Not Reynard. Too far away. Jack crept to the edge of the trees. A man road down the road Jack had come, a large man wearing armor, followed by two mounted squires and a small pack train. He rode with his helm hanging from his saddle, but Jack didn't need to see the man's face to know who he was.

As far as Jack was concerned, he was Death.

"Sir Kevin Grosvenor," whispered Jack to Reynard. "Now it ends."

He looked around. The grove was small, and the path lead right through it; there was no place to hide. There was a chance he could reach the forest proper before Sir Kevin, but there was no point. He was traveling lighter than his pursuers but Reynard was too spent from the previous evening's flight to go far.

Jack considered; Sir Kevin hadn't spotted him yet, but that wouldn't matter in a few moments. He might manage to surprise them, but it was three to one and Jack knew he was no match for the burly knight even if they had been equally armored.

"I suppose," he said, "it's time to show the honor that Sir Kevin claims I do not possess. Do you think the contradiction will give him the slightest pause, Reynard?" The big dun snorted and Jack was forced to agree. "I didn't think so."

Jack loosened his sword in its scabbard and started to mount.

"You chose death, then."

The woman sat on a stone by the stream. She hadn't been there a moment before, Jack was sure of it. It took him a moment before he was sure of something else he knew her. The long dark hair and dimpled smile was very familiar from the tiring but blissful prior evening.

"Edyth? How did you get here?"

"Aren't you pleased to see me, Jack?" she asked.

Actually he was indeed pleased, though Jack had never expected to see her again. When they had met the previous evening in the Houndsfoot Tavern it was Edyth who had sought him out. Likewise, there was nothing in her manner or conversation in the time they'd spent together that led him to think that she expected more from him than his company for that little time. She had been quite unexpected that way, as in others. Jack in turn surprised himself to think that he might have been quite content to spend a good portion of his life perhaps all of it delving her mysteries, if that had been at all possible.

Jack glanced back at the road; Sir Kevin was coming uncomfortably close. "Certainly, but your timing could be better."

She laughed then. It was probably not quite loud enough for Sir Kevin to hear over the clink and flap of his accoutrements, but almost. "I think my timing is perfect as it is. You are about to die," she said.

Jack blinked. "So it seems, though I never thought you would savor the idea. I thought you were somewhat fond of me."

"I am quite fond of you, and there's my meaning," she said. "I offer you this choice: face that angry man out there, and die. Or come with me, and live."

"Come where?"

"With me," she repeated. "It's not necessary that you understand, only that you choose. Know that I do have the power to save your life, but I wouldn't dawdle if I were you."

Jack glanced back at the road. "That's no choice at all. Lead on."

There was a white palfrey, fully comparisoned, standing beside the woman. Jack was sure it hadn't been there a moment before, either, but in a moment Edyth was mounted and reining her horse toward the far end of the grove. Jack climbed back on Reynard and trotted after her.

"We can't reach the forest before Sir Kevin sees us; I'd already considered that," Jack said as he caught up.

"He's not as close as you think," she said.

Jack glanced back, and got an even bigger surprise.

By Our Lady....

There was nothing behind them but trees, as far and as wide as Jack could see: no sign of the road, no sign of Sir Kevin, though both, as Jack was certain, were only a few yards away a moment before. As far as Jack could tell they were out of the grove and into the main forest now, though in truth the trees seemed both thicker and larger than he'd expected.

"What just happened, Edyth?"

The woman just smiled at him, and Jack realized dully that she had changed, too. The hair and the smile had not changed, but her face was more angular than he remembered; her frame, slighter. There was also something different about the eyes, something...older.

"Edyth, who are you?"

She smiled at him. "You may call me Lady Devoted. I am the humble servant of my mistress, the Queen of the Sidhe."

Jack reined in. "Not another step," he said, "until I know what this is about."

The woman's horse stopped too, though she gave no command that Jack could see. The palfrey turned slowly, elegantly, like a dancer. When the woman he had known as Edyth faced him again she looked even more different. He could still see Edyth there, in this stranger's face, but it was no village maid who sat before him. She wore a gown of fine green brocade; gold spurs were strapped to the heels of her soft leather boots. Edyth had been pretty; this woman was not containable in such a pitiful word, or indeed any other Jack knew.

"I am Lady Devoted, as I told you. I just saved your life."

Jack nodded. "Yes. Why?"

She studied him in a way that was a little disconcerting. "Most men would assume it had something to do with our idyll of last night, and my affection for you. Why are you not making that assumption?"

"I am, in that I do believe it has something to do with the previous evening. But what? There's the question. You are not what you seemed, Lady, and thus it follows that our time together was not what it seemed, and so I must ask: why did you seek me out?"

smiled approval. "You're a clever man, Jack, and not as blinded by pride as some. That will help. I sought you out to test you, to make certain you were the man I thought you. Nor was I disappointed. I think you will do nicely."

"For what?"

"For the Queen of the Sidhe's lover."

•

Running Jack was beginning to wonder if, perhaps, Sir Grosvenor was the lesser of the two threats confronting him now. They had been riding for a while, and though Sir Kevin was still out of sight, the edge of the forest, dimly visible ahead, had not gotten any closer.

"How much farther, Lady?"

"A little or a lot. It varies."

That wasn't very helpful. Jack pictured himself riding for an eternity through this dark forest which, Jack was pretty certain, was not Dunby Wood. The company was pleasant enough but the situation did seem uncomfortably short of options.

"Lady, if I ask a question, will you tell me the truth?"

"Anything you ask in my lady's name, I will answer so," she replied. "But, since you don't really know Her Majesty's given name and I've no inclination to reveal it, that doesn't help you much."

"No," said Jack.

She smiled then. "However, you are free to ask as man to woman for such I am, whatever else I may be and you may believe what you will. Isn't that how you mortals normally conduct business?"

Jack had to admit it was. "Very well then: you said you were testing me last night. What was the test? That I could lie with a woman?"

She laughed then. "By the Glamour, no. The meanest lout in that tavern could have managed that, even the few whose tastes don't run to women. I wasn't looking for ability," she said, then added, "or skill, come to that. Though you were... passable, I'd say."

"You are too kind," Jack said, a little wounded.

She shook her head, and she wasn't smiling. "No, Jack. I am not kind. If you don't believe anything else I tell you, believe that. I chose you for our advantage and not for yours. Leaving you to that large angry man back there," she glanced back down the path, "might have been kinder. A sword blade in the head or heart isn't the worst thing that can happen to a person. What you face now is a sort of war, Jack, and we of the Sidhe have been at it a very long time. You're in more danger than you can possibly know."

"You said I was to be the Queen's lover!"

She nodded. "It's the same thing."

•

It was as if Lady Devoted had been waiting for something, Jack thought, and he'd just given it to her. The forest around them grew even thicker for a moment, as if they were riding in night. Then there was a definite lightening of the path ahead. Another few minutes' riding and they crossed the border.

It was the most beautiful country Jack had ever seen.

He looked around with a rising sense of futility, trying to imagine a time, if any, when he would look back on the moment he was now in. What would he tell himself? What images, sounds or emotions filtered through imperfect memory could recapture what he saw, what he heard, what he felt right now? Could there actually be a truth so strong or a lie so golden to be a match for it?

"I couldn't even imagine a place like this."

"What do you see?" Lady Devoted asked.

"What...?" The question sounded ludicrous, but one look at his companion told him she was deadly serious. There was almost no other word quite fit a hunger in her expression as she waited for his answer.

"I see a stream with water clear as glass. I see a palace with turrets shining like finest marble, whiter than snow and taller than any mountain I have ever seen. I see folk of such quality that the meanest among them puts the finest mortal king on his throne to shame. I see such that, if I were to see much more, I would burst into flame like that Greek maiden who saw Zeus in his Glory and could not contain it."

She nodded, and her eyes closed as if she savored each word like some rare and delicate pastry. "Thank you."

"I don't understand," he said. "What do you see?"

"The same," she admitted. "And ever the same, for millennia past counting. Look at the finest emerald in creation long enough and sooner or later a dung heap will become the most fascinating change of pace." She sighed. "But to see, for a moment, with new eyes...that was a gift, and so I thanked you. Simple courtesy, and manners. Understand that proper behavior is life and death here."

"I would consider the debt paid if you would teach me," he said.

"As much as can be done for you, I will. Pray it's enough."

•

There was so much that was new and strange to Jack, but a few things seemed to stand out. For instance, all the grand palaces and castles he saw upon crossing the border were still there, but no one seemed to be using them. No matter where he and Lady Devoted rode none of the fine buildings ever seemed to get any closer. So when Lady Devoted brought him a change of clothing he bathed in a cold water stream, shaved using a bronze mirror hung on a tree. A gilt bucket appeared with oats beside the stream for Reynard, who didn't seem inclined to question farther than his stomach. Jack was different. When Lady Devoted reappeared, Jack finally had to remark upon it.

"You are not deceived; the buildings are but aspects of the Glamour."

"You mean they're not real?"

"They're real enough, but they're not what you think they are. They suit their purpose by doing what they were envisioned to do."

"And what is that?"

"To attest to the glory of my mistress and her kingdom. Aren't they fine?"

"Yes, but what good are they if no one can use them?"

She looked at him as if he was a dull-witted child. "What good is a human palace? It's a testament to the wealth and power of the crown, but as a place to live? Most are somewhat lacking; they're drafty and cold and impossible to clean. These are different. They never age or need repair; they do not gather dust and they do not wall us off from the natural world. Which, as you said yourself, is a splendid place indeed."

"Yes, but what about rain? Or winter chill?"

Lady Devoted smiled then. "Sometimes I think you forget where you are. We are the Changeless, Jack. The Not Born of Eve. What are such things to us? What is a palace but something to admire, as you would a mountain or a fine horse? All the same."

Jack shrugged. "My expectations rule me, My Lady, and they are poor masters at best. So. What happens now?"

"Now we go to see my mistress. What 'happens' remains to be seen."

•

"Lady Devoted, you did not tell me she had a husband!"

Jack kept his voice down to a harsh whisper, but barely. Lady Devoted seemed more amused than chagrined. "I didn't tell you that earth should be under you and sky above, either. Some things you take for granted."

They stood at the edge of a clearing: Jack in his borrowed finery, Lady Devoted in a new gown that was as delicate as a garment of moonbeams and cobwebs, and about as substantial. It had been difficult to take his eyes off her when she directed him to look at the approaching company. Now it wasn't difficult at all. Jack's mouth had dropped open at the sight.

The lords and ladies of the sidhe walked hand in hand, their entrance a pavanne to hidden music. At the head of the column walked a lady of indescribable beauty, a creature not so much perfect of form as something beyond the notion of form, and the ethereal fashions of beauty. She was beauty, and whatever came closest to her in even the palest imitation would be beauty, too. Her hair was whiter than snow, her eyes the faint blue of glaciers. She was at once ancient as earth and new as springtime. Jack lost his heart to her at once. He really had no choice.

It was several long moments before Jack was able to even notice the lord at her side, and then for a moment he had all of Jack's faltering attention. In some ways the lord of the Sidhe reminded Jack of Sir Kevin. Besides the comparisons of size and strength, there was the same sense of implacability about him. He looked otherwise human except for two fine horns springing from his brow like those of a yearling buck. He wore a tunic of silvered thread; his hose was sky blue. He carried a jeweled longsword in his right hand as he held his lady's with his left hand. The blade was hidden in its scabbard and wrapped in a fine jeweled belt, but Jack had no doubt there was nothing of delicacy and show in the blade. It was for using. The fairie lord, for his part, looked as if he knew how to use it, had used it, and would again at the slightest provocation.

"Who is that?" Jack had asked.

"My lady's consort, of course. The King of this realm."

After she seemed certain that Jack's outburst was over, she took him by the hand and led him out into the open, before the dancers and the magnificent couple who led them.

"Keep silent unless directly addressed, and try to follow as I direct."

Jack felt every single glance as they company turned their eyes on him. No one spoke, but the hidden music ended, and so did the dance. All stood watching them approach. Every instinct in Jack's soul told him to break Lady Devoted's grip if he could and flee to whatever safe haven he could find. His wits told him differently: that Lady Devoted's delicate grip was more than he thought, and there were no safe places for him there. He remembered Lady Devoted's words, kept silent, and tried to follow her lead.

The Queen of the Sidhe was the first to speak, in a voice that was the source of all music as far as Jack could tell.

"You have returned to us, Lady Devoted, and you bring company! Most welcome. Who is our guest?"

Lady Devoted bowed low, and Jack copied her. "Your Majesties, may I present Lord Teaser."

Lord...?

In his surprise Jack almost spoke then, but managed to prevent it. The gaze from the massed company seemed even more intense now, if such a thing was possible, and the last thing he wanted was to draw more attention than he could help. If anything, he wanted to make himself very small and hide someplace inconspicuous, such as the nearest rock. But then, he reasoned, he would not be able to hear that voice again, nor see that wonderful face.

The Queen extended one perfect gloved hand. Jack had presence of mind enough to glance at his companion before he accepted it, but brushing the delicate lace with his lips made him a bit light-headed. He caught a scent of something undefinable, but fascinating. When the Queen withdrew her hand it was all Jack could do to let it go. Indeed, he wasn't sure if he'd have been able to release her hand, had not the King of Fairie caught his eye. The sidhe lord nodded once, and Jack found himself bowing again. When he straightened up, the King's eyes were still on him.

"You must join us at the feast this evening," said the Queen. It was a polite enough request, but Jack realized he would have fought armies to be anywhere she wanted him to be, do anything she wanted him to do. In a moment the music began again and, two by two, the dancers passed by. As the royal couple pavonned away from him, Jack heard the King speak to his lady.

"And thus it begins?"

At least that's what it sounded like; the Queen made no answer that he could hear. One thing Jack did know for certain the King's horns were definitely larger now than they were just a few moments before.

•

"You're not eating," Lady Devoted said.

The feast was laid out on three tables, the head table and two others turned at right angles to it. Jack and Lady Devoted sat opposite each other at the head of the rightmost table, close but not too close to the royal couple seated at the center of the head table.

Lady Devoted had risen and gone to speak to her mistress on several occasions as if summoned, though Jack heard nothing. After the last time she acted as if something had been settled, and designed to enjoy the feast herself. There was a great deal to enjoy: venison, turbot, compotes of great delicacy and the most delicious scents. Jack's mouth was practically watering, but all he allowed himself was a little wine. A very little, well mixed with water. Jack wanted his wits about him.

"I dare not," he said.

"That old story about eating the food of fairyland and being trapped forever?" She smiled. "Would that really be such a terrible thing?"

"Being trapped anywhere is a terrible thing," he said. "And though your perspective is far vaster than mine, I can see the same thought in you."

Lady Devoted denied nothing, admitted nothing. She merely looked thoughtful. "Why does Sir Kevin seek your death? What did you do to him?"

Jack allowed himself another sip of wine. "I lived."

"That's all?"

"Even simple things have roots past counting. Specifically, I lived and his brother died. At Charcross."

"Charcross..." Lady Devoted frowned briefly. "I remember hearing something of that. A border skirmish between two barons, was it not? Hardly more than a trifle."

"Normally, yes. One lord claims a serf's croft is on his fief, another disputes. Sometimes they fight, more often it's a brave show and bluster, a little gold changes hands and all is agreed. Unfortunately, there was already bad blood between the Grosvenors and Percys going back some years. They were just looking for an excuse."

"What happened?"

"They fought," Jack said simply. "I was squire to Sir Francois, Kevin's brother. During the melee his banner was torn. Another bloody trifle, but he sent me back to Grosvenor Castle to get a new one. I think the fool still thought it was some grand show. He was wrong. By the time I returned it was over; Sir Francois was dead on the field. I don't think old Percy himself meant it to go as far as that."

"Fools, to squander such wealth," was all Lady Devoted said.

Jack shrugged. "Wealth was squandered, and that's the truth. The Percy family paid a heavy fine to Sir Kevin and the king took a larger one. I wasn't so lucky. Sir Kevin couldn't believe his brother had been so foolish. Easier to believe I had betrayed Sir Francois and fled."

"That wasn't what I meant, Jack. I meant wealth. What does one value more than the thing one does not possess? There's not a fay at this table who wouldn't pay more gold than the world has seen for a moment with such depth of feeling, and humans waste it on nothing." She shook her head in disgust.

Jack didn't understand at first, then he looked around him. He remembered what Lady Devoted had told him about seeing this kingdom with new eyes, and now he tried now to see the company around him with a different perspective. He tried to see the fays as Lady Devoted must, one who had beheld the same tableau for ages past counting. For several long moments he could not get past the jeweled flash, the colors, the glamour. Then he noticed something he had not noticed before.

What's wrong with their eyes?

The fays were laughing, but not with their eyes. They were flirting, but the broad smiles and coy expressions were only on their faces. What spoke of joy and life at their feasting and merriment spoke only on the surface. Jack tried to understand what was in their eyes, instead of all the things that should have been there.

All he could sort out of it was boredom, weariness, a kind of hopeless sameness that did not change whatever fair face he looked at.

"Is everyone here really so weary of existence?"

"It's not as simple as that, but I get your meaning. And the answer is 'no.' For instance, at the head table just now."

Jack looked where Lady Devoted was looking. The queen and her king were in a discussion that was quite animated, even, if Jack could believe such a thing were possible now, heated. There was a definite reddish cast to the king's features, and the queen's fine mouth was set in a hard firm line. For a moment the king looked directly at Jack, and their eyes met briefly. Then the king was smiling at something a courtier had said, the queen had risen from her place, and Jack was trying to remember how to breathe. He had seen something in the king's eyes and no mistake, and it certainly wasn't boredom. Jack shivered.

"Prepare yourself," Lady Devoted said.

"For what?"

"For the first skirmish. This is a war, remember?"

Jack didn't know what to say, nor did he really get a chance. He sensed rather than saw someone behind him, and he rose from his chair to find the Queen of Fairie standing behind him, smiling radiantly as the hidden music began again.

"My Lord Teaser, will you consent to dance with me?"

•

The dance was no stately pavanne this time; it was more like a braisle but not quite as energetic. There was time to talk. The Queen of Fairie seemed perfect in every way, and her conversation was no exception. Jack couldn't remember the last time his wit had been so clearly matched, except perhaps with Lady Devoted. She asked him riddles, and he felt fortunate to get one or two of the lot. She asked him to speak of himself, which was never very hard.

Soon others joined them in the moonlit glade that was their feast hall and ballroom. The dance could have lasted for minutes, hours or days; Jack didn't know or care. Almost the only thing that mattered was the queen did not find him foolish, or clumsy, or slow witted, or any of the things Jack felt he most certainly was in her presence. The "almost" came to mind whenever Jack happened to notice the king, standing with a group of his pale knights, looking at him. The king's hand had crept closer and closer to the pommel of his dagger until it rested there, and Jack was pretty sure he never took his eyes off him the entire time he danced with the man's lady.

Finally it was Lady Devoted who interrupted. She appeared at the queen's side and made a graceful curtsey. "Your Majesty, the hour grows long. Perhaps our guest is fatigued."

Jack almost protested, despite the Fairie King's darkening mood, but a glance from Lady Devoted stopped him. He merely bowed low and took the queen's hand as she offered it, and again brushed the glove with his lips before Lady Devoted and several other attendants escorted the queen away.

Just before she left, Lady Devoted whispered in his ear in parting. "You will be afraid soon, Jack. Try not to show it."

She was gone before Jack had a chance to ask what she meant. Another moment and he didn't have to. The King of Fairie was at his elbow, smiling a smile like burning ice. "My knights and I are going on a hunt. Will you attend? I think you'll enjoy the sport, Lord Teaser."

Jack barely managed to keep his teeth from chattering. "If you insist, Your Majesty."

The chasm of his smile grew even wider. "Oh, I certainly do."

•

Jack had heard enough stories about the Wild Hunt to wonder if he himself or his soul might be the quarry, but the hunt was nothing so straightforward. They hunted no creature that Jack had ever seen, or imagined. It could have been a unicorn, or a pegasus, or something more snakelike than cloven footed. Indeed, it seemed to be all those things, at one time or another.

The fays rode long legged creatures with red eyes that might, at first glance, pass for horses. They carried barbed spears and blew curling horns that made the country echo with their blasts. Reynard gave a good enough account of himself as he carried his master over thickets and through thick woodland, now in sight of the quarry or other hunters, now in a forest so dark and still that Jack and his mount could well have been the only living creatures for leagues.

In time Jack noticed that, one by one, the other hunters turned back. Soon it was only Jack and the king. Jack wanted to turn back himself, but a small quiet voice inside told him that this was a very bad idea.

Jack caught up with the king at the crest of a wooded hill. He arrived just in time to see the rump of their prey if indeed it was a rump disappear into a narrow valley before them. He started after it, but the king did not. Jack drew rein beside the fairie lord.

"What manner of creature did we hunt, My Lord?"

"The same thing we always hunt, and have for a very long time," said the king. "Which is to say: I don't know."

Jack blinked. "Surely you could have caught up to it before now, whatever it is."

The king smiled grimly. "Then what would we hunt?" The smile went away. "I know why you are here, My Lord Teaser."

Jack studied the far rise as if it were the most interesting piece of earth he had ever seen. "Then you are most certainly wiser than I," Jack said.

"Look at me, Mortal."

Jack did as he was told, and immediately wondered if he had ever truly seen the fay king before that moment. The face was much the same as Jack remembered, though the horns had now sprouted into what was becoming an impressive set of antlers. No yearling now, but an almost grown stag. Jack could almost hear the trumpeting of the fall rut as the king let out one gusty breath on the chill air, and watched it drift away like smoke.

"I am the king of no common domain, My Lord Teaser. I command folk the least of whom could make any mortal power quake in its boots. What I rule, I rule. What I claim as mine, is mine. Lady Devoted brought you as a guest, and such you are, but there is more to it as I think you know. Do not presume that guest protection means safe passage in all things. That would be a mistake."

Jack looked at the king's eyes. Time still nestled there, heavy as it did for all the fays, but there was something else, something that was not in the least bit weary. And it was getting stronger by the moment.

"I would not presume," Jack said, bowing slightly.

"You do," the king said, "and you will. It is always thus."

Then, as if he had been no more than the mist of breath he left behind, the Fairie King was gone.

•

Jack could not sleep.

He was weary beyond telling, but that seemed to work against him. Worse, when sleep did briefly touch him, his dreams were full of the face and image of the Fairie Queen; it was at once a sweet image and a nightmare, a font of reverence, desire, and fear. Sleep and the burden of her, imagined, was like a weight he could not hold for long. He came to himself again in his green bower, full awake.

At least, he thought he was awake.

So why did he still hear her laughter? Jack rose from his shadowed bed, dressed quickly. He slipped through the thicket; after years of running it was almost second nature. He emerged from the trees into the open meadow that had been their feast and revel hall, now a darkened expanse vaulted over with stars.

Jack wandered around. The tables were gone now; in the darkness Jack couldn't even find definite sign that they had ever been there.

Is this the dream now, or was the dream before?

For all Jack could tell, he had fallen asleep in the forest by the stream, and all that had happened since the narrow escape from Sir Kevin, the transformation of Edyth, the visit to the Fairie realm was just the imaginings of a guilty brain.

Jack knew better. He knew that someone was waiting for him, someone very close. Nor was he wrong. She stepped out of the trees across the meadow from where he himself had emerged, and stood there, just outside the dark wood. The Fairie Queen, veiled in gossamer and crowned in starlight. She smiled at him, and his knees shook. She held out her hand to him, and it was not an invitation.

"Come."

Jack started toward her. He really didn't have any choice. He was just a little past midway when he heard a new voice.

"So. It happens."

The speaker sounded like Death itself given mouth and tongue to speak. Even so, it took every ounce of will that Jack possessed to turn his head far enough to see who spoke.

The Fairie King stood at the far side of the meadow. Jack almost didn't recognize him; he had a full set of antlers like a rutting stag, and if anything his ears had grown larger and more pointed. His eyes were as red as an animal's reflected in torchlight, but there was no torchlight. The king held two great white hounds at leash, and they strained toward Jack, snarling.

Jack turned back, saw the Fairie Queen disappear into the woods. Jack felt his life in the balance, but when he ran it was toward the Fairie Queen, and not away from anything. He sensed rather than saw when the king released the hounds. Not that it mattered; he couldn't run any faster than he already was.

He got a glimpse of a figure in white, just ahead, and ran toward it. It was the Fairie Queen, waiting for him.

"Your Majesty, the hounds "

"I know. Seek the Fairie Queen, Jack. It's your only chance."

He stared at her. "But you...?"

She wasn't the Fairie Queen. Another moment and she had changed enough that he could see who she was, though by then he had already figured it out.

"Lady Devoted, you have just deceived and betrayed me. Why should I trust you?"

"Because you're not the only one at risk here."

In a moment she changed again, and it was no woman at all, but a graceful doe standing before him, looking at him with familiar eyes. She raised one dainty hoof, indicated the way he should run. "I'll distract the hounds; the rest is up to you. Go!"

Jack heard the baying hounds, closer now. "What shall I tell her?"

"Nothing. She'll either save you, or she won't."

Jack heard a thrashing in the undergrowth and he turned and fled the way Lady Devoted had said. For a moment the hounds were so close he was certain he felt their hot breath at his back, then the sounds faded, their baying grew fainter as the fairie hounds followed new prey. Jack kept running.

Something else pursued Jack then. Something that ran like a human and yet was not much like a human at all. This time he did feel hot breath behind him, and a harsh, sensuous whisper at his ear.

"What shall we hunt now, Lord Teaser?"

Jack saved his breath for running. Now the Fairie King was more stag than man, now something like a will o wisp, now something very much like the beast they had hunted together earlier that evening. Always changing, but at heart the same, and all focussed on him. Jack's foot caught on a log and he almost fell, but managed to catch himself on a sapling just long enough get his feet under him again.

Pointed tines raked his left shoulder and Jack almost fell from the blow. He staggered on. The second blow caught him in the thigh, and he stumbled.

"Now it ends."

Jack's motion carried him through one last thicket, into an open space diffused with white light. He sprawled headlong before a pair of dainty feet. He looked up, gasping, into the radiant face of the Fairie Queen.

"My Lord Teaser, to what do I owe the pleasure?"

She spoke the words, but she wasn't looking at him at all. The Fairie King stood just inside the bower, his chest heaving, his eyes glowing bright.

"He's mine," the king said. "You were together. I saw it. If you love him, he must die!"

The Fairie Queen did look at Jack now. She smiled at him, but only for a moment. All her attention from then on was for the king alone. "I do not, My Lord."

Jack heard the words, and he heard the truth in them. He wanted to die. He thought, perhaps, if he stood up just then the Fairy King would grant his wish. He started to rise, when he felt a hand on his shoulder, restraining him.

"Follow me, if you want to live," Lady Devoted whispered. Jack didn't see where she had come from; he was pretty certain she had not been present a moment before.

"I don't want to live," Jack said. "She doesn't love me."

"She never did, and never would. Look."

Jack did look. He saw the king meet his queen halfway and, if anything was lacking in their embrace, it was not passion.

"Come."

Jack still wanted to die, but it was clear that the Fairie King had things on his mind besides murder now. Jack allowed himself to be hustled away, half running, half crawling, by Lady Devoted. Jack was pretty sure that neither the king nor the queen even bothered to notice.

•

Lady Devoted led Jack to where Reynard was settled for the night. The gelding took his rousting stoically enough. Lady Devoted stood by as Jack saddled and bridled him. He finally noticed the bandage on Lady Devoted's arm.

"You're hurt."

"I said you weren't the only one at risk. War, remember? No matter. We heal quickly. Far faster than you will, I fancy." She sighed. "We did use you ill, didn't we, Jack?"

"'My Lord Teaser.' I should have guessed."

She shrugged. "Perhaps. The word has many meanings."

"One of which is to refer to the farm stallion that, though he is not allowed to mate, is the one who raises the passion of the mares."

"Or in this case, both stallion and mare." Lady Devoted shrugged. "A little novelty, a little jealousy...a little reminder, if you will, and the two Powers of our realm remain committed and in balance. When marriages last for millennia, and every day has the curse of immortal sameness, sometimes even love needs help. And they do love each other, Jack. Despite the occasional indiscretion."

"But I love her too," Jack said softly. He stopped to loosen the saddle girth, which, in his anger, he had tightened a little too much. Reynard whinnied his gratitude. Jack sighed. "Well, it wasn't a very kind thing you did, but you did warn me. I'll take my leave now, if there's no objection."

"Sir Kevin is out there," Lady Devoted pointed out.

Jack almost smiled. "There was a time when that would have terrified me."

"So you still want to die?"

Jack thought about it for a moment, then sighed. "No. But with the Fairy King within and Sir Kevin without, how can I live?"

"Let me ride with you a bit. Perhaps I can think of an answer."

•

When they reached the border, the King and Queen of Fairie were waiting for them.

"One last betrayal, Lady Devoted?" Jack asked.

"As I am not in your service, I can hardly betray you," she said primly. "But, like so much here, this is not what it seems. Dismount."

Jack, seeing no other option, did as he was told. Lady Devoted walked beside him as they approached the royal couple. The king's expression would have done a statue proud, but the queen smiled at him. Jack thought of being out of sight of that smile for as long as he lived and remembered that he didn't want to live very long at all.

The queen turned to Lady Devoted, looking somewhat petulant. "Must I?"

"You did promise me, Your Majesty. And it is such a little thing."

The queen did not look happy, but she nodded. "Very well." She turned to Jack. "A parting gift, Lord Teaser."

The queen changed. It was like the first time Jack had seen transformation in Lady Devoted, only the queen did not change into a different person. She was still the queen. She was still lovely past all understanding.

She was not however, perfection.

Jack saw the age in her eyes. He saw the faint tracings of veins under skin so delicate it seemed worn smooth, like stone. Jack realized that he was seeing her as she really was, and the goddess that he had loved because he had no choice was now only what she was and no more. The spell was broken. Jack's soul was his own again. He kissed the hand she offered and bowed low.

Now the king reached out and took her hand from him, holding it close. "That was my queen's gift. Mine is that I will not finish the hunt I began last night."

The queen smiled almost shyly. "My Lord, you already have. Or have you forgotten already?"

He smiled too. "That," he said, "I have not."

Without another word the royal couple turned away, walking together off into the forest where they were joined by other members of their entourage. As they disappeared Jack heard one final time the soft chords of the hidden music.

"The king's anger seems to have passed. Could I remain here?" Jack asked.

"Certainly," Lady Devoted said. "And the next time you see Her Majesty the Glamour will be in place and you will be hers again. She will make you love her and you will go to her, and sooner or later the king will catch you. In fact, I'd help him."

Jack wondered if that was a trace of jealousy in Lady Devoted's eyes. Jack sighed. "I'm a fool."

She smiled then. "I know. It's part of why I chose you."

"What was the other part? You never did answer me."

"Because you like women, Jack," she said frankly, "and that's rarer than you think. It was never conquest with you, no matter what the number. I knew you would look on my mistress and love her. Any man would desire her, but desire is fleeting and, in the fullness of time, meaningless." Lady Devoted smiled again, and it was the smile of a cat—all teeth. "But love? That's very different. Love is a proper threat. One that would rouse the Queen to ardor and the King to defend his rights. That was what my test at the inn was all about. Now let's be gone."

They reached the edge of the woods in no time at all. Jack looked out into the sunshine, which seemed almost impossibly bright compared to the twilight of fairie.

"You've received gifts from my Lord and Lady," Lady Devoted said. "But I have a gift for you too, Lord Teaser. It waits for you beyond these woods. You will know it when you find it. I hope you will use it wisely."

"Will I see you again?" he asked.

She smiled a bit sadly. "Do you want to?"

Jack thought about it. "Yes."

"Then the answer is 'no.' You will never see me again. And that's kinder than you can possibly imagine."

She raised a hand in farewell, and then Lady Devoted was gone. Jack looked about for a bit, though he knew he would not see her.

Sir Kevin be damned.

He rode out into the sunlight. There was no sign of Sir Kevin, either. It was a beautiful day. Running Jack pointed Reynard back down the road he had come two days before, but otherwise let the horse set the pace. There was no hurry.

•

No hurry at all, as it happened.

It wasn't until he reached Grosvenor Castle that he discovered Lady Devoted's gift. The current Master of Grosvenor was away, but the affable cook was more than happy to tell of Sir Kevin.

"He's dead, young man. Killed on Crusade nearly fifteen years ago. He took the Cross five years after he'd given up the search for the man called Running Jack. He was never the same, after. Just between us two I think he sought his death in the Holy Land."

Jack was too human not to feel a great relief, even with the slight regret that came with it. Sir Kevin had deserved better but then, Jack reminded himself, so had he.

Jack was surprised to find gold in his saddle pouch when he got around to opening it later, but he knew the gold was a mere token. The real gift was time. The King of the Sidhe may have spared Jack's life but it was Lady Devoted who had really given his life back to him.

To truly honor this gift, I need to make the best use of it.

So he did. Jack used the gold to buy himself an inn, since he knew most of the tricks of avoiding payment and could prevent them. In time he found another woman to his liking and married and had a family. He made mistakes enough, over the years, but unlike before they were mostly new ones. Which, Jack decided, was about as much wisdom as he could hope for.

As the years went by, Jack found his memory of the glorious Fairie Queen starting to fade. It was Lady Devoted's face that remained with him, hers that he remembered best. If there was any meaning to that beyond a trick of memory he never knew, but to Jack's everlasting relief and regret the Lady Devoted remained true to the only promise she ever made to him—he never saw her again.

Doppels

Kent's first thought was *They can't be serious*, but he knew he was wrong. One look showed that each and every one of them, from the nameless studio lawyers in their pinstriped Armanis to John Taylor, the studio exec in his carefully feigned 'casual/creative' look, was as serious as a tiger with a toothache. Even the immaculately tailored Liz Taglia, his own alleged agent, wasn't smiling.

"It's in your contract, Kent," Liz said. "It's in all the contracts now. The studio is simply exercising its option under section 12, paragraph 2."

Kent Doolan, daytime holo star and talk show personality, was being doppeled. Duplicated. Worst of all, he had to help the studio do it. The contract said so.

"Kent, you gotta understand the studio's position," John said. He'd turned his infamous smile back on to full power.

"I do? Well, I don't. Not a bit," Kent said. "Is the studio unhappy with my work? Wouldn't it be cheaper just to ask me to make any changes, rather than programming a machine?"

"It's not a machine, Kent. It's a genetic reconstruction of you. And we're not unhappy," John said. "That's the whole point."

Kent gave Liz his best soulful gaze. Liz shook her head. "I can see I didn't do a good job of explaining this, Kent. It's precisely because the studio values your work that it's invoking paragraph 2. They want to protect their investment."

"How do you know the—whatever it is, will be able to act? There's more to it than face and mannerisms."

John's smile never wavered. "Don't worry about that, Kent. Besides, this is to your benefit—the licensing bonuses will make your contract even more lucrative, plus you get a 10% gross royalty on the studio's use of your image and mannerisms in perpetuity. I would think you'd want the studio to be able to exploit those rights for a long, long time."

Liz made a shushing noise, but the damage was done.

"You think I'm too old!" Kent said. He didn't need the awkward silence that followed to know he'd nailed that particular Dorian portrait squarely to the attic wall.

Liz was all calm reason. "Kent, you know I'm on your side, but this is simple reality. You're a leading man," she said. "You're also forty-five as of last Wednesday. Even if you can or want to make the transition to character roles, that's not where your value to the studio lies. This way you and the studio are both protected, plus you can solve your immediate financial difficulties and retire a wealthy man, whenever you're ready."

"You mean as soon as my doppel is ready," Kent said. "Or do I get a year or two yet, just to make sure all the juice is wrung out of the old prune?"

Liz sighed. "You always sulk when I tell you the truth, Kent, but it always turns out for the best. This will too."

"It starts now?" Kent asked. He looked at the doppel, sitting in its chair across the room. Don Mattson, the studio's boy wonder technical expert, stood beside it furiously scribbling notes, but the doppel didn't look at him. Its eyes hadn't left Kent since he entered the room. Kent had the sinking feeling that the process had already begun. The doppel's silvery skin shimmered and rippled like a pool of mercury as its skin color slowly changed and its biomass rearranged itself.

From what Kent understood of the process, the nanomech engines had completed the inner systems and were now beginning their work within the outer layer of its body, starting to match skin tone and general build, using Kent's own DNA as their blueprint. Not a clone—nothing so crude as that— but rather a made from scratch genetic reconstruction of all that Kent Doolan was, minus a few flaws and plus a few enhancements. Kent Doolan Mark II. New. Improved. The technique was very new, and to call it expensive was to understate the facts by an order of magnitude. Kent would have been flattered, if he hadn't felt so...violated.

Damn.

The thing was already sitting like him, both feet planted squarely on the floor, body leaning slightly forward. It was slowly rubbing its thighs with the palms of its hands as if it were sweating, and Kent suddenly realized he'd been doing the same. He stopped. It stopped.

"It starts now," John confirmed. "You don't have to do anything, other than just be you. It'll do the rest."

•

So John lied. Just a little, of course. Kent would have really wondered if things had, for once, turned out exactly the way the studio had promised. The Doppel's imitation turned out a little too slavish when it tried to enter the vehicle on the same side as Kent when he caught a floater cab downtown. Kent finally got it shooed into the opposite door, then he sat back, trying not to think about what had just happened in John's office. That proved impossible when he saw the doppel slide onto the seat beside him, study him for a moment, then lean back in exactly the same way.

It felt strange having someone sitting with him now, even a doppel. It hadn't been easy, even after he gave up his private car, but Kent had managed to lose his entourage over the last several months. The reason for that wasn't anything he could put into words; just the sight of so many people around him had become unpleasant. It was good to be alone now and then.

No one spoke the entire trip. The floater pilot, a burly Turk, finally broke the silence when they arrived downtown and he was returning Kent's money chip. "Doppel, huh? They're talking about replacing all transport operators with those things, but the Union's stopped it so far."

Kent grimaced in sympathy as he tucked the chip away. "Your union must be better than mine."

The floater pulled away from the curb and Kent checked his watch; only ten minutes late. He walked into the restaurant with his doppel close behind. Somehow he'd expected the pair of them to attract more attention, but the few glances sent his way seemed no more than what he usually got upon being recognized. Polite interest from the other patrons, a slight rise in the buzz of conversation, but little more than that in a town packed to the fashionable rent controlled lofts with stars brighter in the firmament than Kent.

Kent didn't know whether to be relieved or annoyed. He still felt almost as if he or at least parts of him, his looks, his mannerisms were being kidnaped, and no one offered to help, or even noticed. Kent's entire career and life was based on public perception. Seeing the reaction, he had to wonder if his concerns were as important as he'd thought. He nodded to the pretty blonde hostess. "I'm meeting someone." He walked past the foyer and then spotted Cassie sitting alone at a table on the patio section.

The noon sun was muted through a polarized glass ceiling but was still fairly bright, and in that sunlight Cassie practically glowed. There were hints of red in her dark hair; her dress was something very white and summery. She looked even more gorgeous than he remembered, though Kent didn't believe it possible. How long had it been? Six months? Longer? It was very good to see her again, better even than he had expected.

Kent smiled and reached for her hand. "Sorry I'm late, Cassie. I got stuck in a meeting."

The hand was not extended. There was a frown on her face. "Do I know you?" she asked.

For a moment he thought she was punishing him for his tardiness, but he quickly discarded the notion. Whatever else Cassie was, she wasn't an actress. A world class model, yes, with a smile to turn any hetero male weak at the knees, but not an actress. Kent was certain that Cassie was not pretending; she honestly did not recognize him.

"Kent," he finally managed. "I'm Kent."

"You're also late."

He turned. Cassie was standing behind him, smiling a bit hesitantly. She was not nearly so radiant as the Cassie sitting at the restaurant table, nor was she wearing the white summer dress. This Cassie was dressed much more casually in a pair of blue sweat pants and tee shirt; she wore her hair in a long braid that fell halfway down her back.

"Glad you could make it. How's Melody these days? Or have you changed dance partners again?"

Kent barely reacted to the dig. "She's fine...uh, Cassie? Then who is that?"

She smiled at him. Damn, he remembered that smile. "Kent, I'd like you to meet Cassie II. She's my doppel." Cassie slid into the seat beside Cassie II. "Sit."

Kent sat down. His own doppel took the chair beside him without invitation or prompting; it was learning quickly.

Cassie glanced at Kent's companion. "He's new."

"I just got him today." Kent kept looking at Cassie II, who regarded him with polite disinterest. "You're being replaced? I thought you'd already retired," he said finally.

Cassie signaled to a waiter and ordered a white wine. Kent mumbled "Scotch" almost from habit. "Scotch," repeated Kent's doppel. The voice wasn't near right yet, but the construct's tense posture was dead on. Kent tried to ignore it.

"I did," she said. "Nearly a year ago. Not that the Agency would have bothered with a doppel. Sweet young things come in by the busload every day, and face/mannerism recognition still isn't quite as important in my work as yours. It's a miracle I lasted as long as I did."

"Then who's replacing you?"

She looked solemn. "I am."

There was a long silence, broken only by the waiter returning with their drinks and menus. He placed a scotch in front of Kent's doppel. Kent almost told him to take it back, but there was something about young, good looking waiters that reminded him too much of himself at a certain time of his life; they made him uncomfortable. He also thought about the obstruction clause in his contract and decided to just let the matter go.

Kent took a sip of his scotch and the doppel mimicked him, motion for motion, but a bit awkwardly. It spilled several drops on the glass top table. Kent watched in fascination as the amber drops in turn broke down into smaller and smaller drops and flowed away toward a small port in the middle of the table near the rose center piece. In a moment the table was spotless.

Cassie frowned. "Where have you been for the last two years? Most commercial food surfaces are nano-enabled these days."

"Strange. I never noticed."

She smiled again, a little wistfully. "You always had a knack for not noticing anything until it was a personal inconvenience. You just don't change, Kent."

Kent took a deep drink, almost emptying the tumbler. He nodded toward his silent companion. "If that were so..." He sighed. "Why did you get a doppel, Cassie? If it had been the Agency, that would at least make sense."

Cassie put an arm around her doppel, gazing at it with affection. "Here you are asking about me rather than why I wanted to see you after all this time. I'm surprised."

Arguing with Cassie was something Kent understood; it was easy and familiar. "Let's take the conversation back to me, if that makes you feel better: you haven't answered my question. Was it a pre emptive strike against the modeling agency?"

Cassie laughed. "You idiot. Modeling was just something I did, Kent. I knew my career wouldn't last forever and never wanted it to. I hired a good broker and an even better accountant. I was prepared."

Unlike some people. Cassie didn't say it. Kent heard it anyway. "Why, then?"

"I'm dying, Kent."

Kent started to say something, anything, but nothing would come out. He just stared at her. She shrugged. "It's an artificial virus. The Agency's idea; not mine. It was supposed to repair the skin surface, give me a few more years to work. Blame my vanity that I went along, but somebody at Lifetech Ink screwed up big time. The virus migrated into deep tissue and it's fixing things that don't need fixing. In a month or two they might have something to stop it, but that probably won't do me any good." She toyed with her drink. "Lifetech and the Agency settled well and quickly to avoid the bad press. I used the money for Cassie II."

Kent looked at Cassie II, perfect and serene and heart breakingly gorgeous. "Was this Koji's idea?" he asked. "Remind me to punch him out next time we meet."

She glared at him. "Oh, you are about the biggest fool that ever walked the earth! If I'd known that when I married you..." She stopped, and the smile came back. "I probably would have done it anyway."

"Cassie, I really would like to understand."

"Since when?" Cassie glared at him, but she was too weary to keep the hostility up for long. "Sorry. Koji doesn't know about Cassie II or the virus. He's been on an extended business trip for over six months. He keeps asking me to join him and I've stalled so much he's starting to worry. I'll make it up to him." Cassie hugged the doppel's shoulders again. "Or rather she will."

Kent just stared for a moment, and when he spoke again he was a little surprised at what came out. "Cassie, you can't do that. You have to tell him!"

Cassie grinned fiercely. "Like hell. Kent, you have no idea what kind of shape I was in when we finally split. I was a mess." She held up a hand when Kent started to protest. "This isn't about blame, you twirk! Let me finish. When I met Koji-san I was suicidal. He saved my life literally. I owe him everything, and that's exactly what I'm going to give him even if it takes more time than I have. Cassie II will take over for me and Koji will never know the difference."

"When he's seventy and Cassie II still looks twenty nine, he might get suspicious," Kent said dryly.

"Suspicious," repeated his doppel. The voice was still too high, and a bit slurred, but it was getting better. Kent ignored it.

"That's all taken care of. Cassie II's outward adaptation was halted six weeks ago. Her nanomech's are programmed for very gradual deterioration. She'll outlive Koji, but she won't look much better or worse than she's supposed to."

"Unless someone else screwed up big time," Kent said dryly. "That still doesn't explain why you wanted to see me."

She laughed. "I didn't. I wanted her to see you. Cassie II's almost finished but there are gaps in her education. You're going to fill them. After we're done, she takes the six o'clock hyper shuttle to Jakarta."

"Why didn't you tell me before?"

"Would you have come if I had?"

Kent thought about it a moment. "I don't know. What now?"

Cassie II signaled the waiter, and for that instant even Kent wasn't sure that this creation wasn't the girl he'd once loved. "We have lunch, of course," it said. "And we talk about old times."

•

It was late afternoon when Cassie was finished with him. He'd done all she'd asked: reminisced, answered questions, and talked about himself. Strangely, it was that last bit that made him the most self conscious. It was something he'd done thousands of times over the years in interviews; normally he enjoyed it. Not when he was with Cassie. For some reason, he just didn't feel that important then, or rather that there were things beside himself that mattered, and why weren't they getting the attention they deserved?

Kent walked outside, his doppel following. Cassies I and II were already gone, probably on their way to La Guardia. Kent thought of calling for a floater, but there was nowhere he particularly wanted to go. There was a cool edge to the breeze, something high and clean and only a little tainted with smoke and chemical stench. Kent turned up his collar and started walking.

There was a holo ad on 42nd Street; the actors walked and declaimed in a phantom set floating about thirty feet off the pavement. Kent started to walk past, but he heard a familiar voice.

That sounded like...me!

He glanced up again, and there he was involved in a tense romantic confrontation with a woman he had never, as far as he could tell, met. Kent glanced at the trailer: KENT DOOLAN AND MARY SOTHLING IN "THE SWEET BETRAYAL." COMING SOON!

"I never played that part," he said.

"Never," repeated the doppel. Its voice was getting a lot better. The time spent with Cassie had probably sped up his own replacement, but Kent hadn't minded that. He'd regretted only when it was over, and there was nothing more Cassie needed from him.

Kent looked long and hard at the holo ad, trying to remember something that, as far as he could tell, had never happened.

I don't understand this. But I know who might.

Kent flagged down a floater cab. He finally had somewhere he wanted to go.

•

"Of course it wasn't you. It was a digital animation of you."

Don Mattson was head graphics technician, plus several other things Kent was only now starting to realize. He was also a boyish young man probably not yet thirty. They weren't exactly friends—Kent couldn't think of anyone off hand who held that title—but their working relationship had been pleasant enough. Don's green eyes lit up with pride when he spoke about the holo ad.

"You worked on that?" Kent asked.

"Sure. I had to borrow Sothling's specs from our west coast office, but you were already in. I did the initial specs for your doppel, too."

"I don't understand this, Don. If the studio already has the actors digitized, what do they keep us? And why bother with doppels?"

Don smiled. "Mr. Doolan, pardon me for saying, but you sure don't know much about the history of your medium."

Kent was beginning to see that there were a great many things he didn't know much about. Not that it had really mattered before. "Enlighten me, then. Please? I just don't understand why they'd go to all the trouble."

The young man's eyes were shining. "That's the beauty part: it's no trouble at all. We have thousands of hours of digitape to draw from, and the interpolation software is very advanced. There are no logistics, no crew, no personalities to deal with. Direction alone is required. It was quite a fad in the late 20's. The studios brought back a lot of dead actors and actresses and made movies. Didn't last long."

"I remember those. Novel for a bit but I didn't miss them. Why did it stop?"

"You just said," Don replied, grinning. "No one missed them. It's the Cult of Personality, this business's One True Religion. The studios discovered that it wasn't enough to show a star on the screen. The public had to believe that there was a living, breathing person behind the person on the holo screen. One they could meet and get autographs from and fantasize about and have affairs with and gossip about. Take all that away, and the only thing left is a cartoon. People like cartoons, but they don't mistake them for life, as a rule. And life vicarious life is what the studios are really selling."

"Or at least their versions of it." Kent finally understood why John wasn't worried about the doppel's acting ability. With the digital version to use in the holos if need be, it just didn't matter.

Don sat back. "Does that answer your question?"

"Thoroughly. Thanks, Don. You do good work."

"So do you."

Kent sighed. *Too damn good.*

•

If anyone needs to fill the role of a haunted man, I'm sure as hell ready.

The days and weeks that followed were one continuous adjustment to his new shadow. For the first time in years, Kent felt self-conscious in front of the camera. It was difficult to work at first; after a while it was merely uncomfortable. He studied the holos the first few times, looking for signs that it was interfering with his performance, but he didn't notice any. It looked as if nothing that he felt as an individual showed up in the projections; everything came from the script and character. Kent knew he should have been relieved, but as he watched the doppel become less like a construct and more like a person with every passing day, that was not the way Kent felt.

Strange, but the only time Kent did feel relief was when the doppel actually went before the camera. It was only for brief stints at first, and with mixed but slowly improving results, but Kent felt a profound relief that he simply could not explain, relief that it was the doppel in front of the camera and not him. Given that his time on camera was all his life had been about, Kent found that more than a little odd.

Kent relaxed even more when the doppel showed its first signs of independence, striking out on its own around the studio and finally out onto the city streets. It felt good to be alone again. That good feeling ended the day he came home and found Melody and the doppel in bed together.

Melody Diega was the...fourth? fifth? in a line of temporary relationships he'd fallen into since Cassie left him, a lovely brunette half his age with dark skin and darker eyes. She seemed surprised when she saw him standing there in the doorway. Not shocked, not afraid, just...surprised. She glanced slowly from the doorway to the doppel lying beside her and then back again. She didn't bother to cover herself.

"It's you, isn't it?" she asked.

Kent almost laughed. "Are you really going to tell me that you didn't know what that was?" he asked.

She shook her head. "It's you," she repeated. "Down to the funny look you get on your face when...well, you know. Everything you are, he is. I wasn't sure before. Now I am."

Kent wanted to be furious, but he was too numb to feel anything. "Get out," he said.

"All right." Melody calmly slipped out of bed and began to pull on the clothes scattered on the floor. She put her purse over her shoulder and smiled at him. "Good bye, Kent." Then she glanced back at the doppel. "Later."

Kent searched for the perfect thing to say, but could only manage to repeat himself. "Get out."

He thought of making an unscheduled appointment with his therapist. In the end he'd called Cassie instead.

•

Cassie met him at the door to her apartment. She'd lost weight in the weeks since he'd seen her last. She looked tired. She was a little light on sympathy, too. She led him inside and sat him down in an overstuffed wing chair, then curled up on the sofa, her legs tucked beneath her in the way that Kent, flexible as a construction girder, still considered a marvel. His doppelganger stood just inside the door, watching and listening, as Kent told the story.

"What the hell did you expect?" Cassie said finally.

"I didn't expect my girlfriend to boff a robot!"

Cassie sighed. "It's not a robot, as you damn well know. Doppels will be considered people one day." Cassie looked thoughtful. "In fact, one day they may be all the people there are. I wonder what that will be like..."

Kent didn't want to think about that. He had enough on his shoulders. "Melody already considers this one a person. Or an autonomous sex toy. She said he was me. Of all the—"

"In a way, she's exactly right."

Kent stared for a moment. "He he just looks like me, and sounds like me. That's not the same thing!"

"The hell. Did you actually think that primo young thing loved you for your soul? No. She was after Kent Doolan, daytime holo star. She got him...well, everything that counted anyway. In our line of work what you show the world is what matters. You took that a step further your entire life has been about how you look, and how you sound. How you talk and how you move. Maybe once you were a person, Kent. Not now— you're a commodity."

"That's a crummy thing to say." Even if it is the truth, he finished silently.

"Yes, but I've got no particular reason to spare your feelings. Deal with it. Was that all you wanted to talk to me about?"

Kent sighed. "You're right. About everything. And I don't blame you for being impatient. I've got no claim on you now."

Cassie managed a tentative smile. "We shared a good part of a life, Kent. Even a divorce doesn't erase that."

He put his head in his hands. "This isn't about Melody, really. I just wanted to tell you something, Cassie. For a while...you know, after we split...well, I blamed you. I don't suppose that's a surprise?"

"I'm passing out from shock even as we speak. Can't you tell?" Cassie's mouth was a hard little line in her face.

Kent smiled. "Sarcasm. I remember that one."

Cassie shrugged. "We fight with the weapons we're given, Kent."

"What were you fighting for? I don't think I ever asked you."

She shrugged again. "You. Me. Us. It doesn't matter now."

He smiled sadly. "No, I suppose not. I started seeing a therapist after we broke up. I thought it was because I'd lost you, to deal with the pain, but I was fooling myself. I really did it to have someone to listen to me the way you did. To let me be the center of attention always. Maybe that was what I was looking for in Melody and the others. I got it too. For a while."

Cassie sighed. "I fell in love with the image too, Kent. The difference being I honestly thought there was something more in there that was you. Every now and then I seemed to get a glimpse of it, and every time I tried to get closer you blocked me. At first I thought it wasn't deliberate, that I could reach you, but now I think, deep down, you knew exactly what you were doing."

He nodded. "Maybe you're right. Maybe I believed that the image was all I needed to be, Cassie. That if you saw anything beyond that...well, maybe you wouldn't love that part so much. I was afraid, and I couldn't stop being afraid. Even when I knew you were going to leave. Even when I knew I was going to lose you... I just couldn't stop!"

Cassie was almost in tears. "Why? Dammit, why now?"

He nodded toward his doppel. "It." He hesitated, then amended, "Him. When he's done he'll be as much "me" as I've been for the last several years. But will I? No. And if all I am is surface, then what's left when that belongs to him?" he nodded at the doppel. "Where does that leave me?"

"That's up to you. You could try building a life," Cassie said. "That's what I'd do if I had the time. But if I had the time I'd have kept the life I had."

"Interesting notion. Making a life. How does one do that?"

"You'll have plenty of time—figure it out. I have my own problems, thanks for asking."

Kent sighed. "Old habits, Cassie, but then I always did take from you. I am sorry. For everything. I just wanted you to know."

"For your conscience's sake?" Cassie asked, oddly intent.

Kent shrugged, and then he smiled. "Maybe. I haven't had one long enough to know," he said.

Cassie smiled too, but she didn't look at him. "Thank you," she said finally, and that was all she said. Kent waited a moment or two, then let himself and the doppel out.

•

"We've been very pleased with your progress, I must say."

John smiled from behind his desk while three of the studio techs, including Don, checked out the doppel.

"Thank you, sir," the doppel said.

Kent, sitting against the wall beside Liz, leaned over to whisper in her ear. "I suppose that obedience chip was John's idea?"

"Standard component of the neural net," Liz said, a little too shortly. She had been in a mood since the start of the meeting; Kent had a pretty good idea as to why. Liz might be misguided but she was no fool she knew something was up.

Everything will be clear soon enough, Liz.

Kent knew her complicity in all this was shortsighted in the extreme, but he wasn't angry with her now. That was past. "How long until he's ready?" Kent asked aloud. Liz shot him a glance but said nothing.

Don Mattson glanced at John, who shrugged. "About two weeks," Don said. "A month to be safe."

Kent nodded. "In six weeks I'd like to invoke my retirement clause, John, but of course I'll need your permission. Is that a problem?" Kent tried not to smile at the relief he saw on John's face before the executive mask reasserted itself.

"Kent, you still have a few good years left," he said.

Kent nodded agreement. "I know. That's why I'm leaving now."

Liz started to rise out of her chair. "Kent, I really feel we need to discuss this—"

"Sit down, Liz. You're here to iron out the final details, and that's all. The discussion was over the day I signed my last contract. For your own sake, try to remember that the next time you're negotiating someone's life," Kent said. He turned back to John. "Well?"

The infamous smile was now one of pure regret. "We'll respect your wishes of course," John said.

"Thanks. Keep a lunch date free for me a month from now. Till then..." He got up and headed for the door. "Come along, Kent."

After a bare fraction of hesitation, the doppel followed.

•

Kent was used to the disinfectant smell now; he barely noticed it. The hospital room was dim, lit only by a faint glow from the dampening field Cassie's doctors were trying as a last resort. Probably useless. The flesh would try to heal itself with or without it, but in either case the nano virus was like a battering ram, striking the cell walls again and again till they had no choice but to give way.

Kent's new contact at Lifetech Ink had explained all that. Also that a specific antigen construct would probably be ready in a week or so. Probably a week or so too late, though neither Kent nor his contact had felt the need to say it out loud.

"You fight with the weapons you have." That's what Cassie said. Kent wondered what he had left to use, and hoped he would know it when he saw it. He leaned back in the plastiform chair, yawning.

Cassie moaned softly and then woke up. "Koji...no. Kent? Kent, is that you?" She sounded puzzled.

He went to the bedside. "Yes. How do you feel?"

Cassie tried to sit up, thought better of it. "Like hell; what'd you think? What time is it?"

"A little after midnight."

She groaned. "Almost didn't recognize you in that beard you look like crap. How long have you been here?"

"Two days. You've been asleep a lot."

"Two..? Get out, Kent. Better yet, give me the call button; I'll have that cute orderly with the muscles throw you out."

"Why?" he asked. "I've been quiet."

"I don't want you to see me like this!"

He smiled at her. "A little late for that. Besides, I thought it was Koji you didn't want to see you like this. Wasn't that the point?"

Cassie yawned. "Don't be jealous; you don't have the right."

Kent nodded. "I know. But I'm staying anyway."

Cassie glanced toward heaven. "Only Kent Doolan would try to upstage his own ex wife's death. You're such a bastard."

He nodded amiably. "Maybe, but I'm not Kent Doolan. Not anymore. He's the guy on the holo. The guy living in what used to be my apartment with what used to be my Melody Diega. The guy who inherited the mess I made of my life. And you want to know something? I'm grateful."

She frowned. "So you've lost your mind. That still doesn't explain the beard."

"I grew the beard so people wouldn't confuse me with that other guy; no one even recognizes me now. I just told the staff I was your husband."

"You're not. And that thing on your face looks like roadkill."

He shrugged. "True as always, but right now you're stuck with both." Kent leaned forward and took her hand. He had to ask the question, no matter how much he feared the answer. "Do you really want me to leave, Cassie? I mean...I will, if that's what you want."

Cassie's hands clenched into emaciated fists. "So ask her what she really wants, if you can find her. You're not Kent and I'm not Cassie," she said, sounding resigned. "Not now. Kent's on the Holo and Cassie is in Jakarta with Koji san. Probably parboiling his hormones even as we speak, the slut." She grinned weakly. "Ok, so that was my idea. Doesn't mean I have to like it."

"Koji has your gratitude. He has Cassie II. Fine, he's welcome to both. I want you. Call yourself whatever you want, I don't care."

Cassie barely managed to smile. "You can be the sweetest thing when you try. Made it that much harder to leave you."

Kent pulled his chair closer to the bed and sat back down. "I still think you should have told him, Cassie. He's bound to find out the truth sooner or later, and maybe he won't like the fact that he never had the chance to be where I am right now."

She shook her head in exasperation. "Kent, when you develop a conscience you don't kid around. Damned inconvenient " She winced through a new wave of pain. After a few moments she managed to smile again. "Maybe you're right, but I won't have to deal with it either way. My choice. My turn to be selfish, Kent. I'm damn well due."

"Yes," he said. "You are."

Cassie really looked at him then, for the first time since awakening. "All right, I admit it—I'm scared, Kent," she said at last. "Please don't go."

"No chance, no way, no how. Call me Paul, by the way. It was my middle name; I haven't used it since my college theater days. I'm trying it on for size."

She squeezed his hand. "Pleased to meet you, Paul. Finally."

Wrecks

Eli Mothersbaugh checked the readings again. The station manager didn't bother to conceal her impatience.

"Mr. Mothersbaugh, I'm falling behind schedule. Can you tell me what's wrong with this platform or not?"

Eli shut off the Sensic and put it away in its fake leather case. "Yes," he said, but chose not to elaborate just then. The manager for the South/Central maglev station had shown open hostility to his investigation from the first, and without any reason that Eli could see; he considered it his duty now to supply just a little bit of provocation.

"Well? Do you honestly believe the platform is haunted?"

Eli pulled out his hand held workstation, unfolded the thin film screen to its full extent and punched the scan button. "Yes and no," he said, concealing a hint of vicious glee.

The call from AmLev to the Bureau of BioRemnant Reconciliation had seemed routine enough: check out a platform on the South/Central maglev hub station. There were reports of unexplained events, suspicious accidents, the usual now that the departed body's residual biomechanical energy signature was partly understood and easily detected, the presence of ghosts, real, verifiable ghosts, could actually be called "usual." But what Eli had found was not usual, not in the least. He'd even go so far as to say it was rapidly approaching "unusual," which, for Eli's line of work, was saying something.

"What kind of answer is that?" demanded the station manager. A slim, fortyish woman with graying black hair and hard dark eyes, she hadn't even bothered to introduce herself, but had herded Eli out to Platform Seven immediately on his arrival.

For someone so anxious to start the investigation you'd think she'd be more supportive.

That had not been the case. She made it clear that she thought little of Eli's methods and less of him. Eli tried to imagine her frustration as an excuse for her behavior, but he saw the way her subordinates walked on invisible eggshells whenever they were in her presence, and guessed that the station manager's personality was more consistent than the present crisis might indicate. Either that or the problem had been going on longer than she'd cared to admit.

A reluctance to admit the truth wasn't unusual either. Dr. Nigel Flagard's discovery and studies of residual organic energies were still only a few decades old; the human attitudes towards ghosts believer and non had been around for millennia. The fact that ghosts were demonstrably, repeatably under controlled conditions real didn't change as many minds as you'd think.

"It's the correct answer, of course," he said. "Ms.? I do wish you'd tell me your name; it's like talking to a holo."

Was that an actual hint of a blush? It was over so quickly Eli wasn't sure. "Cartwright," she said. "Amanda Cartwright. I'm sorry, Mr. Mothersbaugh, but the passengers have been complaining. I need an answer I can use."

Eli conceded the point. "So do I, Ms. Cartwright. Towards that end, I need to see what happens when the train leaves." Eli still wasn't sure about the blush, but there was no question that Amanda Cartwright's face was now a shade paler than it had been a moment before.

"All right," she said. "I'll clear the 3PM for departure. She spoke into a lapel mike as Eli glanced at the time window on his workstation. It was 3:23 already. He glanced about the station, taking note now of the living passengers milling about, glancing at timepieces, muttering. He began to get a better idea of what Amanda Cartwright was up against. In a moment the announcement came over the intercom and the passengers mostly commuters from the Memphis/New Orleans corridor, he gathered—moved forward with the symmetry of a school of three-piece fish and headed toward the opening doors on the maglev.

Eli turned his attention to his workstation screen. The mini Sensic built into it was feeding data which hundreds of genetic algorithm generators grabbed raw and sent on refined, filling the screen with a two dimensional interpretation of the energy signatures on the platform The passengers were strongest of course. Too strong. Each one glowed on the screen like a walking sun.

Eli knew he wouldn't be able to sort out what he wanted from the background noise. He waited, taking a moment to admire the sleek lines of the maglev train. It looked like a white bullet with windows, and had a top speed in excess of five hundred mph. How far in excess wasn't commonly known, though rumor was the thing could break the sound barrier at sea level. It wasn't done, which Eli considered a good thing. Otherwise there wouldn't be an unbroken window between Memphis and New Orleans.

"It's happening," he heard Amanda Cartwright say. Eli looked up. The doors on the maglev had just closed with a pneumatic hiss and the train swayed briefly as the magnetic coils activated.

"Where?"

She pointed at the edge of the platform. It wasn't much, really. A piece of a discarded memo floated into the air and then fell to the side as if caught in a sudden breeze. Eli turned the scan port in that direction. There was still a great deal of interference from around the train; the magnetic field there was enormous. Eli adjusted the scaling a bit and finally saw what he was looking for. He thumbed VOC and said "Record," then looked up from the screen. There would be plenty of time for analysis later.

Papers were flying all around the train, as if every bit of trash in the entire station had been gathered and thrown at the train. Eli thought about commenting on the station's housekeeping level, but one glance at the station manager and he thought better of it. Passengers were looking through the windows and pointing at the tornado of trash surrounding them; then the train started forward as alternating coils activated in turn, developing the magnetic rhythm that moved the train forward. It slid slowly out of the station, picking up speed as it went. The access doors irised open and the maglev exited the station. It was nearly a quarter of a mile down the rails by the time the doors closed again. After a moment the paper cyclone subsided.

"Does that happen every time?"

"Except when it's worse," she said, glumly. "I've been deliberately delaying boarding. If I don't it starts up before everyone's off the train and the platform is full. Sometimes it's not just paper that gets thrown an older gentleman was hit with a trashcan yesterday and badly shaken up. That's when I called you people. I can't keep up the delays any longer and I can't risk my passengers' safety."

"Ms. Cartwright, forgive me for asking, but why did you wait so long to report this?"

"Because," she said, "I don't believe in ghosts."

•

Eli was having coffee with someone he'd never met before. At least, that's how it felt. Oh, she looked like Amanda Cartwright, sounded like her or how he had imagined she might sound, without the anger in her voice. She didn't much act like her. Right now, as they sat together in the station cafe, she seemed close to human. A tired human near the end of her rope, but maybe that was what Eli saw now that he didn't see before.

Eli started on his second cup. "Ghosts are against your religion?"

She nodded, looking just a little defensive. "We were taught that souls lie in the grave until the Resurrection. If I stop believing that..."

Eli shrugged. "Still, so what if this one bit of dogma is wrong? A few details at most. Does that change the underlying truth of your beliefs? I wouldn't think so."

She smiled then. It was the first time he'd seen her smile since they met. Eli rather liked it. "I can see this has come up before," she said.

Eli nodded. "I've met clients with religious proscriptions against 'intercourse with spirits' or some such before, yes. It's not the first time 'facts' and 'truths' have been in seeming opposition."

She paused, holding her cup halfway between the table and her lips. "Seeming?"

"Facts are the realities of the world as best we understand them. Truth is how you interpret the same world according to your own unique understanding. They're not the same thing."

She sipped her coffee. "This isn't Looking Glass Land, and I'm not the Red Queen, Mr. Mothersbaugh. I can't believe in six impossible things before breakfast. My faith does not allow ghosts. Evil spirits, perhaps. Demons, certainly, though they seem rather redundant considering how well we torture one another these days. But Ghosts? No. Not unless everything I believe is wrong."

"There are ghosts, whether you believe in them or not. They are a fact."

"So you say," she said.

Eli didn't press the matter. There didn't seem to be any need, and much potential harm. The last thing he needed was Amanda Cartwright any more uncooperative than she had been already. Neither one spoke for a long time. The silence wasn't nearly as awkward as Eli thought it should be. She wasn't convinced, clearly, and it seemed important to her that she not be convinced. He knew there was more to than she was saying, but he didn't know how important that was to the work at hand. He found himself wondering anyway.

"What happens now?" she asked finally.

"I have to make contact with the ghost...or whatever it is."

She smiled again, accepting the gift of his qualifier for the conciliatory gesture it was. "All right. Besides staying out of the way, what do you need from me?"

•

Amanda met Eli later that evening in the station platform after the last scheduled run. The maglev train sat in its maintenance cradle, its huge electromagnets powered down and silent.

When Eli explained what he had in mind Amanda sighed gustily. "I'd rather you just asked me to stay out of the way, Mr. Mothersbaugh."

Eli, thinking of the hunted look in Amanda's eyes when he'd first explained his plan, regretted the matter a bit as well. Yet there always came a point in any investigation where Eli's instrumentation could do no more and the rest was up to instinct and intuition, and every instinct he possessed told him that Amanda might be needed.

"Please, call me Eli. You know more about this station and its history than anyone." Eli held up the headset, twin of his own.

"All right, Eli tell me how this works," she said. Her voice was very quiet and even. Eli could see that she was afraid, though he was pretty sure it wasn't the clumsy looking instrument that worried her.

"Despite the energy spikes that sometimes appear, most revenants don't have a very big energy field; my workstation has a modified scanning sensor with a three-eighty degree field and special software to enhance whatever it finds into a three dimensional portrait. IR ports in the workstation accept positional data from the visors."

"You mean, if we wear these we'll be able to see it?"

"That's the idea," Eli said, pausing to help her adjust the eyepieces. "We could already talk to it, but it helps to be in close proximity, and to address it as you would another person, including proper facial expression and eye contact, if possible. It helps the revenants remember that they're human, or were."

Amanda did not smile. "Assuming we can see it, whatever it is, how does this help?"

Eli shrugged. "Sometimes it doesn't help at all," he admitted. "We won't know till we try."

Amanda looked dubious, but allowed Eli to continue his adjustments. When she was all set he dropped his own visor into place and punched in the activation code.

The artificial platform created by the workstation looked exactly like the real one, only not quite as good. There was a faint pixelation affect near boundary edges that was a little disconcerting at first, but Eli had gotten used to it. Amanda looked like an actress in an old fashioned movie that had been "colorized." There was a pastel appearance to her face and clothes; her colors were muted.

"You look like a cartoon," she said.

"So do you. How are you doing with the visor?"

"Not bad," she looked slowly around the platform. "I don't see your ghost." There was a hint of "I told you so" in her voice.

Eli didn't see the ghost either, nor did his instruments. There was nothing to indicate a revenant energy signature anywhere. He fired up the Sensic and its mirror image in the looking-glass artificial world gave back the confirming reading: nada.

What's different?

Eli considered. There were no or very few people on the platform now. There had been cases of revenants "borrowing" bio electric energy from living people in a vampiric manner, but Eli didn't think that was the case here. The ghost had clearly been angry about something, and the energy spike Eli had detected didn't coincide with a lessening of any other signature at the time. But if the spirit didn't need people to manifest, why wasn't it here now? A ghost, unlike the living, couldn't just wander off on a whim; it was confined to the area of manifestation as surely as if it had been chained there.

It has to be here. "The conditions are wrong," Eli said.

"Oh, please "

Eli shook his head. "I'm serious. This isn't a controlled experiment; some of the conditions are out of our hands. So, besides the fact that this platform isn't crawling with commuters, what's different now compared to earlier today?"

Amanda still looked skeptical, but after a moment she sighed. Another moment and a slight frown of concentration appeared. "Well...some of the lights have been switched off. Our power consumption is up "

Eli blinked. "Wait. Why would the power levels be greater now than earlier?"

"Because the systems batteries on the maglev are recharging. We don't actually put current into the rail until the train is ready to depart. There's a surge then as the train leaves the station, but we use more power overall during downtime."

"The magnets are off," Eli said. Then he smacked himself in the forehead, nearly dislodging his eyepieces in the process. "Of course. I'm an idiot."

"That may be, but what are you talking about?"

"Amanda, can we activate the maglev now? It's important." It was only a little later that he realized he'd called the station master by her given name, but she didn't seem to notice. Amanda seemed to catch a little of Eli's excitement, despite herself.

She nodded. "Give me a minute." She went to one of the access doors in front of the glassed in control booth and palmed it open. After a moment Eli heard a change in the electrical hum in the air; one tone seemed to diminish as a slightly different one appeared, stabilized, increased. As Amanda rejoined him on the platform the maglev train shuddered once and raised ever so slightly.

"I can't get full lift with it cradled like that; the electromagnets are only at thirty percent."

"Rate that in teslas for me."

She frowned. "About twenty thousand, give or take."

He nodded, grinning. "And the average household magnet is what? .01?"

"Yes, but I still don't see..."

"You will if you look." Eli pointed toward the train.

The Sensic data as interpreted by the visors showed the maglev train glowing with a pale blue aura representing its now substantial magnetic field. The fluctuations showed up as flashes of green, like patches of shallower water against a translucent blue sea. They flowed together as if compelled, at the same time the blue glow of the maglev seemed to push them away. The green reformed again and again, only to batter itself against the remorseless blue of the train's magnetic field. After a very short time the green glow gave up and moved away from the train. As it did it coalesced, reformed, until it was a lot less like the glow of an energy field, and much more like a man.

A very angry man. A trash can a few feet away from the manifesting spectre suddenly lifted off its base and flew end over end to crash against the platform wall thirty feet away.

Eli couldn't keep from smiling. "I have to admit you were right about one thing, Amanda: neither your train nor this platform is haunted. And that is precisely the problem."

Amanda didn't look at him. "Bastard," she said.

She was still looking at the spectre, given shape and form by the Sensic data, and for a moment he thought she was referring to it, but when she turned to face him he knew beyond a doubt that this wasn't the case at all. There was cold fury in her eyes and it was all for him.

"Of all the despicable stunts...."

"What are you talking about?"

Amanda's hands had balled into fists. Eli realized dully that Amanda wanted very much to strike him. "You knew," she said.

The ghost was on the move again. Small pieces of paper, cigarette butts, a discarded cup, all lifted and spiraled up before flying away, as if the ghost was the center of a small tornado. Eli noted that the tornado was heading straight for them; there was no time for discussion. He was forced to shut down the visor's datalink as he closed up his workstation to protect it. Eli didn't see the ghost now as it moved past, no, through him on its way to a spot near the entranceway where the paint was slightly discolored. He felt it. The air, for just that instant, turned suddenly cooler and denser, as if he'd just stepped under an air conditioning vent or into a cold fog. Another moment and it was gone. A glance told him that Amanda had felt it too. Then she turned away from him and marched out the door, dropping her visor on the floor by the door.

"Amanda, wait!"

She did not. Eli hurried, but by the time he got his own visor off and had taken care of his instruments, Amanda was gone.

●

The house was an older section of the city, but well kept. As Eli drove under the shadowing oak trees the next morning he almost felt as if he'd gone back in time to this place of stately Victorian homes and ancient trees, though it was only a half hour drive from the gleaming towers and mini rails of the city center. He found the address he was looking for and parked on the street.

Amanda met him at the door, before he could even touch the knocker. There were traces of anger left on her face, but they were poor, pitiful things compared to what he had seen there earlier. She looked like she'd been crying.

"I suppose my address was in that computer of yours, too?"

Eli smiled tentatively. "Actually, I called Directory Assistance when you didn't report for work this morning. May I come in?"

She stood a little to one side, and Eli figured that was all the invitation he was going to get. She followed him in.

"Have you come to apologize?" she asked. "Not that it matters."

"Gladly, if you'll tell me what it is I'm apologizing for."

She glared at him. Eli sensed her anger waiting just under the surface. He looked about, wondering if it would help to change the subject and least for a while and found that Amanda Cartwright's house was a shrine to trains. Memorabilia was all over the room, but a few pieces drew attention immediately: the lamp by the overpadded chair was made from an antique brakeman's light; there was a crossed-R warning sign mounted on the wall. Over the fireplace mantel was a large picture of a man in old fashioned Engineer's garb; Eli could see it was no mere decoration. It was a portrait, and there was something familiar about it.

Eli stared at it for several long moments, studying the height and build and the face of the man looking back at him from the canvas while the silence grew so thick he could feel it settling down on him like a blanket. After a moment or two it came to him where he had seen that face before, or rather, a poor shadow of it. In the Sensic.

"It's him, isn't it? This is our ghost."

"That's my grandfather, Matthew Daniel Cartwright. As you well know."

Eli finally understood. "You think I rigged the display as some kind of sick joke, don't you? That's why you're so angry."

She looked disgusted. "I wouldn't have thought it of you. I really wouldn't."

"You'd have been right," he said softly.

"Are you going to deny it?"

Eli sighed. "I like to consider myself a fairly talented man, Amanda I'm a decent woodworker and better than fair gardner, when I get the chance. But I'm a lousy actor, and a worse liar, and I'm telling you straight out: I didn't know."

She looked at him for several long moments, looking increasingly miserable. "I want to believe you." She paused then, and managed a tentative smile. "No, that's a lie. I don't want to believe you, since that would mean..." She didn't finish. Amanda sat down in the big wingchair, and for a moment Eli thought she would start crying again, but she didn't. "It couldn't be," she said. "It just couldn't."

•

Amanda put the kettle on, and Eli didn't protest, though he really wasn't in the mood for tea. Amanda seemed to need the distraction, the fiddling with cups and tea bags and paraphernalia. He remembered the way she drank coffee in the AmLev station's cafe the day before; drinking coffee was clearly just something she did out of habit, or for want of something better. Tea was different. Tea was a ritual.

"Your grandfather was a tea drinker, I bet."

She gave him another hard look, but it quickly softened. "You're good; I have to give you that. You know people. Part of your job, I guess. Yes, I learned it from him. He was from Yorkshire originally."

"He must have been very important to you."

"He was my life," she said simply. She didn't say anything for a moment, just watched the kettle fail to come to a boil. "I wanted to be just like him: an engineer.

By the time I was old enough the maglevs were coming on line and they're all automation and fuzzy logic control systems. So I did the next best thing...I don't know why I'm telling you this, but I don't know what else to do. I mean, I saw...what I saw. It looked like Papaw."

Eli nodded, but he didn't say anything. He waited for Amanda to tell the rest and, as the kettle finally began to come to a boil, she did. "My mother died right after I was born. After that my father wasn't good for much. He drank. Sometimes he hit me. He just disappeared one day when I was six, and I was glad. My grandfather raised me."

"Who was he?"

She glanced down the hallway, where the portrait was still visible from the kitchen. "He was the engineer on the last diesel passenger train to operate out of this station. The maglev still follows the same track path; the old rails were mostly torn up when the station was refitted, except for those in the roundhouse where the museum is now. Anyway, when I was eighteen Papaw was killed in an accident on the platform."

"Can you tell me what happened?"

She shrugged. "It was just a stupid accident. Papaw was in a hurry; he'd overslept. It was the last scheduled run of the diesel train and mostly empty. Just a mail run, really. It didn't matter, I thought. He felt differently. 'I've never missed a run in twenty seven years,' he said, 'and I'm not starting now.'"

Eli didn't say anything but he did make a mental note: Compulsive personality. The profile fit so far. He waited until Amanda continued.

"Anyway, he was starting up the steps to the engine cabin, when his assistant, not knowing he was coming, released the brake. Papaw lost his balance and fell just as the engine shifted. His leg was badly crushed in the coupling; he bled to death before anyone could do anything."

"I'm sorry," Eli said.

She shrugged. "It was years ago. At Papaw's church, at the funeral, the preacher said that Papaw wasn't gone forever. That as long as I kept faith, sooner or later I'd be with him. I'd gone to church with Papaw now and then, because he wanted me to; he attended when the schedule let him. I couldn't see that much use in church before then."

"And your mother and father had already left you," Eli said.

Amanda set the leaves to steeping. "No need to look so wise, Eli; I know all about 'the psychology of abandonment.' But yes, I'd already lost my mother and father. My mother I didn't know at all, but it was a safe bet dear old Dad wouldn't be waiting for me in Heaven. I figured I'd given up enough, that it was time to hold onto something, and I damn well did. I know where my grandfather is now. I take your word that you weren't trying to trick me. That means someone or something else is. I'm being tested, perhaps. I hear it happens. But whatever that thing on the station is, it's not my grandfather."

"I understand you were transferred to this assignment only recently. Within the last few months."

"This was my grandfather's old station. I'd been trying to get back here for years, and finally got the seniority to do it. So?"

"So why is it only now that these manifestations occur?"

"That's for you to answer," she snapped.

"Well then," Eli said. "We have a problem."

"I know that!"

Eli shook his head. "No, I don't think you do. You were right about me, Amanda. I'm a specialist, and I'm very good at what I do. Part of that is because I do understand people, at least a little. People that used to be and," he added pointedly, "People who are."

She poured the tea, not looking at him. "Your point is?"

"My point is that it's not your religion that keeps you from accepting that your grandfather is trying to haunt that train. It's you."

"That's nonsense!"

"Is it? Does a soul quiet in its grave awaiting resurrection really make any more sense than one trying to do what it always tried to do in life? Habits are very hard to break."

"My grandfather is safe. He's waiting " Amanda began, but Eli wouldn't let her finish.

"Your grandfather is in *Hell*, Amanda. He's still trying to keep his appointment with that damned train; that's what his eternity looks like. Without your help, that's where he stays. It's possible that, at some level, he knows that."

"No," she said, and that was all.

"You think I'm full of horseshine, but what if I'm not? Will you really take that chance?"

"This is a test," she said, calmly pouring the tea.

Eli nodded. "Yes, but not the one you think. You have to decide what's more important: your cold comfort or your grandfather's freedom."

She finally looked at him; her eyes were glistening but her voice was even and strong. "Assuming I believe a word of this and I don't what can I do? I don't know anything about ghosts."

Eli touched her hand then. It was a risk, and he knew it, but there was no time for hesitation now and his instincts were all he had to trust. Human to human, he made contact with Amanda and she did not pull away. "You know a great deal about this one," he said, "I'm asking you to help me help him."

Amanda broke the contact. "Drink your tea," she said.

•

Eli thought the faint shimmer that suddenly appeared beside him was the ghost at first, refuting all expectation of its habits. Then the image resolved itself like the image in a camera being focussed. Amanda stood beside him on the recreated station platform. The resolution wasn't ideal, but Eli could still see the scowl on her face.

"I'm not here because I believe you," she said. "I'm here because this is my station, and my responsibility to see that it's fixed."

He nodded. "And because you'd still like to prove me wrong," Eli said. He regretted saying it, but only a little.

She turned to look at him then. "Eli Mothersbaugh, you are the most insufferable know it all I've ever met."

"I'll have to take your word for that. Come on."

The maglev nestled in its cradle, recharging as it had the night before. Eli walked across the platform towards it and, after a hesitation, so did Amanda. The passenger entrance was open for access to the cleaning crew that was to come later. To the left was the hallway leading to the crew cabin in the forward compartment; the maglevs still had manual controls for emergencies but, according to Amanda, they had never been used.

Eli activated the Sensic and, after a short delay, the simulated display came up on the visual field of his visor. He studied the readings, well aware that Amanda was doing the same.

"It's not here," she said, relieved. "Whatever it is, your theory about the haunting and the way the magnetic fields interfere is wrong. Your infernal device doesn't say otherwise."

Eli shook his head. "That's because you're looking for a definable locus. There isn't one, but he's here; the energy field is diffusing across the entire train." He showed her the faint traces of residual energy as the Sensic plotted them against the axis of the simulated train, made her see what he was seeing.

"Damn," she said.

"I'm sorry, Amanda, but it all fits. I admit we really don't know how residual energy is dissipated since we're not sure how it remains coherent in the first place. But from what I'm seeing here it's clear that, left alone long enough, the current rate of diffusion in the station revenant would continue to the point of full dispersal. He'd be free. As it is, the magnetic field is reactivated and throws him out before that can happen, over and over. No wonder he's angry."

"What do we do?"

"We have to break the cycle somehow. Don't ask me how."

She smiled then, weakly. "Something you don't know, Eli. I'm astonished."

•

Amanda had brought an assistant this time. She gave him the signal through the window, remaining on the platform with Eli as the maglev suddenly lurched and shifted in its cradle, then rose just the slightest bit, like a cat stretching.

The ghost scattered to the four winds and then reformed almost immediately.

"Amanda, speak to him."

"No. Don't ask me that again!"

Eli didn't. There was no more time for argument, no more time for more persuasion. If the problem proved intractable, then that's the way he would have to report it. But it was his duty to do the best he could first. He left his equipment and exposed and approached the developing whirlwind.

"Matthew Cartwright, I want to speak to you "

Eli hadn't taken two steps before he knew he'd just made a very serious mistake. Before then the anger the spectre carried was pervasive but unfocussed. Now it was as if giving the spectre its name put a spark of intelligence into its energy and a direction for that anger, and it was all turned on him.

Eli felt the cold again but it was not like before. This was a numbing, cold, a blistering cold, so cold it burned him like fire. He couldn't move, couldn't cry out, and then the creature was on him, in him, smothering every part of him inside and out with pure cold rage. Eli felt his mind giving way beneath the shock, his personality and identify tearing like gauze in a high wind. The revenant's emotions raged through him, carrying something else, something that might have been thought with a little more coherence.

Fight it...

Eli tried, but he was carried away, helpless. What identity was left to him he turned this way and that in the mindstorm, trying to find something of the revenant's own identity to fight against, or to hold on to. There wasn't very much but images, memories, an occasionally word or two. He tried to sort them out but it was like trying to catch dust motes in a hurricane. He finally found something, but it wasn't a weapon. It was a cry for help.

"Little Bit..." he said, then everything began going black.

"Papaw!"

The storm eased. Eli blinked trying to clear his vision. The visor image wobbled and danced as if from radio interference; it was a moment before Eli could make sense of what he was seeing.

The revenant had moved away from him. It now stood halfway between himself and Amanda. She looked at it with a mixture of fear and astonishment. And, finally, recognition. "It is you, isn't it?" Eli thought he saw the image of Matthew

Daniel Cartwright nod, but he couldn't be sure.

Amanda spoke again. "This isn't the way," she said. "Let me show you."

Amanda walked slowly toward the back of the platform. She passed the maglev at a respectable distance and then worked her way behind it toward a small door in the far wall. The revenant followed. After his knees stopped shaking quite so badly, so did Eli.

They stepped out the door together into a starry night; a cool breeze touched the sweat on Eli's face and he shivered. It was getting near the range limit of Eli's workstation; the image of Matthew Cartwright flickered like a bad candle.

"This way," she said. She led them both across a small parking lot to a brick building with old fashioned steel rails intersecting into it as if it were the hub of a spider's web.

The Roundhouse, thought Eli dully. Something Amanda said earlier...turned it into a museum? The notion was fuzzy. He couldn't quite bring it into view. Amanda stepped forward, but the ghost held back.

"It may not be able to leave the platform area," Eli managed to say. "It's like a mental block, only worse."

Amanda held out her hand. "This way."

Eli watched as the image extended its hand to meet hers. Amanda shuddered slightly at the contact, but did not break it. She stepped backwards slowly and the ghost followed under one of the arched entrances to the old station Roundhouse. There, on polished rails, sat the engine for the last of the Amtrack trains. It was freshly painted and gleamed even in the poor light.

The ghost's hand parted from Amanda's as it walked forward, fading out as it went. The visor was useless now; Eli took his off. Amanda had already removed hers. Eli brought up the Sensic. "He's inside," he said. What happened next, happened quickly. Eli checked the readings twice. Whatever the substitute maglev had meant to Matthew Cartwright, this old diesel engine meant a great deal more.

"He's gone," Eli said.

Amanda nodded. "I know."

•

Amanda and Eli sat together at a table in the condo AmLev had set aside for Eli's use during the investigation, and they tried to decide if they liked each other. The jury was still out on that, but not on the tea. This time Eli did the brewing and Amanda was impressed.

Amanda savored the steaming tea. "Another thing you know about, I see."

"What made you change your mind?"

"About coming here?" she asked shyly.

"Well, that too. But mostly about the ghost."

"He called me 'Little Bit.' Right there on the platform."

Eli laughed. "That was me."

She shook her head. "No it wasn't. It was him. It was even his voice, calling me. Do you know what 'Little Bit' means?"

"No," replied Eli honestly.

"It was my nickname. My grandfather was the only one who ever called me that. When he was dying, they told me he called out for me. I guess I finally heard."

"Lucky for me. Thank you."

She shrugged then, and her smile made Eli wondert what he had not seen in her, until now. "Lucky for Papaw, too. And for me. I think my grandfather had been haunting me for a very long time."

The thought had occurred to Eli too, but this time he kept his mouth shut. He merely raised his cup, and after a moment Amanda followed. Together they drank a toast to freedom, and the memory of all ghosts now at rest.

The God of Children

The old bullet train was an hour out of Narita. Eli Mothersbaugh checked his portable sensic now and then, out of habit. Mostly he watched the scenery blur by and wished he'd brought more paperwork with him. It wasn't a good time to be in Japan; his caseload at home was getting out of hand as it was. Still, it's not as if he could turn his old friend down.

"Obaasan is haunted."

That was all Hiro Yamada said. It was all he had to say.

"Excuse me, please."

The words were halting but clear enough. Eli glanced up to find a very pretty young girl in her high school uniform standing beside his seat. A few rows down, two more girls in identical blue sailor-suit uniforms were giggling encouragement to their classmate.

"Hai. Nan deshou?" Eli allowed himself a slight smile at the girl's evident embarrassment, then slipped back into English. "I'm sorry. My Japanese is very rusty and I don't get to practice often."

It turned out the girl in turn wanted to practice her English with the gaijin, probably on a dare from her classmates. Eli suspected as much; similar thngs happened on his one previous trip to Japan years before. But then, at that age he'd expected such things to happen to him. Now it was more of a treat.

The girl glanced at the object on his lap. "Very cute computer," she said, looking somewhat pleased with herself.

"It's called a 'sensic,' actually," Eli said. "An instrument to find things."

"Things? What sort of things, Ojii-san?"

Ojii-san. Eli didn't need a dictionary for that one. It was a generic polite term meaning anything from "Grandfather" to "Old guy I met on the train." Eli sighed. Forty-three seemed ancient to sixteen. He remembered. "Spirits," Eli said to her. "Ghosts."

The girl's eyes got very big. For a moment he thought she was going to run back to her friends right then and there without another word. She managed to be more polite than that. "You must be very brave," she said, then retreated, whispering excitedly to her friends. Eli sighed. He didn't feel brave. Just old and tired and a long way from home. He started running diagnostics on the sensic again as the train patiently devoured the miles through Honshu.

•

Hiro Yamada met him at the station. Hiro had gained a little weight since the last photo and letter; he looked quite well and prosperous, though there was a dullness about his eyes that suggested he hadn't been sleeping well. The two men exchanged bows just to see who would crack first. That proved to be Eli. He stepped forward and grabbed his old friend in a bearhug.

"Wonderful to see you," Eli said, "whatever the reason."

Hiro managed a weak smile. "We won't talk of that right now, Eli-san. How was your trip?"

Eli told him about the girls on the train, and Yamada laughed. "Once we were as green in the vine as they are, and thought as they did. Now we are older; it's the way of things. So. Let's get you settled in. Tomoko's expecting us."

Eli had never met Yamada's housekeeper, but one thing was clear immediately when they reached his apartment: Tomoko Sowa did not look to "Madame Butterfly" for inspiration. A thirtyish woman, heavy-set, she eschewed kimono for jeans, blouse, and apron, smoked like a furnace, and made one fine t-bone steak. When supper was finished, she brought two cold beers into the room where Hiro and Eli sat by a low table and then left them there with dire threats of what would happen should any of that beer spill on the mats.

Eli watched her go. "So this is the infamous Tomoko. Quite a character," he said.

Hiro shrugged. "She takes care of me. Men are so helpless that way, or so they would have us believe. That is one tradition that does not change." He paused, seeming to consider. "Perhaps I should marry her."

"She wouldn't have you. Besides, since when do your tastes run to women?"

His friend smiled, slipping into the more familiar form of address now that they were alone. "Eli, duty and my interests are often at odds. It's nothing new."

Eli didn't know what to say to that, so he didn't say anything. Supper had been at a western-style table but now they were in the tatami room, with low tables, no chairs, and mats for cushions. Eli was having a little trouble with the kneeling on the floor tradition. He finally stretched out into a half-reclining position which worked fairly well. He took a sip of his beer, then nodded in grudging appreciation. "Good stuff. So. It's just us now. Tell me what's wrong with Obaasan."

Hiro smiled weakly. "That directness of addressing the issue...it took me years to unlearn that after I came home." He sighed. "She's fading, Eli, and not because of her age."

"What then? Have you seen something?"

"Iya. But Miss Tanaka says Obaasan goes to her apartments behind the Shrine at a certain time of day, prepares two cups of tea, opens her doors, and waits. Miss Tanaka says my grandmother is waiting for someone that no one else can see."

"I mean no offense, but she must be in her eighties by now. Have you ruled out dementia?"

Hiro smiled. "Do you remember my grandmother at all?"

Eli reddened just a bit. "I see your point."

"To answer what must come next: yes, she has seen a doctor on my insistence. And yes, purification of her rooms and wards against spirits have been posted at all corners of Yamada Shrine. Nothing has helped."

Hiro's family were the caretakers of one of the oldest and most revered shrines in the district. Eli didn't know a great deal about Shinto, but he did know that something was very wrong if Hiro's own grandmother and the shrine priests couldn't deal with the matter themselves. There was one more question, though.

"Forgive me for asking, but why me? Nakamura and Saito at Tokyo University were students of Dr. Nigel Flagard himself. They're two of the finest experts on bio-energy residues in the world!"

"True, but they are not friends. Moreover, they are Japanese."

Eli blinked. "I don't understand."

Hiro looked unhappy. "My grandmother is old and frail, but her mind is sharp as ever. She knows what you do now since she often asks about you. She will know why you have come, whatever story I tell her." He hesitated, then went on, "She is the product of a different generation, Eli. She would not forgive me if I shamed her by bringing in spirit hunters from our own country."

Eli nodded, understanding dawning. "Ah. I'm a gaijin. Outside the tribe. When I am gone, any tales of what happened go with me. I don't count."

"Well. . . .."

Hiro put his hand behind his head. Eli didn't need the ubiquitous gesture to know he had embarrassed his friend with the truth. He waved it away. "You were only thinking of Obaasan. I am not offended."

"I am grateful for that. Yes, there is truth in what you say, but don't discount yourself. My grandmother became quite fond of you, and that might make a difference now. That is my hope, at least."

"And mine too. She's a remarkable woman. I will do what I can."

•

The Yamada Shrine was located on what looked like an acre of parkland near the edge of the city proper. One turn past the first bright red torii spirit gate and, except for an occasional murmur of traffic, they could have been in another time. The shrine was on a hill of maples, pines, and mossy stones. They walked up a wide stone path flanked by maples, the leaves just beginning to turn for fall. A short flight of steps led up to a wider approach, this marked by another torii that framed the sweeping curved roofline of Yamada Shrine.

"Wow," was all Eli said at first. "What's. . . different?"

Hiro frowned. "We have changed very little since your last visit. . . when? Twenty years ago?"

"About. I remember how lovely the shrine is. But I don't—" Eli struggled to put his reaction into words. "I don't remember being so aware of it."

That sense of timelessness settled over Eli even stronger now. The building style was several hundred years old, though Hiro had told him the current shrine building itself only dated to just before World War II, and was one of the few structures to survive the Allied firebombing late in the war.

Eli groped for the words to express how he was feeling, couldn't quite reach them. The best he could do was a comparison. "I visited Chartres Cathedral in France about five years ago. It felt a lot like this."

Hiro looked at him. "Perhaps it is you who has changed. I would have thought reducing ghosts to a graph on a computer would have gone far to remove what sense of awe you might have had at the mysteries of the world."

Eli smiled at him. "Quite the opposite. The more I learn of spirits the more I am reminded of just how much I do not understand."

They came closer to the shrine, walking towards the side of the path rather than the middle, as Hiro directed. There was a reason for that, but Eli didn't ask just then. He was more interested in everything else around him: the trees, the hill, the stones, the shrine. It was only when they reached the last terrace before the shrine doors that Eli remembered his sensic. He paused for a moment to switch it on. As the flat panel screen warmed up, he made a test sweep of his immediate surroundings.

The path through the woods was full of ghosts.

Eli checked and rechecked the readings the sensic gave him, but there was no mistake. He changed the display from charting to mapping and individual figures resolved themselves on his screen, as if he was looking at the monitor of a miniature camera. Some figures were so hazy as to be almost invisible, even to the sensic's finely tuned sensors. Others became very distinct as they drew nearer, like a solemn young woman in a bright blue kimono, normal appearing in all respects save for a slash of red at her throat. For a moment it was like standing on a busy street; Eli instinctively stepped back from the path to avoid colliding with her.

"What do you see?" Hiro asked.

Eli said nothing, just showed him the screen.

Hiro sighed deeply. "This will make it difficult."

Eli stared at his friend for a moment. "You're not at all surprised about this, are you?"

"No, Eli. The Shrine is a source of comfort and stability in many people's lives, even in these modern times. Why wouldn't their unhappy spirits look to it now?"

They both paused to watch a pair of soldiers approach, their uniforms and faces alike burned almost beyond recognition. At the last moment Eli handed the sensic to Hiro and stepped directly into their path. They trudged through and past him, taking no notice at all.

Eli touched his chest, frowning. "This isn't right. I didn't feel them."

Now Hiro frowned. "I don't understand. What did you expect?"

"I'm physically sensitive to the bio-energy signatures that mark a ghost; have been since I was a kid, though at the time I didn't know what they were. To make matters worse, our house was haunted. If Flagard hadn't published when he did, my folks might have had me committed. In any case, I should have felt those two."

"Not necessarily so. Didn't you just say that the presence of the shrine was near overwhelming? You forget that this is a sacred place. A kami lives here. Not a ghost as you understand it, but a spirit nonetheless. Your device tells you ghosts are here, but wouldn't they get lost in the...how should I say, 'background noise?' Frankly I was afraid your device also would not be able to separate the two. Its sensitivity seems to exceed your own."

Eli nodded, though he couldn't help feeling a little annoyed. "That could be. I felt no individual spirits when I was here before, nor at Chartres, now that you mention it. I'd expect a few in a site that old. I didn't have my sensic with me then, though."

"Just so. It's the same principle," Hiro said.

"You know more about this subject than I realized, Hiro."

His friend chuckled. "I was in training to be a priest, up until and during the time we were at University. I still might be, one day. If Obaasan has her way."

Eli changed the subject. "Since the presence of ghosts as such doesn't trouble you, I'm assuming it doesn't trouble your grandmother either."

"Yes, I would think that is so."

"So we're clearly looking for one particular ghost, if indeed such is the source of her misfortune. Something must set that spirit apart, perhaps something we can recognize."

Hiro shrugged. "My understanding of these matters is limited to traditional concepts. We have legends of spirits of many kinds. Those of people who have died are called yuurei, and they are often bound to earth for the purpose of revenge. Yet I saw nothing in those wretched spirits on the path that spoke to me of anger, or malice at least not directed at the shrine. I still believe they come here for comfort."

"Perhaps, but if you're right about Obaasan there is at least one spirit that does not. Despite the fact that Obaasan waits for it at tea every day." Eli didn't speak for a moment. "Let's go see your grandmother," he said finally.

"All right."

Hiro turned to go and Eli shut down the sensic and started to follow when a flash of white in the shadowed woods caught his eye. Eli watched as a little girl made her way along a dirt path he hadn't noticed before, some distance to the east of the shrine. She was too far away for Eli to make out her face, but she was wearing a formal kimono of white, with sash and sandals to match. Her hair was bobbed short in a style Eli hadn't seen before. She carried another pair of plain straw sandals of the old-fashioned sort that were still common in tourist shops along the coast. Eli looked back into the woods but there was no one with her. She walked the trail slowly, looking very solemn. Then she came to a small stone figure along the trail and very carefully placed the sandals by the image.

"Eli? What are you looking at?"

"A little girl. She's making an offering of some kind. I'm sorry, but something about it struck me as odd."

"Where? I don't see her."

Eli glanced at his friend and pointed back at the trail. "There."

"There's no one there, Eli."

Hiro was right. The trail was there, and the small statue, but there was no little girl in white or any other color to be seen. Eli wondered for just a moment if he was breaking some unwritten rule before he left the marked road and set off toward the trail, with Hiro close behind him.

The statue by the path was real enough. It was about two feet high, a little bald man with long, almost comical-looking earlobes. The sandals that Eli had seen the girl carry hung from a string around his neck. Eli stared at it for several long moments. "What is this?"

"It's OJizou-sama," Hiro said. He sounded surprised. The ghosts had not rattled him. This little statue had.

"Who is he?"

Hiro looked thoughtful. "Jizou is an Enlightened Being, one who chose to stay behind to fulfill some worthy function in this world rather than pass into transcendence."

"That sounds more Buddhist than Shinto."

Hiro raised an eyebrow. "You've been studying, haven't you? Yes, it is Buddhist. The two work together in many ways, but I don't recall seeing this statue before."

"It's here now. So why would someone be offering sandals?"

"Jizou is a protective deity in general, but he's mainly known as 'The God of Children.' He guides and cares for the spirits of departed children in their journey in the River of Souls. The dry stream bed is hard there, and full of stones. Jizou wears out many shoes in his work, so offerings of sandals are traditional. Also toys, clothes, things to help the little ones."

Eli considered. "May I touch the offering?" Hiro nodded and Eli carefully prodded one sandal with his finger, confirming its reality. He turned it over, and found a small inscription circled in red.

"It's a maker's mark," Hiro said, looking over his shoulder. "The Hinao family has made sandals of this type for hundreds of years."

There was a faint sound behind them, almost like a whisper. When he turned around all Eli saw was the shrine proper and a few outbuildings behind it. One of them had a small porch and a sliding panel for a door. What he'd heard sounded a bit like a sliding door closing. Eli looked back down the path away from the shrine. As far as he could tell, it ended in trees and shadows. "Let's go see your grandmother," he repeated.

•

There was a ceremony in progress. Miss Tanaka, the shrine's elderly secretary, brought them through a side hall to Mrs. Yamada's rooms at the rear of the shrine. She reappeared only long enough to bring tea and then disappeared again. Eli still wasn't bending easily, but he was getting used to the mats. Hiro sat formally at the table, but he just stared at his tea, waiting.

Eli looked around.

It's as if I never left.

Eli had wondered how well he would remember this place, but it turned out he didn't need to remember it at all. The calligraphed scrolls, the single bonsai by an eastern window, the delicate paper screens, even the small squares of handmade yellow paper Obaasan always had close to hand on her table were all in place, everything almost exactly as it had been when he met Mrs. Yamada on his first and only visit right after college. Even then Eli had known that there were few places in Japan which still looked like this, unchanged in style and function for hundreds of years. He imagined there were fewer still, now.

"Eli, what are you doing?"

"Huh?"

Eli looked down. He'd picked up one of the small squares of paper without even thinking about it and began to fold it as Obaasan had taught him back then. He'd assumed he'd forgotten how, but apparently his fingers remembered. He set the paper crane down on the table in front of him. It wasn't very good, but then his origami never had been.

"You need more practice, Mr. Mothersbaugh."

Kumiko Yamada entered the room. To say she looked older than Eli remembered wouldn't have been true. Old was a binary condition to him then, you either were or weren't, and Kumiko Yamada was then and was now. Her face was lined and she looked frail and small in her blue silk robes; there was a weariness in her eyes that almost frightened Eli. That said, she certainly did not act frail. Her iron-grey hair had been pulled back and braided like a warrior preparing for battle, plus she had a sheer presence that made the air in her small apartment fairly crackle as if it were playing host to a coming storm.

If this lady ever becomes a ghost, you won't need a sensic to find her.

She served them more green tea; she expressed her pleasure at seeing Eli again. She asked about his health. She asked about his work at the Bureau. Talk was cordial and polite and nowhere near the point. After a while Mrs. Yamada seemed to remember something.

"Grandson, Tanaka-san was having a problem with the shrine's phone charges. Would you check with her on the matter?"

"Now?"

"Since you're here, now would seem appropriate."

Hiro excused himself and hurried out with no more argument. Eli shot a wistful glance at his retreating friend.

"Now then, Eli," Mrs. Yamada said in perfect English, "We can talk freely for a moment. I know why you have come. I appreciate my grandson's concern, but it is pointless."

Eli chose his words with caution. "But not, as you were careful not to say, 'groundless'?"

Mrs. Yamada sipped her tea. "It changes nothing."

"Would it change anything if I told you I've seen the ghost?"

"I know what you have seen."

"You know. . ? Ah. That was you I heard, wasn't it? Does the ghost come every day at that time?"

Mrs. Yamada didn't yield an inch. "You saw something you did not understand."

Eli persisted. "I understand some of it. The old style white kimono, for one. Hiro said it's the type sometimes used for funeral rites. For another, even a very quick little girl couldn't have vanished from the time I moved my head a bare ninety degrees. Can I prove any of this? No. My instrument wasn't reading. Yet I hardly think that matters. You are in some kind of difficulty. Why would you refuse help when offered? Yes, your grandson is concerned." Eli hesitated, then added, "as am I, Obaasan."

Mrs. Yamada's face was unreadable. "You are kind. And a clever young man, as I recall. Curious and quick to learn. I hope you are still, for there is something else you must learn now."

"What is that, Obaasan?"

"That I am an old woman, and not long for this world no matter what happens. How well I face my death is for me to choose. I will not say I am sorry you have come so far, for it was very good to see you once more. But believe me when I tell you there's nothing you can do."

Hiro returned shortly afterwards, and they finished their tea in a haze of polite chatter. Afterwards, Hiro gave Eli his promised tour of the shrine, and that, it appeared, was that.

Later, back at his apartment, Hiro was gloomily resigned as Eli told him what had happened. "The term 'stubborn' might have been invented for my grandmother, though it does not do her justice. I am truly sorry to have wasted your time."

Eli shook his head. "I'm not giving up just yet. There may be limits to what we can do, but that doesn't mean we can't do anything."

Hiro looked at him. "I'm listening."

"The fact that the apparition is a child may be significant. Your grandmother lost her family in the Second World War, didn't she? I need access to local records from that period. Can you help?"

"I'll try, but I understand there are very few. The firebombing at the end of that war destroyed almost everything; most date from the time of the Occupation and later."

"It'll have to do. Also, though this may sound presumptuous, do you have any family albums?"

Hiro blinked. "Pictures? Certainly, and you're welcome to see them. Yet I have to ask: why?"

Eli didn't have much more to go on than instinct. A ghost was a pallid, frail thing most of the time and no physical danger to anyone. There were exceptions but not many; Eli had a feeling that Mrs. Yamada knew that, yet she was terrified of this one. And the fact that Eli had been able to see it without his sensic made him wonder if, perhaps, her fear was more than justified.

"I don't know," Eli said, and he sighed. "I'm sorry; if I could explain it better I would."

"You have a suspicion," Hiro said.

Eli shrugged. "It's more of a question. I saw the ghost without the sensic and that's unusual. It makes me wonder what sort of ghost we're looking for."

•

The next morning Eli was back at the Shrine. Hiro had to report to work at the Ministry and Eli was a little relieved; one person fumbling in the dark seemed quite enough. He checked his watch. Almost time. There were a few visitors to the shrine this morning who were not ghosts; Eli got a few curious looks but that was all as he moved off the path to stand some distance behind Jizou, his sensic tuned and ready.

The little girl appeared at the foot of the path.

She emerged suddenly from the tree shadows and Eli almost jumped, startled despite himself. He quickly looked away from the girl as he checked his readings. An even quicker glance at the main path showed that no one else was taking any notice of them. He looked back at his instrument and the look lengthened into a stare.

That can't be right.

There was a whisper of sound behind him but he did not turn. He glanced from the sensic to the apparition then back again, almost hoping for a change in either of them, but there was none. After a moment Eli closed down his instruments and zipped the case. He just watched as the little girl came closer.

There was something in her hands today, too. Eli watched as she came closer, torn between his desire to see her better and his desire not to see her at all. He'd seen many ghosts in his work, but there was something very different about this one. It was all he could do to keep from stepping back and putting as much distance as he could between himself and the appearance of one little girl.

She's carrying a doll.

That was what the girl brought today. A little doll in a red and white polka-dotted kimono. She did not carry it as any ordinary little girl would, cradled in her arms or holding its hand. She carried it on the palms of both hands. An offering. She placed it at the base of Jizou and bowed. Then, for a moment, she looked up at the shrine. A feeling of black dread washed over Eli, so strong that it seemed to blot out the shrine's peaceful influence; for a moment the sun went dark as if blotted by clouds. In the distance the forest beyond the path seemed on fire and Eli coughed; the air was thick with smoke. In another instant both the vision and the fear began to ebb. The apparition turned back down the path. Eli thought about going after it, but that was useless. Even if there had been a reason, even if he'd thought there was something, anything, he could do, he could not take a step. He did finally find his voice.

"What do you think she will bring tomorrow, Obaasan?"

She answered from the building behind him, where he'd known she was since hearing the shoji screen slide open. "A toy, probably, to aid in his work. Before you came she brought a cap. OJizou-sama's bald head gets cold, you know."

"A very thoughtful and pious ghost. What happens when she has given all that is right and proper?"

"I think you know. Go home, Eli san," Mrs. Yamada said. Then, "Please."

Eli heard another whisper as the screen was carefully but firmly closed, but he didn't bother to look behind him. Instead he walked down the path the way the girl had gone. He did not see her, which was probably the only reason he was able to follow. Now it seemed a pleasant trail through the woods and nothing more.

The path shortly ended at a place where some of the stones on the hillside were blackened and cracked under their moss as if by intense heat. Beyond that was a drainage channel beside a busy downtown street. There was a small stone footbridge over the channel, but it was nearly blocked by undergrowth and clearly had not been used in some time. Eli looked out into the modern city for a moment, trying without much success to picture it as it might have looked in 1945. After a moment he made his way back to the shrine.

•

Later, in Hiro's apartment, Eli wondered if there was anyone he could call. There was no one at the Bureau he could think of. A bit frustrated, Eli still felt honor bound for his friend's sake not to contact either Saito or Nakamura. There had been a hint in one of Saito's last papers that might have been relevant had it, as Eli suspected, referred to a similar phenomenon. Now he couldn't find out; Eli's presence in Japan alone would raise questions he'd rather not answer.

Honor isn't always convenient.

He had made a stop at the Ministry office to keep an appointment Hiro made for him, but the archivist could offer little help. The records were even scantier than Hiro had believed. Now Eli contented himself with looking through the Yamada family albums.

Most of the photographs dated from the late nineteen nineties and before. Hiro hadn't been much for photography after college, and apparently Hiro and his grandmother were all the family remaining. The pictures of his friend as a young man were amusing enough, but Eli quickly put them aside in favor of the older albums.

The last thing he examined wasn't an album but a very old shoebox filled with curling photographs. There was writing on the backs of many of them, most of which he could not read.

"The period's right, at least."

He found photographs of soldiers in uniform, including one stern looking man seated stiffly in a plain wooden chair. A pretty woman in formal kimono kneeled beside the chair, and a smiling little girl stood at the soldier's knee. The child's hair style looked very familiar. Eli looked at the picture for a long time, then put it aside. Deeper into the box he dug, until finally he came to a slightly larger photo of the same little girl standing beside another girl who looked to be the same age, and then another of the first little girl by herself. He stared at this one even longer, though his doubts by then had long since fled.

When Hiro returned from work Eli didn't even wait for "good evening" as he held up the last picture he had found.

"Hiro, who is this child?" He waited impatiently, ready for whatever Hiro might have to tell him. Ready, that is, for anything except what Hiro did say.

"My grandmother, of course. As a child. Can you tell me what this is all about?"

Eli shook his head. "Not yet I can't. But I think my question has become a suspicion after all."

•

The next morning Eli went to the shrine early, even before Hiro left for work. He went to the shrine entrance and stopped at the basin, using the water to cleanse his hands and mouth as Hiro had shown him two days before. Then he went inside and asked to see Mrs. Yamada. While he waited he looked at the calligraphed scrolls and the delicate carvings on the supporting columns. As the time stretched into several minutes Eli wondered if she would refuse. She did not. She came out of her apartments herself.

"Eli-san, there is nothing more to discuss."

"Gomen nasai, but I believe you are mistaken, Obaasan."

She raised an eyebrow. "Oh?"

"I know who your ghost is."

She shook her head. "You cannot."

"I didn't say it was possible, Obaasan. I said it was true."

She looked at him for a moment. Eli was careful not to turn away from her gaze.

"Come with me," she said, and that was all. She led the way back into her apartment at the rear of the shrine where a low table was already set out for tea.

"Please sit," she said. Eli managed as best he could while the old woman slowly lowered herself to her knees and slid the screen aside. It took Eli several long moments looking out into the trees to realize where he was.

"Good morning, OJizou-sama," he said, when he finally noticed the statue.

The path still glistened from droplets of dew, caught in the morning light filtering through the trees. The table was set with two cups for tea, just as Miss Tanaka had said. It was only then that Mrs. Yamada brought another for Eli.

"This is where you wait for her every morning. I assume OJizou-sama was your idea."

"A delay, nothing more. I discovered I needed more time to get my affairs in order, but that's all done now. She will not come more than once more, I think."

"What was her name?"

Mrs. Yamada glared at him. "You said—"

Eli chose his words more carefully. "And I told you the truth I did and I do know who she is. That's not the same thing."

Mrs. Yamada drank her tea. "Kozue. She was a friend of mine. My best friend. I killed her, as you must know."

"Records are sketchy. I'd appreciate it if you could fill in the details."

"It doesn't matter now."

Eli raised his own cup. "If that were so, you wouldn't have agreed to see me." He paused, then pressed on. "I presume to think after all this time you want to tell someone. I also presume that someone might be me."

"Indeed? Why is that?"

"For the same reason your grandson sought my help in the first place," Eli said simply, without elaborating.

Hiro's grandmother smiled so that every wrinkle on her face stood in sharp relief. "You are a careful man, Eli san. Perhaps that is why I will tell you."

The ghost appeared at the foot of the path. Eli kept his nervousness out of his voice with difficulty. "I am listening."

"It was during the War. I was just a child, but I was not strong and I broke under the burden of lies, Eli-san."

"I don't understand." Eli sighed. He'd been saying that a lot.

"Simple: we were told we would not be bombed. We were. We were told that American cities were being bombed. They were not. We were told our fathers and husbands and brothers would bring home a glorious victory. Many did not come home at all. My brother did not. Now it was father's turn."

Eli started to say something about truth being the first casualty of war, but the platitude would not come. He kept silent. Obaasan watched the ghost getting closer; Eli could not tell which was the more patient.

"He was an old man, even when I was born; he was not able to fight! I was only five, but I knew the soldiers lied and the war was lost and my father would die just as my brother did and my mother and I would be alone."

"What happened to Kozue?" Eli regretted the question as soon as he'd spoken it, afraid he'd played his hand too far, but Mrs. Yamada didn't even blink.

"There was to be a ceremony at the barracks, with children of the soldier's families dressed in their best kimonos. We were to thank the soldiers and send them off to victory with flowers and song. I would not go. No matter what my father threatened or how my mother pleaded, I would not. When the time came, I hid. Kozue's mother was dead and her father was in the army; she was staying with my family. She went in my place."

"That's when the city was firebombed, wasn't it?"

She nodded. "It had happened before, but this was worse. Their main target was the barracks, and my mother was there. My father. Kozue. She was the only one I ever saw again. . . for a little while. She made it back to the shrine, somehow. She walked through the fire, burned as she was, burned horribly. Her face...She came up the path. She made a sound. Not crying. Not like anything I've heard before or since, and then she fell right where OJizou-sama is now, calling my name. I screamed and ran from her. As if she were the monster then that she is now. I did that to her. I made her."

Eli nodded. "I think you are right, Obaasan."

She smiled weakly. "Well then," she said, finishing her tea. "At least you don't presume to argue from false hope. It was my place to die with my family, not Kozue's. I have had a good, long life but it did not belong to me. Now I must give it up to its rightful owner; I won't hide from her any more."

Eli watched for a moment as the apparition lay down one final offering: a toy soldier standing proudly at attention. Then she smiled with entirely too many pointed teeth, bowed to OJizou sama, and walked right past him. They were out of time.

Eli put down his own empty cup. All offerings are made. It's now or never.

"You were never hiding from Kozue. Kozue is not the ghost."

Mrs. Yamada's surprise actually pulled her sight from the little demon advancing on her. "Masaka... What are you talking about??"

Eli reached into the pocket of his shirt and pulled out an old photograph. He reached over the table and held it up, so that the ghost and the photograph were, in perspective, almost exactly the same size. "Look at her, Obaasan. Look very carefully."

"K-Kozue...."

"You may have forgotten what you looked like then. Maybe you wanted to forget, but whoever wrote the names on the back of those pictures certainly knew who was in them. That is not Kozue on the path, Obaasan. That is you."

For a long moment she stared at him, as did the ghost on the path, as if, for that one thought and moment, they were of the same mind.

Mrs. Yamada broke the spell. "I am not long for this world but I am certainly not a ghost!"

Eli shrugged. "Perhaps not, but you created something like one. What is it called? A spirit, yet not a ghost. Not the *yuurei* that your grandson told me about. Something else, something created, transformed. A bit of your soul, all of your guilt. An idea given form and purpose. That purpose here being your own death."

"*Yokai*," Mrs. Yamada said, softly. "That's the word you're looking for. And not guilt, really. Shame. Even if no one else knew, I did."

"You blamed yourself, and you continued every day from then until now, and little by little, day by day you made this dreadful thing and you called it Kozue."

Mrs. Yamada looked into the small dark eyes of death, and she smiled. She looked almost proud. "Yes."

The pit of Eli's stomach grew cold; he could not believe what he was hearing. "You knew!?"

She looked at him. "Always. Why did you think otherwise? Yet you got beyond the surface of the matter, for all your blundering. I am impressed," she said.

Eli realized to his horror that Obaasan had been right all along—he had seen something he did not understand. Now he knew that all of his digging and cleverness, everything he had done and said was not going to change a damn thing. He was too late. He had been too late for a very long time.

Mrs. Yamada took pity on him and touched his hand, briefly. "Do not fret, Eli-san there was no other way. I could not take my own life in atonement. As I said, it wasn't mine to take."

"I'm a fool. I thought I could make a difference. Obaasan, I'm so sorry."

"No need to apologize. You acted as a friend. And you did make a difference. I am grateful."

Eli blinked; his vision was getting blurry. "How? For what?"

"Just because I knew what I was doing didn't mean I wasn't afraid of what was to come. Afraid and very much alone. Now, thanks to you, I am neither." She then spoke to the spirit on the path. "Just a little more, Kozue chan. Just a little more."

There was nothing else to do but wait. Knowing what was about to happen brought responsibility with it, and Eli did not intend to shirk the burden he'd made for himself. He sat there beside the old woman and waited with her for death to arrive at its own tiny pace.

Mrs. Yamada sighed. "I didn't tell my grandson to spare him this. I didn't tell you for much the same reason, Eli san. Yet now that you are here there is one small favor I must ask of you."

"Anything," Eli said, and meant it.

"Tell my grandson that I know why he would not marry, and I'm sorry I could not bring myself to tell him so before. Or to stop hounding him about it. He will understand. I think you do, too."

The apparition stood on the step. "Ikimashou ka?" it asked, in a small sweet voice very much like that of the child it was not. Obaasan took its small hand in hers.

"Yes, we shall go now, little one. Sorry to keep you waiting for so very long."

•

Eli stayed until the funeral rites were done. The day after that Hiro saw Eli off at the train station for his ride back to Narita and the flight home.

"Perhaps this comes too late, but the ghost is at rest now and will not return. What will you do now?"

Hiro shrugged. "I will take over management of the shrine, of course. As my grandmother wished. Perhaps I will marry and try to have a family before it's too late. She wished that, too. Let it not be said that Obaasan did not get her way in all things."

"She knew about you, Hiro. She was sorry she never told you, and made you pretend all these years. That was on her mind at the end."

Hiro looked surprised, but only a little. "There are always fewer secrets than one thinks. I'm sure Tomoko knows also, and yet she remains with me. Perhaps it must be her decision as well." Hiro bowed. "I am grateful for everything you have done."

"Since this wasn't a Bureau matter there will be no record. I'll destroy the sensic data. We need not speak of it again."

After Hiro left, Eli changed his ticket to a later train and walked alone back to Yamada Shrine. He couldn't say why it was important to come here to do as he had promised, but it was before the statue of OJizou-sama that he kept his word. First he erased all readings from the time index when he'd first arrived on the shrine's main path. Then he pulled out the printout of all his data on the creature called Kozue. It consisted of one long column of numbers.

All zeroes.

This he carefully folded into the best paper crane he had ever made and placed it as an offering at Jizou's feet. Eli had never thought of himself as a religious man. He still did not. Later he would wonder what had moved him to perform this rite, but for now he needed no justification other than, within the understanding of that one moment, a sense of what needed to be done.

Eli clapped twice as he had seen Hiro do. Then he put his hands together and said a silent prayer on behalf of one more small soul given at last into the care of the God of Children.

A Respectful Silence

Eli Mothersbaugh glanced at the case log scrolling by on the screen of his handheld. Three new ones so far this week alone, and there had already been a two-month backlog. Eli activated the voc recorder and made himself a note: "Either the Bureau hires more investigators next fiscal or I'm taking early retirement. There are only so many ghosts a man can hunt."

He wasn't sure if he meant it or not, but it felt good to say. Even so, there were some interesting cases waiting for him, and he still felt some of the old eagerness remaining despite it all. That didn't explain why he was driving through miles of scrubby desert to the middle of nowhere, for a case that had been added to his load by the Director just that morning. Highest priority, meaning "now."

Eli groaned. Doubtless some Congressman owed a constituent a favor. Eli pulled over for a moment and a huge cloud of dust rolled past his windows. He took the time to take a closer look at the travel map on his dashboard, comparing what the location indicator told him with the information on the last signpost. Two military jets roared high overhead, chasing each other through a pale blue sky like a pair of black dragonflies.

Only about three more miles.

Eli checked the time and the height of the sun over the nearby mountains. There were still about two hours of daylight left. He smiled.

Good.

Hunting ghosts was a task for the light of day. Eli hated working at night.

•

The file said Sayer's Field was abandoned, but that was a lame word compared to the stark reality. Eli got out and made one round of the cracked, weedy tarmac and rusting hangers, checking the calibration of his sensory integrator and compilation device not so affectionately known as sensic—when he came across the old man sweeping the concrete floor of an abandoned hangar. Maintaining an abandoned airfield, just as the file had said.

Well, at least that explains how this case got high priority.

Eli hadn't made the connection with the urgency and the name in his file until he saw the old man — Conrad Stallings. He tapped a few keys on the sensic to request a confirmation, but he didn't really need it. The profile was unmistakable.

"You're Senator Nathaniel Stallings' father, aren't you?"

The man nodded. "I don't suppose it would do any good to deny it. So. My son sent you, did he?"

Stallings leaned on his broom for a moment, studying Eli without expression as Eli in turn studied him. He was old, of course. There was a pinkness to his cheeks and a shine on his skin that suggested telomere therapy, and perhaps other treatments as well. Physically he looked about sixty. Just a little older than his son, and the resemblance was unmistakable.

Eli broke the silence. "Why would you think your son sent me?"

"There's no reason for anyone else to come here, except me, or because of me. My son thinks I'm crazy. Are you a doctor?"

"Of medicine? No. Do you need one?"

The old man smiled. His teeth were perfect, though probably not those he'd been born with. "Not at all. Yet Nate keeps sending me to them. He means well." The old man stuck out his hand. "Conrad Stallings, but of course you know that."

Eli accepted the handshake. "Eli Mothersbaugh. And you're right; I'm here because of Senator Stallings."

"Thought as much. You've come to take me home, then? I woulda guessed doctor first, really. You don't look like the muscle type."

"I'm not here to force you to do anything."

"Well, well. Then why are you here?"

"I'm looking for ghosts. Your son is apparently of the opinion that you are haunted."

Conrad stared at him, and drew back a bit. Eli nodded almost imperceptibly.

He's afraid, but not of me. What, then?

"How could Nate know...." he stopped himself, but Eli knew a trail when he saw one.

"How could Nate know what?" he asked.

Stallings didn't answer. After a moment he asked a question of his own. "How old were you when people found out ghosts were real? I mean, those who didn't already know."

Eli frowned. "Oh, about twelve, I think. Why do you ask?"

"Don't you think it's strange that it took so little time for everyone to accept such an astounding revelation?"

Eli wasn't sure where Stallings senior was going with this, but he knew his job would be a lot easier if the old man cooperated.

"Not really," Eli said. "Before Flagard published his first papers there were people who believed and people who did not. After he published, there were still those who did and those who did not. To most people, though, it wasn't something they gave much thought to. Once the proof was there, the reaction was more like 'Oh, that's interesting' and then they went on with their lives."

Stallings nodded. "Yes, I can see that. But there's a group you're leaving out. A small one, maybe, but it does exist."

"What group is that?"

"The ones who had gone their whole lives not knowing one way or another," he said, "yet really, really hoped that the stories were true."

•

Night was falling rapidly. A room of sorts had been arranged for him not too far away, but Eli wasn't ready to leave just yet. He stood on the cooling tarmac and made a calibration sweep of the buildings and surrounding desert, his sensic humming quietly to itself as it digested the readings. Eli had been briefed on how residual heat could interfere with the detection of bio-energy signatures, but this was the first time he'd gotten the chance to put that knowledge into practice.

Let's try it now.

Eli watched the ebb and flow as the desert heat registered on his screen almost like ripples of water. Then he applied the calibration to mask it. Another moment and the heat signatures disappeared.

Wow.

The desert was blooming right there on his screen. Life was everywhere. Not the faintness of a specter's bio energy reading, wan and pale as a fading memory, but bright, white hot life. Eli enjoyed the show for a moment or two, then applied another calibration, masking out the living readings in turn. So whatever was left had to be what he was looking for, except, right now, there was nothing left. Eli did a slow scan along the horizon, and the lengthening shadows where a mountain range rose to the west.

"See anything?"

Eli almost jumped. He hadn't seen or heard the old man approach. "N-not yet. I was just calibrating, mostly."

Stallings nodded. "What's that thing?"

"This?" Eli held it up. "It's called a sensic. It detects the bio-energy signatures that identify a ghost."

"You'd see...what? Numbers on a graph?"

Eli shrugged. "Data is data. You can look at it any way you want. In mapping mode, for instance, you can see them."

Stallings studied the shadows. "What do they look like?"

"Like they did when they were alive, mostly."

"It's a funny thing, isn't it? If this is life after death, if the spirit survives, why would it have to look like the mortal coil?"

Eli shrugged. "Then again, why not? If you see the same face in the mirror for seventy years, why wouldn't you expect to see that same face the next time? Even, perhaps, if you're dead?"

Stallings laughed. "Good point, I guess."

"Besides, we're not sure that what we're seeing is the 'spirit' or anything of the sort. We can detect it, quantify it, study it, but what is it? No one knows. I certainly don't."

"Ghosts, souls, gods... Down through the centuries the questions don't change much, do they?" Stallings said. "Wise folk disagree and the numbers keep a respectful silence. You have to make up your own mind."

Eli stopped looking at his instrument. He started to say something, he wasn't sure what, but the old man was already walking toward a beat up old pickup. "It gets chilly at night around here," he said. "I'd wait for morning to go any farther, if I were you."

Eli felt an edge on the breeze and decided to take Stallings' advice. Any ghosts in Sayers Field that night were left to themselves.

•

"Why do you come here?" Eli asked.

"What part of the investigation is this?" Stallings asked in turn.

They sat together by a rickety wooden table in what, Eli guessed, had once been an airmen's barracks. Stallings had used a can of Sterno and bottled water to make coffee; Eli gratefully accepted a cup.

"This is the part of the investigation," Eli said, "where I ask you simple questions and hope I get straight answers."

"You're with the Bureau, aren't you? I thought you came to hunt ghosts. Isn't that what you said?"

"Yes, but which ones?"

Stalling smiled. "For a person who wants straight answers you're fairly cryptic."

Eli shook his head. "It's just the truth. I might find a ghost, or not. I might find several. In any case, how would I know if a ghost or lack of one has anything to do with your presence here?"

Stallings nodded. "You wouldn't, would you?"

"Well, then. You see my dilemma. So. How about a trade, then? I ask a question, you answer. Then you ask. I answer."

"Sounds fair."

"All right: why do you come here?"

"I like it here. I was stationed here."

"Stationed? But they told me Sayers Field was closed in 1947. That's over eighty years ago."

"So it was. Now then, my turn: what is the purpose of finding a ghost?"

"There's more than one answer to that question, Mr. Stallings."

"I only want one. I'm not greedy."

Eli thought about it. "All right: to settle business."

Stallings looked at him rather intently. "So that part of the legends is true."

"My turn: Mr. Stallings, how old are you?"

"One hundred and seven...next Wednesday. And so: is the business that of the dead or of the living?"

"Sometimes one, sometimes the other. Mostly? The living. Now me: are you haunted?"

"Yes."

"By what, may I ask?"

"Memories, for one thing."

"Mr. Stallings..."

Stallings raised his hand. "You're two ahead already, and I'm too tired of questions to catch up. Anyway, time for my rounds." He got up and left Eli to finish his coffee. Eli took his time. He'd already decided that "as quickly as you can" wasn't going to be all that fast, the Director's wishes and his own notwithstanding. He finally put down his empty cup and picked up his sensic once more.

Eli scanned the barracks first, using his calibrations from the previous day. He made a slight adjustment for the temperature difference, but the screen remained blank. Even manifestations of a periodic nature always showed a faint glow, like a mark on stage awaiting a player's entrance, but there was nothing.

If there is a ghost, it isn't here.

Eli took his instruments out into the morning light. The sun was well above the horizon now; the mountains to the west glowed in reflected sunrise. There was still a hint of coolness in the breeze, left over from the desert night, but Eli knew it would not last long. He adjusted the sensic and started scanning.

Noon found him back in the barracks and out of the sun, staring at the blank screen of the sensic. Stallings finally reappeared and stopped to pour himself a glass of cold water from the cooler he kept in the far corner. He took a good long drink; it was hot outside and the man was nearly soaked through with sweat. Eli wasn't much better; he'd traded his coat and slacks from the day before for jeans and a white cotton shirt, but it hadn't helped deal with the heat.

"Drink something," Stallings said. "You don't want to get dehydrated out here."

"I did," Eli said though, when he thought back, he couldn't remember if it was the truth or not. He tended to get like that when he was "on the trail," as he called it. He paused to drink from the canteen he'd brought, just in case. The water was warm and didn't bring much virtue with it. Eli grimaced. Stallings rinsed out his coffee mug and poured that full of cold water for Eli without comment. Eli accepted it gratefully.

"So," Stallings said. "You found anything?"

Eli drained his cup. "Yes. I just don't know what yet."

Stallings' eyebrows went up. "Oh?"

Eli tapped a few keys on the sensic and then turned the instrument's screen so Stallings could see. "If I had one of the newer holo-capable models you could see this better, but here's the layout of the airbase."

The image on the sensic's screen wasn't quite three dimensional, but with perspective, color, and shading the illusion was close enough. Eli had scanned in most of the main hanger area and what was left of the runways that morning. Now he mapped his data onto the backdrop those scans provided. "Do you see it?" he asked.

"A faint bluish glow...rather like a motion blur."

Eli smiled. "Good guess. These are bio energy trails. There's a small but definite and very measurable effect those things have on ambient air. Sometimes the traces are apparent for as much as twenty-four hours."

"So these are a ghost's footprints?"

"Something like that. Does the path it took mean anything to you?"

Stallings leaned close, then shook his head. "Hanger seven to the CO's office...or what used to be. The trail doesn't start there, though."

Eli stared at him. "How did you know that?"

The old man just shrugged his shoulders. "Take me to the ghost," he said. "And I'll tell you."

●

They were nearing the north end of the second runway. The tarmac was badly broken there, pushed up by weeds and scrub and undercut by the occasional hard rain. A little further and the tarmac surrendered entirely to scrub and cactus.

Eli looked up from his sensic. "There's nothing left to follow," he said. "It's faded."

Stallings looked out over the vast expanse of nothing. "What time is it?"

Eli checked the time index on the sensic. "Four thirty five. Why?"

"I think we need to wait about fifteen minutes," Stalling said.

"Wait for what, may I ask?"

Stalling smiled. "If you've got a brain in your head, you already know."

Eli didn't bother to ask any more questions. He adjusted the gain of the sensic and pointed it in the last known direction the ghost's path had taken. Stallings stood beside him, his eyes now turned toward the sensic's screen. They waited, but not for very long. At time index sixteen the screen flickered to life.

"It's coming," Eli said.

Stallings didn't say anything. He just looked at the sensic's screen as the image resolved from a faint glow to a human outline. The closer the apparition came, the finer the detail on the screen until the flight jacket and helmet were clearly visible.

"It's a pilot," Eli said. "The Second World War, from the look of his uniform."

Stallings grunted. "People died in that war. Some of them even died stateside. I was there, remember? No surprise about that."

Eli glanced at Stallings but the old man's face was hard and unreadable. Eli finally shrugged and turned his attention back to the screen.

"No, I suppose not. I've been dealing with the ghosts of that war since I started with the Bureau."

"Then I guess very little would surprise you."

"It doesn't happen often," Eli admitted.

"It's about to."

"What...? Oh." Eli's breath left him in a little gasp. "That pilot...she's a woman!"

"Surprise."

•

"You knew," Eli said. It wasn't a question.

They sat back in the barracks in the shade. The sun still had a few hours before it was due to set behind the hills and let the heat of the day fade. Eli passed on the coffee and drank water alone as the sweat on his collar began to cool. Stallings had produced a bottle of very old scotch from his bag and he was drinking that. He seemed more than a little cheerful.

"I hoped," Stallings said. "Strange as that may sound."

"You've been mysterious far too long, Mr. Stallings. Who was she?"

"Jane Somersby. And put yourself in my place, Mr. Mothersbaugh: All knew for certain was that my son sent you. I played it close to the vest until I knew for sure why you were here. Now I know my boy got it right for once."

"I'll take that as a compliment, but that doesn't answer my question. The only female flyers in your branch in 1943 were the Women Airforce Service Pilots. Just to be sure, I've downloaded their stats and they told me my recollection is correct: thirty seven were killed either in training or on duty. One is missing to this day. Jane Somersby was not among them."

The old man looked at him with something like admiration. "You've done your homework, that's for sure. Or has the subject come up before?"

Eli shrugged. "Bureau matters are confidential, but it's no secret that war creates a lot of ghosts. Now, then. Why did you lie to me? Who was Jane Somersby?"

"I didn't lie. She was a pilot, like I said. Only she wasn't a WASP. Do you know why the WASPs were organized in the first place?"

"To free male pilots from aircraft ferrying duty and other non-combat roles so they could be placed where they were most needed. That was the official line, as I understand it. It was an experiment. One that worked very well by most accounts."

Stallings stared off at nothing. "It was a different world then. Maybe hard to understand now, but there were many who were dead set against the whole idea. At least one of the WASPs died because her plane was sabotaged, maybe even by her own groundcrew. They don't teach that in the history books, do they?"

Eli remembered reading about the incident. "It was never officially confirmed," he said, and realized then how weak that sounded.

Stallings laughed. "No. It wouldn't have been. Well, Jane was another experiment, back when we didn't know for certain which way the war was going to turn and how much it might take to win it: A female combat pilot. All top secret, of course. People might have thought we were desperate if word got out. Bad for morale. The whole project is still classified and buried so deep it'll probably never be found."

"Then why are you telling me?"

"Because I'm one hundred and seven years old and I no longer give a damn about secrets."

"If that were so," Eli said, "you wouldn't be chasing this one. Or haunting this airfield even more thoroughly than Jane Somersby."

Stallings looked at him with such a lack of expression that he seemed, for an instant, to be made of painted stone. "And which one would that be?"

"The one that Jane Somersby took to her grave back in 1943. Or are you going to claim that Miss Somersby has nothing to do with your obsession with this place?"

"No. She's got everything to do with it. But what good does knowing that she's the ghost do me? It's not as if I can change..." His voice trailed off.

"Change what?"

"Anything! I said I'd hoped that she was still here, but that's not really true. I knew she was. Just knew it. That's the real reason I came back. I thought perhaps if I could see her that I would know, that maybe it would make a difference. It didn't."

Eli considered. "Mr. Stallings...Conrad. I still don't know what you're trying to accomplish here, but I will say you're wrong that there's nothing you can do. There is one more thing, if you'd like to try."

Stallings looked at Eli then, and his face was anything but stony. "What?"

Eli almost regretted speaking, but he couldn't bring himself to dash a hope so newly raised. "If we're very lucky, you can talk to her."

•

Eli looked at the two old style VR helmets ruefully. *Next year I'm getting a sensic with true holo projection capability, and the budget be damned.*

Stallings, for his part, stared at his own helmet with deep suspicion. "Is this contraption really necessary?"

"It's a bit primitive, I'm afraid, but 'twill serve. The sensic will read from two staggered ports on your helmet and map those readings to the right and left display on your goggles. Full depth perception."

Stallings slowly eased the helmet on. "That explains seeing. How can she talk to me without breath?"

"The sensic's neural net runs pattern-recognition algorithms on the apparition's facial expressions, assuming she's aware of you enough to try talking. There's a slight latency, and of course she has to be looking right at you for it to work."

Stallings smiled. "Reads lips, eh? Clever."

"Just remember that not all ghosts are created equal. Some are little more than an imperfect memory of the person they used to be. Not even self-aware. This is a chance, Conrad. That's all."

"That's more than I had. Let's do it."

Eli lowered his own helmet into place and blinked up the command menu. He didn't use the voice input; he'd always found it two distracting when trying to make contact. The desert rose around them in a three-dimensional construct created by the sensic. There was a bit of pixelation towards the horizon, especially if you turned your head quickly, and the scene had that shiny, plastic look of older computer animations. Eli adjusted the phong shading and light controls a bit, and the scene improved. It still wouldn't quite pass for reality, but it was good enough. Eli and Stallings stood together on the stage, looking like little more than mannequins.

"Is this how we'll look to her?"

"No one's really sure how we look to a ghost. They don't like being interviewed as a rule." Eli checked the chronometer on the display, then set the sensic for auto response and blinked off the menu. "It's time."

And it was. The ghost was visible in the distance, but not as a blue smear this time. There was a definite human shape walking down the runway from the old crash site. Eli wondered, for a moment, at the uncanny time sense of this sort of apparition. Always manifesting at the same moment, down to the second. The instant they died, he assumed. But why these, when others died in situations equally sudden, and yet manifested entirely differently? There always seemed, in any field, that there was so much you could know for certain, and so much you might never know. The trick was learning one from the other before you let a mystery drive you mad.

Maybe it has nothing to do with time sense or being punctual. Maybe they don't have a choice.

Unfortunately, periodic apparitions—repeaters—were those least likely to be contactable. Sometimes they didn't even qualify as a memory at all. They were more like a recording that was simply played at the same time index every day, no more self-aware than the images on film. What they were calling Jane Somersby might be no more Jane Somersby than old photograph.

We'll know soon enough.

She was getting closer; the image was quite clear now, moving past and sometimes through bushes and saguaro. The sensic, tuned to her specific bioenergy signatures, cast her image more clearly than Eli's or Conrad's. Perhaps she was no more than a picture, but she was a very clear one and not at all what Eli had deduced from the first blurred images. Jane Somersby strode through the scrub and rocks, her bearing erect, her eyes focused straight ahead. There was nothing of pain and regret on her face, things Eli was quite used to seeing on a ghost. Nor was there anger, or fear, or confusion any one of the number of things past experience had told him to expect. She moved with poise and confidence, intent on something but giving no hint as to what that might be.

Appearances can be deceiving, but I'd be willing to bet she's definitely not "earthbound" in any traditional sense. Why is she here at all?

The apparition gave no clues that he could see, and when Conrad walked ahead to meet her and spoke her name she gave no response at all. She walked past him as if he weren't there. In another moment she passed Eli the saw way.

"I'm sorry, Conrad. It doesn't look like we'll be able to reach her."

Conrad shook his head. "I will. I have to. There's got to be a way."

"She seems very focused. If we knew what she wanted..." Eli thought about it. "Wait a minute. That first time she appeared, where did you say she was heading?"

Conrad frowned. "It looked like she was heading for the CO's office."

"I never saw anything like that."

"That's because it's not there anymore. It used to sit across the street from the barracks. It was struck by lightning and burned down years ago."

"Why would she go there?"

Conrad grimaced. "Of course. That's exactly where she would go. Come on."

Stallings sprinted ahead, rather spry for a man of his years. Eli hurried to catch up. When he reached the apparition he didn't even hesitate but ran past her, with Eli close behind.

"I don't understand. Why is she going... to the CO's office?" Eli asked, in between gasps for air.

Stallings wasn't even winded. "She wouldn't go anywhere else. Damn me for not realizing it sooner!"

"You didn't answer."

"No time. Can that contraption of yours recreate a building so she could see it?"

"Why? She saw us and it didn't make any difference."

"That's because she wasn't looking for us, Mr. Mothersbaugh. Can you do it or not?"

"Well...probably. I can...program something crude of the approximate dimensions and project a weak bio-energy field simulation of it, but that's all. She will see it, but we won't without the helmets. I can't do a real projection."

"It might do. Put it there."

Stallings stopped just past the barracks, pointing to a patch of littered patch of desert where the remains of a foundation were just visible. Eli used those to dimensions to rough out the structure while he tried to catch his breath. Stallings called out corrections and suggestions from time to time, all the while keeping a close eye on the path the ghost normally took behind them.

"She's almost here!"

"I'm done."

It wasn't much, little more than a three dimensional shaded blueprint, but the walls were in place and matched the foundations.

"I'd better open the door," Eli said. "She can't and neither can we."

Eli made a few quick adjustments. Stallings went inside, with Eli only a step behind. Jane Somersby stood across the road.

"She's stopping," Eli said.

"Fade out," Stallings said. "I know you can. Let me handle this."

"I hope you know what you're doing."

Stallings smiled a wistful smile. "Me too."

Eli took himself out of the projections, though he kept the helmet in place so he could follow what was happening. The apparition still stood on the far side of the road. There was a hesitance to her that had not been apparent before.

Maybe it's what she expects to see, Eli thought, but it can't look right.

"What are you waiting for, Lieutenant?"

Eli was startled. It took him a moment to realize it was Stallings speaking, and in a tone Eli had never heard the old man use before.

"Well? You think I've got nothing better to do than wait for you?"

The hesitation was gone. Jane Somersby crossed the road and snapped to attention in front of Stallings.

"Report, Lieutenant. We've both waited long enough."

•

They were back in the barracks. This time Stallings drank coffee and Eli borrowed the man's bottle of whiskey. He took a good long pull.

"You didn't tell me you were the CO of this airbase," he said. "Among other things."

Stallings shrugged. "I'm not...or rather I wasn't. I was the chief of Jane Somersby's groundcrew."

"But why did you need her to tell you what had happened? Wasn't there an investigation at the time?"

Stallings drank his coffee. "Of course there was. Inconclusive. It was all the excuse the brass needed to pull the plug on the project though."

"And you believed in the project."

Stallings shrugged again. "Let's just say I believed in Jane."

Eli remembered the way Stallings had looked the apparition when she first appeared and didn't ask any more about that. "All right, but why were you so determined to learn the truth? Training crashes were nothing unusual."

"They are when the crewchief catches one of his own men trying to sabotage a plane."

Eli just looked at him. "Jane's?"

Stallings nodded. "Corporal Parsons had an explanation which I didn't believe. I had no real proof, but I know what I saw, so I had him transferred since that was all I could do short of killing the sumbitch. Then..." He didn't finish.

"Then Jane's plane went down on a routine training flight."

"I had to know the truth, Mr. Mothersbaugh. I had to know if that jackass Parsons or somebody else murdered Jane. I had no reason to suspect anyone else, but then I had no reason to suspect Parsons until I caught him."

"You were in love with her, weren't you?"

He looked wistful. "Sure I was. I don't think she loved me. Oh, we dated even though we weren't supposed to, but I don't think she loved anything but flying. Then she died and all I had left of her was the question of how and why. It took me eighty years to answer that."

"The crash was an accident. Jane said so. Was it worth so much of your life to know that for certain?"

Stallings looked grim. "She wasn't killed because of me, because of something my crew did or failed to do. Yes, I'd say that was worth knowing."

Eli hesitated. "Did it ever occur to you that maybe it was your obsession that kept Jane here in the first place? That all this time you've held her memory here so it could give you what you wanted?"

Stallings didn't answer for a long time. Then: "Maybe it did. Maybe I thought about that for a very long time. Call it obsession on my part; that's fair. Yet she did remain. What would you call it on her part?"

"I don't know," Eli said, after a long pause. "But I do know it was a great deal more than nothing. Go home, Mr. Stallings. For Jane's sake. For your own."

Stallings smiled. "You have a good heart, Mr. Mothersbaugh."

Eli waited until Conrad Stallings got into his truck and drove away. Eli thought of making one last sweep with the sensic, but there was no point. He got into his car and left Sayers Field to emptiness and respectful silence.

The Trickster's Wife

It was Thursday, as near as Sigyn could tell. She had no calendar, but usually a rumbly, brooding sort of atmosphere filled the air of the cave on a Thursday. She had come to be pretty good at seeing the differences in days, down in the cave where her husband, albeit greatly against his will, resided.

Hel came to visit on Thursday. Sigyn looked forward to those visits though, frankly, she wasn't all that fond of Loki's bastard daughter. No one was, really, but it broke up the day. After so many days, Sigyn had come to appreciate that.

Hel peeked around a bend in the tunnel. "Hello, Sigyn."

Hel looked tired. Being tired would probably make her irritable, not that any of Loki's offspring had ever needed much excuse for that.

"Hello, Hel. Come to visit your father?"

Hel walked out into the chamber. Sigyn no longer winced at the girl's black and blue complexion; one got used to that. Otherwise she was a tall, skinny thing, with just enough of the height of her giantess mother to make her too tall for the slimness she got from her father's side of the family.

Slightly-built Loki had never been a particularly strong god, even in his prime. Thor could have snapped him like a twig. Sometimes Sigyn wondered why he hadn't. The Vanir and Aesir alike knew Loki had given the thunder god enough provocation. Sigyn didn't wonder long; she knew the reason—fate. Wyrd, destiny, all the words for the Way Things Had to Be. It wasn't Thor's destiny to kill Loki; Thor had other eels to fry. As did Loki, for that matter. Or so the Norns had said.

"Father looks better today," Hel said.

"No, he doesn't."

Drip.

Hel glanced up at the serpent on its tree, a tree that had no business being where it was, and yet was, because it needed to be, to hold the serpent that dripped venom onto Loki's bound form. Or would have, if not for Sigyn's intervention with her bowl. Sigyn glanced down at her husband. Loki's eyes were open. His limbs were bound by iron chains formed from the entrails of his butchered son. Her son too, Sigyn remembered, though it was hard. She tried to remember his face. Failed.

"I can't even remember his name," she said aloud.

Hel looked confused. "Loki."

Sigyn shook her head. "Someone else. A long time ago."

Hel sat down on a stone fairly close but far enough away to avoid a splash, should there be one. "Has he spoken?"

"No, child."

Sigyn rather doubted that Loki could speak any more. One look into her father's wild eyes should have told Hel that much. There had been little to Loki to begin with except mischief and well-concealed rage. Now the mischief was gone and rage was all that remained, and not well-concealed at all.

"I'm no child," Hel said. "I am Queen of the Underworld and Lady of the Dead!"

Because no one else wants to be, Sigyn thought. Well, the Aesir had regretted that detail soon enough when Woden's dear son Balder came under Hel's control.

"You're his child," Sigyn said aloud, with as much diplomacy as she could muster. She didn't want to anger Hel unnecessarily; she would miss their visits if she pushed the girl too far. Not that she'd meant insult; Sigyn just couldn't help thinking of Hel as a child, despite her immortality. What the years didn't touch the years didn't teach. As for herself, well, she had other lesson masters to lean on.

"Not yours," Hel said pointedly.

"For which I'm a bit sorry," Sigyn admitted. "I would love to have a daughter." *Or any child still living*, she thought but didn't say. *Even a monster like you.*

Somewhat mollified, Hel leaned back on the stone. "They're talking about you, you know," she said.

Sigyn steadied the bowl which was heavy and in danger of tipping. "Who is 'they,' if I might ask?"

Hel shrugged. "Everyone."

"What are they saying?"

"No one talks to me," Hel said, sullen. "I listen, though. Always. I hear your name but little else. The Aesir, the Vanir. They sound angry."

Sigyn nodded, then turned her face up, pretending to study the serpent so Hel wouldn't see her smile. "I think they might be."

"Why?"

"For being a good wife to your father."

Hel frowned. "I don't understand."

"I do. I think I have from the beginning," Sigyn said.

Hel didn't say anything or ask what Sigyn meant. Mysteries didn't interest her, or much of anything below the surface of a matter. Sigyn considered that one of Hel's few virtues.

Sigyn's bowl was almost full, and, as she had thousands of times before, she got up to empty it. And, like a thousand times before, Loki twisted in rage and agony in his fetters as the poison, unimpeded, dripped onto his breast. The earth shook.

His strength grows along with his madness. I'll have to be more careful.

Sigyn hurried, but not as much as she could have.

•

It wasn't Thorsday and hadn't been for some time. This day had a different feel to it. Wodensday. Someone was coming to visit, too. Thor didn't come on Thorsday. Who might come on a Wodensday? Sigyn didn't know. Yet so used to her surroundings she was that even a slight change, anywhere, that affected that sameness stood out like a blazing beacon. Something was different today. Someone would visit her. She knew it.

It was Woden. He appeared suddenly, as he was wont to do wherever he went, his floppy traveler's hat pulled low over his face.

And on his own day. How oddly appropriate, Sigyn thought, and nothing else. She wasn't even surprised, really. She just waited patiently with her filling bowl.

"Sigyn," he said. There was a reflection on his face, a reddish cast as if he were illuminated by torches. Only there were no torches there, just the unchanging werelight of that deep place. Little else seemed god like about him. By appearances he might have been an itinerant tradesman.

"All-Father. Welcome. Forgive me for not rising."

Woden glanced at Loki's bound form. "Still suffering, I see."

"As you wished."

Woden shook his head. The phantom light was lost in the blackness where his right eye used to be. "I did not want this. I wanted my son back." There was an unspeakable weariness on his face. Sigyn hadn't seen him for a very long time but seemed to remember that he looked tired then, too.

"I speak to Hel of that now and again," Sigyn said. "She just looks at me, and asks after her father. I don't think she quite understands the connection."

"I think she does, more or less," Woden said.

"Then why doesn't she just let Balder go?"

"Because she made a bargain. We did not fulfil the terms."

"Because of Loki."

Woden looked back at the tightly bound trickster god. "Yes. All because of him. The death, then the loss. All of it."

"So you killed my sons to punish the father and the circle is completed, and here we are again. I had two of them, did I not? Sons? I seem to recall you turned one of them into a wolf to rend the other."

Woden frowned. "That does not matter. It was done."

Sigyn sighed. "Fate, again? It's how we answer everything."

Woden looked at her. "You could release the poison, Sigyn."

"What sort of wife would I be then? How would I serve fate betraying my nature?"

"You refuse?" He didn't sound angry, or disappointed. He just sounded tired.

"How can I do other than what I must do, as you did? Aren't we are all bound to the rock, All-Father? In our own way?"

Woden didn't answer. In another moment he was gone. Sigyn turned to empty the bowl, and again, for a time, the earth shook.

•

Sigyn watched the bowl, wondering who the visitor would be today. It wasn't Wodensday or Thorsday or Freyasday. Not that the day dictated, but Sigyn still liked to look for connections. There was little else to do but hold the bowl and think. She had done this for a long time. Memory faded, but thought did not. It remembered the purpose, if very little of the reason, for all that Sigyn had done since that black day so long ago. It was enough.

•

Three visitors that day. Three hooded crones with faces mostly hidden by cowls blacker than night.

"Greetings, Loki's wife," they said as if there were only one voice among them.

"The sister Norns, greetings. This is an unexpected honor."

"No it isn't," they said. They seemed perturbed. Almost...frantic, for all that they moved and spoke very slowly.

Sigyn was not perturbed or frantic and moved even slower than they did. She had reason to be consistent and constant but seldom had reason to hurry. "Which? Honor or unexpected?"

"You knew we would come. We knew that you would know."

Sigyn nodded. "If you say so, for isn't it true that you know everything?"

"We know...what we must know."

Sigyn couldn't suppress a smile. "Fate rules the Fates? This is a strange world."

They ignored that. "We are tired, Sigyn."

Sigyn nodded. "As am I. So very tired. People come to visit me here in my loneliness, but they never offer to hold the bowl, even for a moment. I'd take it back, of course. No one but me is bound to hold it. Do they offer? No, they do not. Not even Hel, Loki's own dear daughter."

"You are angry," they said.

Sigyn shrugged. "I suppose you could say that. For want of a better word, a more complete word, a word that comes even slightly near describing how I feel. I am, indeed, angry."

"It is far past time," they said. Then, "Please."

"Please? Please what, good Norns?"

Silence.

"Am I to guess then? Or perhaps you cannot say it? Woden could, but then Woden probably has the heart of it worked out now, as is his nature. He always was clever. You merely know what is and what will be. But when? That's a separate matter. You can measure out a mortal life, but that doesn't apply to me, does it? What will happen will happen, but you don't know when any more than I do. Maybe less." Sigyn watched her bowl, nearly full now. "Yes. Rather less, I believe."

"It should have...ended." They stressed the word, perhaps to make sure that Sigyn understood, but there was no question of that. Sigyn understood perfectly.

"Our wyrd decides all. I do what I am fated to do, and so no one may interfere, not even Woden. You knew that. Loki's steadfast and loyal wife. But did anyone know I would be so good at it? So tireless? Did even the Norns know?"

Silence.

Sigyn nodded in satisfaction. "Well, I knew. The moment the Aesir murdered my sons for their silly revenge and bound this damn fool to this rock for being the nithling he is, I knew. Now mankind has turned away from Asgaard and Valhalla and yet we remain. Midgaard Serpent and Fenris Wolf slumber in their dotage and yet we remain."

"It should have ended!" The Norns' united voice was a wail of despair.

Sigyn just nodded. "I know. We're tired, aren't we? Everyone wants Loki to thrash in agony just enough to break his bonds. To break this circle and begin another. To lead the Giants against Asgaard and bring Ragnarok. An end to this weariness, this sameness, this suffering. Destiny cannot be cheated—Ragnarok will happen. Yes, but when will the end come? You don't know. I do. Shall I tell you?"

Silence. Then, "Please."

Sigyn smiled at them. "It ends when I say it ends. And not one moment before."

Silence again. After a few moments, the Norns left. Sigyn watched them shuffling slowly away for a bit, then checked her bowl. Close to spilling it was, and she always spilled a little, just a little, herself. She let the serpent do the rest, but not too much. Not enough.

It was never enough.

Sigyn took the bowl away, and once more the earth shook. But only for a little while.

Sigyn hurried off to empty the bowl, and, despite the weight of the ages, her step was quick and her heart was light. Behind her Loki groaned, and Sigyn smiled.

"Coming, Husband."

A Place to Begin

Long ago, when the wind spoke with a voice you could understand, in a village by the sea there lived a poor girl of almost infinite potential. Her name was Umi, which meant 'ocean.' She had a sweet face, and hair long and glossy black, but so did most of her friends. Umi was hardly worth anyone's notice, to her own way of thinking.

So it was to Umi's great surprise that she returned from gathering wood late one evening to find her mother and father in intense but polite conversation with the most powerful sorceress on the island.

"Umi, this is White Willow-sama. She has come to take you into her service," her father said. "It is a great honor." Her mother said nothing, but merely looked sad.

The next morning Umi made a bundle of her few possessions, bowed to her mother and father, and followed the sorceress, leaving her family, her friends, and the village that had been her home. She never saw any of them again.

As they made their way out of the village, the folk there either bowed to White Willow as they would a priest or noble, or just avoided her gaze altogether, hurrying out of her path as decorously as possible. Umi couldn't decide if there was more respect or fear in their deference; there seemed to be a good measure of both.

Umi studied her companion as best she could while they walked. The sorceress's name fit her well. White Willow was tall and slim, and her hair was white as mountain snow. Umi tried to judge her age and failed. Despite the testament of her hair, White Willow did not look any older than Umi's own mother. Her robes were of fine silk, and silk wrappings cushioned the thongs of her sandals. She carried a stout stick, but so far had merely used it to help balance herself as the road turned into a mountain path as they traveled away from the sea.

"You're staring at me," White Willow said, finally. It was the first time she'd spoken to Umi directly.

"I'm sorry," Umi said, "but I've never met a sorceress before."

"Nor been bound in service to one, I suppose. Are you angry with your parents for selling you to a stranger?"

Umi shrugged. "It is often the lot of girls from poor families. Some fare worse, I hear. No doubt Father did what he thought best."

White Willow smiled then. "Strange how that seems to happen most often when gold and silver are involved. Well, then are you afraid of me?" she asked. There was a pleasant tone in her voice that, for some reason, did not reassure Umi in the least.

"Yes, White Willow-sama," Umi said. Indeed, she was even too afraid to lie about it.

The sorceress nodded in satisfaction. "That's as it should be, but don't worry, Umi I will be fair to you. If you are obedient and work hard, I will not mistreat you. If you prove to be lazy or obstinate I promise you will regret it. Do you understand me?"

"Yes, White Willow sama. I will try to please you."

"Well, then. Let us hope you succeed."

•

White Willow's home was on a small plateau on the side of a great mountain, a place so flat and green it was as if the forces of nature themselves had chosen to rest there before finishing the mountain they'd started. The plateau was high but not so high that trees would not grow; White Willow's home was a rambling collection of buildings nestled into birch, maple, and stone. It seemed part fortress, part temple, part woodland glade, and part cave and den all at once.

At first glance it was hard for Umi to tell where the house ended and the mountain began. After a few weeks it was even more difficult, as spring had come to the land and new leaves were everywhere, hiding stone and timber.

Umi explored whenever her duties allowed, which was fairly often. White Willow required little of her except to sweep a certain stone path once a day and fetch two pails of water from a nearby mountain stream at the end of that path, one in the morning and one at evening. An elderly woman name Kyuko did all the cooking, another slightly younger lady who may have been the cook's daughter served as White Willow's personal body servant. There were three thick bodied men of indeterminate age who saw to the gardens and buildings and did most of the heavier work, including hauling water for the baths. This in itself seemed strange to Umi, since in her own village most of the women worked like donkeys, as hard or harder than the men.

It was very light work, compared to what Umi was used to. She saw no reason to complain on that score and didn't. Yet it was hard not to wonder why White Willow had brought her into service in the first place, to use her so little.

In time, Umi found it beyond her ability not to wonder about this. When the opportunity presented itself, she asked her mistress about it. White Willow had merely looked at her for a moment and said, with no trace of anger or any other emotion Umi could detect, "Starting tomorrow, sweep the maple grove path twice, morning and afternoon too." Not being a particularly foolish girl, Umi did not ask again. Yet still she wondered.

Spring turned into summer as Umi became more at ease in her new home. The questions in her mind were still present, but it was as if the warming days had lulled them to sleep, even as they soon coaxed a nap out of Umi on a particularly

languid afternoon, when the sun was bright and fierce and the shadows of the maple grove were a welcome haven. She finished her sweeping and then rested against a tree. When she opened her eyes again it was nearly dark.

"Mistress will be wanting her water..."

Umi hurried to fetch the pail, then ran up the path to the place where the stream bubbled out of a fissure in the mountain slope and into a shallow rock basin, a quiet place of ferns and shadow. Umi filled the pail, then hesitated. The run and her long nap had left her very thirsty, yet White Willow had warned her against drinking from that particular stream.

"Perhaps it's poison," she said to herself. The water certainly didn't seem tainted: there was no scent to it at all, and indeed it looked so cold and fresh Umi couldn't resist. Rather than disobeying White Willow directly, she took a drink from the pail itself. The water was as cool and sweet as it looked.

"That was reckless of you."

Umi couldn't see who had spoken. For a moment her vision had blurred; indeed she was afraid then that the water had been poisoned. Yet she felt no pain, and in a few moments she could see again.

In truth, she could see better than ever.

Suddenly, and even in the fading light, the leaves on the maples and the ferns growing by the basin looked extremely bright, as they might after a spring rain. Now Umi noticed that there were characters written on the stone basin, though she could not read them.

"Why didn't I notice this before?"

"Because this is the Shiryoku no Mizu, the Water of Sight, and you drank it, silly girl. Or did you think White Willow uses it to bathe her feet?"

Now Umi followed the sound and saw something else she had never noticed before. There was a niche carved into the rock a scant few feet from the fissure, and in that sat a small bamboo cage, and in that sat a small bird. Its feathers were blue and red and gold; it was the prettiest thing Umi had ever seen. Yet when she looked at it closely the feathers and bright colors faded, and something very different sat on the perch. It was horned and taloned and it smiled at her with pointed teeth. Its skin was as red as fire.

Frightened, Umi stepped back. "You're not a bird!"

"Of course not, you ignorant child. Do birds commonly speak, even in this place of magic? I'm a shikigami. A creature summoned by White Willow to do her bidding."

"You look like a devil," Umi said.

"Is it so? I may resemble an oni, but who has heard of one as small as I? Perhaps we're a related folk, I do not know. That does not make me a devil. I looked like a bird a moment ago," the creature pointed out. "That does not mean I was a bird."

Umi could see the truth in that, but she was still careful to keep her distance. The cage looked strong, but the creature inside looked strong, too. "I must go," Umi said. "White Willow is waiting for me."

The creature smiled again. "Do what you must, but a word of caution, girl: until the water leaves your body many things will look quite different, perhaps startling, to you. Do not let White Willow catch you noticing any of it, or she will know you've disobeyed her."

Umi saw the sense in that. "Why are you helping me?"

It didn't look at her when it answered. "Because this time I choose to. Ask me again when the answer is different."

Umi didn't understand what it meant, but she had no time to ask. She took up her pail and hurried back down the path to White Willow's house.

•

"You are late, Umi."

The sorceress sat on a blue silk pillow while her servant unbraided and combed out her long white hair. Umi stood in the open doorway with her pail. There was movement at the edges of her vision, colors, devices, things that she had never noticed before. She tried not to pay attention to them now, but that was surprisingly easy. Umi used most of her concentration trying not to tremble.

It wasn't simple fear at White Willow's obvious displeasure that shook her so; it was the sight of White Willow herself. She didn't look so greatly different now. She was still a human woman, her hair still long and white as the snow on their mountain's top. No, what Umi saw now were things just below the surface of White Willow's face, things hidden to Umi before now.

The first was time, or more correctly, age. White Willow had the surface appearance of a fairly young woman, but Umi now understood this was not true the sorceress was very, very old. Her unlined face now seemed as cold and lifeless to Umi as that of a painted porcelain doll.

That wasn't the worst part. Under White Willow's cool gaze Umi felt herself constantly weighed as if on a merchant's scale, her value falling this way or that, constantly changing, constantly reconsidered.

How long before the scale turns the wrong way?

Umi bowed low. "Gomen nasai, White Willow sama. I foolishly let the warm sun lull me to sleep."

"Is it this, then? Nothing more?"

Umi felt White Willow's gaze on her as a bird might feel a cat's, but she kept her eyes averted and her head bowed. "I didn't wake until nearly dark, and thus am only now come to bring your water."

White Willow said nothing for several very long moments, then sighed wearily. "I've had a long, tiring day. I may not even require the water. Still, failure must bring punishment. Is that just?"

"Yes, mistress."

White Willow contented herself with a sharp blow of her fan across the back of Umi's hand, with dire warnings of what would happen if she proved tardy a second time. Umi left the water and scurried gratefully out of the room, the sting of her punishment already fading. She tried to put as much distance between White Willow's chambers and herself as she could, short of leaving the house. She had seen much to disturb her in White Willow's room, but she had seen more things along the path from the spring, and was in no hurry to encounter them again in the present darkness.

Umi considered what to do for a moment, but only for a moment. She smelled something wonderful coming from the kitchen and remembered she hadn't had supper yet. Kyuko the cook was tending the coals under the grate, which was empty, but there was a bowl of rice and three pickles sitting on the windowsill. The old woman grunted. "About time. I was about to toss this to the foxes."

Umi doubted that; she had yet to see Kyuko express more than mild annoyance at anything, and certainly not to the point of wasting food. Still, she was careful to express her gratitude, and the old woman smiled. With her round face it made Kyuko look something like a melon with teeth.

Umi ate in comfortable silence as Kyuko went on with cleaning up the kitchen. The kitchen seemed safe from the disturbing visions Umi had discovered elsewhere, but Umi found herself studying the old woman now with an intensity that she didn't understand. It was as if Kyuko had been here all this time and Umi had only now noticed her. The way the glow from the embers traced a line of gold along the side of her face, damp with perspiration. The way all her movements seemed practiced and precise, almost unconsciously so. Umi found herself wondering how many times the old cook had done just this, in the very same kitchen, performing these very same duties with gentle good humor.

"If it is not impertinent to ask, how long have you been with Mistress White Willow?"

Kyuko had been looking out at the woods, a distant expression on her face. The question apparently caught her by surprise. She hesitated for several long moments, clearly giving the matter some thought. "Well, I'm not sure one can really be said to be with White Willow, since she is mostly complete unto herself. I've been in her service since I was a little girl."

"Like me?" Umi asked.

Kyuko smiled. "Much like you. I remember the day she came to our village. She looked at many young girls, but she chose me. It was a fine day."

"Weren't you sad to leave your family?"

Kyuko raised an eyebrow. "Weren't you?"

Umi bowed her head. "Forgive me; it was a foolish question."

Kyuko dismissed that. "I hadn't thought of it in such a long time. The days here seem to flow together like currents in a river; there's no separating them."

Umi nodded. Until today, that had been true for her, too.

•

Umi's dreams were vivid and frightening. She woke early and visited the privy; afterwards she felt more than normal relief the world seemed to have lost its strangeness. Now the leaves on the maple trees did not suggest disturbing patterns, hints of things unseen. They were just leaves, the stone wall that ran along one side of the grove path was simply a wall and did not, as it had seemed the evening before, have a section with eyes and small, stout legs. Umi swept the grove path carefully and then went to see Kyuko in the kitchen for her breakfast.

Now it was time to fetch the water.

Umi took her pail and trudged up the grove path. Not dragging her feet, exactly, but not hurrying either. When she came to the spring she filled her pail as usual and then stood there beside the water for several long moments, waiting for she didn't know what, looking for the same. She looked where the writing was, where the shikigami had been, and saw neither. She finally turned her back on the spring and hurried back to White Willow. Umi didn't want to be late a second time.

•

It was three days before Umi drank from the pail again. The little creature was in its cage as before, now regarding her thoughtfully. In fact Umi had taken a little more of the water this time, and she looked at the creature very long and intently when it appeared.

It ignored her scrutiny. "I wondered how long it would be before you took the water again," it said.

"How did you know I would?"

The creature smiled, showing very pointed teeth. "When a person is touched by magic it is hard to let the world go back to the way it was. Some people can do it with no problem at all, like old Kyuko. I did not think you would be like her."

"She's a fine woman and has been very kind to me," Umi said. "I would not have you speak ill of her."

It laughed. "And have I? No, Umi-chan. I merely spoke the truth; I made no judgment. I think that came from you."

"I " Umi blushed crimson. The shikigami was right. "What do you know of Kyuko?" she finally asked.

"Just that she came as a young girl to White Willow's service, as have you, and when her time came to drink the water she drank once and never again. Perhaps that was best for her, who can say? She is content enough with her life...or so one could suppose."

Umi frowned. "You make it sound as if drinking the water was expected!"

The creature showed its teeth again. "Isn't it? In my experience the one infallible way to make sure a certain thing will happen is to forbid it." Another smile. "She'd rather reduce her power than be insecure in the power she does possess. I think White Willow is very wise in that."

"I do not understand," Umi said.

"Of course not. Else you would not be standing here talking to me."

Umi took a deep breath. "Then what should I be doing, save hurrying with my pail to my mistress?" Umi asked. "And, come to that, what does White Willow really want of me? My duties are but few; such that I'm hardly worth even the small price I'm sure she paid my father."

The small creature was grinning from ear to ear, almost literally. "You have little wisdom as yet, but you're a clever enough girl as your kind go. Yes, there is more to this matter as you have guessed. But what? That would be good for you to know."

"Do you know what White Willow really wants from me? Will you tell me?"

"Of course I know." The shikigami seemed to consider. "I might tell you. For a price."

"What do you want?"

"My freedom, of course. Release me."

"Why are you imprisoned?"

"That's my affair," it said, but Umi shook her head.

"If I were to release you then it would be my concern too. I want to know what I am doing by releasing you, if I choose to do so. There may well be more to that than one can guess, as well."

"Clever girl," the creature repeated, almost admiringly. "But there's no time now. Run along to White Willow or you'll be late. And remember what I said about letting her find you out; you'll be no good to me if she suspects. Come back when you are ready to bargain."

•

Umi was almost late again, because she came across a vision that was very startling. She thought about what she had seen as long as she could, then hurried on with the water.

It seemed that White Willow stared at her long and hard for a bit, but in the end she had dismissed Umi without saying anything. Umi was relieved, but also certain that, if she kept drinking the Seeing Water, she wouldn't be able to fool White Willow for much longer. Frankly, she was surprised she'd done it as long as this.

Soon Umi found herself once more in Kyuko's kitchen, where, as usual, her supper waited. Umi was nearly through with her meal before she finally worked up the courage to ask what was on her mind.

"Kyuko-san?"

The old woman didn't look up from her washing. "Hmm?"

"Did you ever wish your life had been different?"

Kyuko paused. "What possesses you to ask such a thing, child?"

"I just wondered...if you ever thought about it."

Now Kyuko did look at her, with an expression lost somewhere between a frown and a smile. "You are a strange child, Umi chan. What should my life have been, other than it is?"

Umi shook her head. "I think your life is a fine one as it is. Yet aren't there choices, or circumstances, that might make one choose or follow one path over another?"

Kyuko smiled. "A passing scholar once tried to seduce me, in my younger days. He spoke of different paths and life's potential, when what he really wanted was me under the maple trees. You sound a lot like he did, Umi chan. Do you want something of me, too?"

Umi blushed, but she did not waver. "I want to know."

Kyuko shrugged. "White Willow bought me from my parents, as she did you. I suppose I might have wound up a farmer's wife, and more likely dead now from work and children. Or perhaps a merchant's concubine, married off or comfortably and discreetly retired. You may not believe this, child, but I was more than a little fair in those days."

Umi, looking at Kyuko's sweet face, had no trouble at all imagining it and said as much, but Kyuko didn't seem to hear. After a bit she went on, but Umi wasn't sure she was speaking to her at all. "What should I have been? I was not born to be a great lady, nor a sorceress like White Willow. Those paths were closed, what was left? White Willow treated me well, my duties were and are easy to bear. What should I have done..?"

Umi bowed her head. "Pardon my foolish curiosity. My head is full of fancies these days."

Kyuko looked up. It was as if she had only now remembered that Umi was in the room. She leaned over and tousled Umi's short black hair. "You are a strange girl, but sweet. I don't know the answer to your question, Umi-chan. I can't remember ever asking it myself. I I guess at the time things seemed well enough as they were. Now run along and get your bath; it's late."

Umi had more questions, but she didn't think they were for Kyuko to answer. She finished her rice and hurried off to the bath house where White Willow's menservants would have already prepared the tubs. This time she didn't avert her eyes from the bits of strangeness her new sight promised to reveal to her. She found herself actually eager for them now, and was a little disappointed when none appeared.

•

Umi drank from the pail the very next morning. "I don't suppose," she said, "that it would do any good for you to swear to tell me the truth?"

The shikigami grinned at her. "By what kami should I swear, that you would believe me?"

Umi considered. "I do not think there is any power that you respect enough to compel truth. Nor do I know that your nature will even allow for the truth."

"My warnings were true enough." The creature actually looked offended. "Consider, Umi the shikigami are as much a part of the Divine as any venerated hero or goddess. We are family, in a way. What sibling really holds another more worthy than himself, proper forms of deference and respect not withstanding? There is no power by which I will swear, so instead I suggest this: test me."

"How?"

"Ask me a question other than the one you really want to know. I'll answer, and you can test the truth of my answer. It's not as compelling as an oath, of course, but it will show that I am at least capable of speaking truth, and, perhaps, wise enough to know the answer you seek. After that, what you choose to believe from me is up to you."

Umi considered. "All right why was Kyuko brought into White Willow's service?"

The creature sighed. "For the same reason you were, silly child, and therefore I won't tell you that. Ask another, and don't try to be so clever this time."

Umi blushed again. "Very well: Do you intend any harm to me or to Mistress White Willow?"

The shikigami frowned. "Why do you care what happens to White Willow?"

"She has been kind to me. You can well say that it only serves her purpose, but I am not certain of that, nor is that less reason to be grateful. I would not do anything to harm her."

"Such loyalty a dog might show its owner. You're welcome to it, Umi, but this question doesn't serve either of us. You will not know my true intentions until I act on them. Such is the way of things. Ask again, and be quick. Neither of us has much time here."

Umi put her hands on her hips. "Well then, tell me this: yesterday by the path I thought I saw a young woman, just for a moment. She was very beautiful, and wore robes of blue silk. I was distracted for a moment. When I turned back, she was gone. Do you know who she was?"

"She was and is a ghost. She often walks the path."

Umi felt a little chill. "Whose ghost?"

"Kyuko's."

Umi stared at the creature. "This is a lie on the face of it! Kyuko is very much alive."

"Kyuko as you see her now? Certainly. But..." the shikigami waved a clawed finger at her, "Kyuko as she was, now that is a different matter. What you saw was an echo, a memory. Something remained after the Kyuko you know moved on down time's river. Caught in an eddy along the shore, perhaps, or stubbornly clinging to a branch, who can say? Yet there it is. Those with eyes to see, will see."

"So how do I know you speak truly of what you understand?"

The creature smiled. "In the hour after breakfast, when Kyuko washes the bowls and her eyes seem to look at a place beyond here and now, then come to the maple grove path where the stream crosses it. Say nothing. Do nothing, save take careful note of what you see. Then come back here and tell me if my words are weeds or blossoms."

•

Umi waited for the right time, and had no trouble seeing it. Kyuko grew distant, as indeed Umi remembered from many times before. She excused herself but doubted Kyuko heard her. She slipped out the back way to the maple grove path. She felt the need to relieve herself now, but she did not; the effect of the Shiryoku no Mizu was already somewhat diminished and she didn't want to lessen it further. At least not yet.

Mists were gathering in the forest, summoned by the waning sun. Umi thought that, perhaps, she could see more than mist in the grayish white wisps if she tried, but she did not try. She walked very quickly to the place the shikigami had spoken of, and there she waited. It did not take long.

Umi watched the ghost approach. She wondered how she would perceive the spirit without the magic water coursing through her now. Perhaps a bit of mist, or the wind blowing leaves along the path; a flash of blue that might have been a bird, but not seen well enough to guess, or even wonder. Perhaps all those things, or none of them. What Umi saw now was a young woman in a blue silk robe, her glistening black hair carefully arranged. There was very little shadowy about her; Umi almost fancied that she could reach out and touch flesh. She remembered the shikigami's instructions and kept her hands still. She waited, and she watched.

The grove seemed very quiet now. Umi heard the sound of her own heartbeat, not even masked by the tickly chatter of the stream flowing beneath the small stone bridge. Now and then she heard something from the water that sounded almost like a word, but she didn't turn her attention away from the vision in front of her.

Umi saw the pail.

She hadn't noticed it before; her attention was on the spectre's face, and clothes. It was Kyuko, or was. Umi was certain of that now; it had taken her a while for that particular seed to sprout, but now it grew fast and strong. When Umi saw the eyes, she knew. They were Kyuko's eyes. Younger, clearer, perhaps not yet so weary, but very familiar. It was only after that certainty had arrived that the pail was clear to her, too.

It's the same as mine....

Umi knew she should not have been surprised by that. The shikigami has said that

Kyuko came into White Willow's service for the same reason Umi had; it wasn't unreasonable that she'd perform the same duties at first.

Until when? Another of her servants dies and everyone moves a step forward, as in a dance?

In her heart Umi did not believe matters were as simple as that, but she put the thought aside to consider later. She needed her attention for what was happening now. She watched Kyuko-rei glide up the path in complete silence; not even the rustle of her silks carried on the faint breeze; it was as if Umi watched a moving reflection. The vision came to where the stream crossed the path under the small stone bridge. Umi looked directly into Kyuko rei's eyes; there was barely an arm's reach between them, but Umi saw no recognition there. The spirit, like Kyuko herself, seemed to be looking at something beyond. In this case, something off the path, deep in the maple grove.

Someone, rather.

Where Kyuko's image was clear and bright, the man stood in shadow. Umi could not make out his face. His robes could have been those of a mountain monk or a scholar; she couldn't be sure. Umi could easily guess, though, after what Kyuko had told her before.

This isn't a memory at all. This is a regret.

Kyuko rei stood on the maple grove path. She didn't move, or speak. She only stared out into the woods at something she obviously saw much more clearly than Umi did. Perhaps because it was only the shadow of a shadow, but it was real for this echo of the Kyuko that had been. Still, even after a while Kyuko's younger image began to fade too. Umi almost let it go. She remembered the shikigami's warning. Yet Umi found that, at the end, she could not do nothing, or at least the "nothing" that the creature had asked of her.

"Why do you stop now?" Umi asked, aloud.

Silence. Umi walked forward, into the spirit's line of vision. Umi didn't know if it could see her, but she wanted to try. "Why do you stop now?" she repeated.

Umi knew the ghost didn't turn its head a fraction, or look directly at her, but she also knew that, somehow, it answered her.

I ALWAYS STOP. ONE CANNOT CHANGE THE PAST.

"That is true," Umi said, "but this is not the past. Is he your regret?"

Now Kyuko rei did look at her. She seemed to peer at Umi as if she were the shadow, fading, hiding. The spirit smiled faintly. THERE ARE TWO SORTS OF REGRETS, CHILD: THOSE THINGS ONES DOES...AND THOSE THINGS ONE DOES NOT DO. THE LATTER ARE THE WORST.

"Then why hold on to it?"

The spirit smiled sadly. BECAUSE IT'S ALL I HAVE OF HIM.

"Then make something else, something better. Go to him. Change what is."

THAT IS NOT POSSIBLE... She stopped.

"This is not the past," Umi repeated. "This is now, and all things are possible."

Umi spoke with a fierce conviction that surprised her. She spoke of things she could not possibly understand, and yet she did not see the mystery in them. She knew what she said was true, and she was certain that Kyuko rei knew that too.

CHILD, THIS DOESN'T CONCERN YOU.

"You are my friend," Umi said. "It does."

The image was fading fast, but not before Umi saw it hesitate for the barest of moments then walk slowly across the small stone bridge and take the side trail into the maple grove where the other shadow waited. Umi almost felt as if it were her will alone that forced the spirit in that direction; she wondered if that were possible.

More than that, she wondered if it was right.

•

Kyuko didn't speak to her that next morning, or to anyone as far as Umi could see; the cook seemed to be in a daze. Umi wanted to speak to her friend, but she couldn't think what she should say. In the end she had gone off to face the shikigami one last time.

Umi stood before the basin at the end of the trail, the taste of the Shiryoku no Mizu still cool and sweet on her tongue. The shikigami sat in its cage. "Did I speak the truth?"

"As far as you did speak, yes," Umi said.

Another fierce grin appeared. "Don't start laying traps and puzzles, Umi. I am far better at it than you are. Are you saying that there is truth I have not spoken?"

"I'm saying that you lied without saying a word."

The creature frowned. "When did I not speak?"

"You always spoke. Of many things and nothing. I think that was part of the problem."

"That's no puzzle, girl. That's a contradiction."

Umi shook her head. "Sitting in that cage, appearing to be what you claimed to be. That was the lie." Umi leaned over and took up a handful of the magic water. With the first drink still working within her, Umi took another. The cage disappeared. Umi took another handful, another drink. The shikigami disappeared.

White Willow stood in its place in a cleft of the rock, her white hair flowing around her like the glory of an albino sun. She was beautiful and terrible all at once. Umi was afraid, but she did not run.

All choices operate in the "now," as I said to Kyuko. This one is mine.

Umi picked up another mouthful of the water.

White Willow raised her hands. "I can't stop you, Umi, but I would not advise it. Mortals were never meant to see that clearly."

Umi thought about it. She finally let the water drip between her fingers to fall back into the basin. "You knew all along, didn't you?"

White Willow opened her fan and considered. "Of course I did," she finally said. "The real question is: how long did you know there was no shikigami?"

"The second time I took a bit more of the water than at first. The edges of the creature were...shadowed, almost like a picture in a lantern. I knew he wasn't what he seemed. I also never really believed that my perception could alter so drastically and still escape your notice, however fervently I might wish to believe that."

White Willow looked grim. "You've disobeyed me, Umi."

Umi bowed, but she did not falter. "As you knew I would. He—you— said as much. If you merely wanted to punish me for that you could have done it the first day. I assume there was something you wanted to know about me. I must be impertinent enough to ask if you found your answer."

"Yes, Umi. I have. Or perhaps more importantly, you have."

"I don't understand."

"I dare say." White Willow smiled again. "You have a great deal to learn. But will I teach you? That is yet to be decided."

Umi bowed again. "You own me," Umi said frankly, "and may do as you will. Yet I think there is something besides obedience you require of me."

"And I would take it from you if I could," White Willow replied with equal frankness. "but that is not the way this particular sort of magic works."

"What magic?"

"Yours," White Willow says. "Or rather, your potential. All human beings have potential all their lives. To be something greater than they are, or something worse. To choose one path and not another. To hone one skill and let another go fallow. Yet, before one path is chosen, all paths have almost equal potential, and are just as real. There is power in that potential, Umi. Power that one such as I knows how to tap, and use. Everyone has it to some degree, as I said, but no one has potential without limit. Some, however, come very close."

"Kyuko," Umi said. "I thought she was my friend. Why didn't she warn me?"

White Willow laughed harshly. "Warn you, child? How could she do so, without steering you toward one path instead of another, even though only you would bear the responsibility if you chose wrong? Do you think her so cruel, to deny you the same choice that she had?"

As cruel as I might have been to her... "No," Umi said. "Kyuko and I are the same?"

White Willow seemed to consider. "In a way. You both have great capacity. As long as it exists, I can use it. In time it fades, since potential is a child of time and as mortal as we, but it never completely leaves so long as breath is in the body. As for us, so for it there is a place to begin, and a place to end."

"So why say anything to me at all? Why test? Why tempt me to interfere, as I did with Kyuko? If I remained ignorant, couldn't you continue to use me all the days of my life?"

"Clever girl. Yes, I could," White Willow admitted. "And there are many of my sort who've chosen that path. Yet if you think of potential as a well, then thwarted potential is poison to that well. Sooner or later I would choke on it. No, Umi. Kyuko drank from the spring as you did, and she made her choice. You'll do the same because, in this one matter, there is no choice. In time you will stay or go, but which path you take will be up to you. Which will it be?"

Umi thought of the ghost of Kyuko's regret. What you do not do is always the greater regret. Perhaps Kyuko did warn me, in the only way she could. Umi looked at White Willow. She was still afraid, but there was something greater than her fear working now. A sort of hunger that Umi hadn't known before. "Will you teach me what you know?"

"Yes. You may not always like the methods I choose, nor what must be learned, but I will teach you. Learning those lessons is also up to you."

"Then I will stay," Umi said, "and I will learn. I have already begun, I think."

White Willow smiled. "I can feel the potentials weaving their tapestry even now."

Umi fancied she could as well, but perhaps that was her imagination. No matter; she would soon know. For the moment, however, she took leave of her mistress and sought out Kyuko. She thought she might have an apology to make and, perhaps, gratitude to show. Umi wasn't really sure, but that, too, seemed worth learning.

Take a Long Step

The Walker had been a god once. He would soon be one again, these things tending to be cyclical. He was already hearing voices. Not the average, everyday kill strangers for no good reason voices. Real voices. Real people.

Soon he would even know what they were saying.

Now the voices were only murmurs in the distance, but they were getting louder by the day. Soon he would know what they wanted, dreamed, felt, were. What had happened before was going to happen again. He wasn't particularly happy about it. Walker did want to be ready, as far as possible, but there just wasn't a lot one could do to prepare for divinity.

Homeless, unemployed, he waited for his new time by walking the streets of Canemill on a regular route, almost never varying, his long skinny legs covering ground much faster than was really possible. His parents had thought him slow in the head, but he wasn't so much slow as quiet, listening to things they did not hear, not inclined to talk though he knew how.

Now his shoulders were always hunched, eyes looking at the ground as if he did not wish to see anyone, but he saw everyone. Sometimes he would break into a run for no reason that anyone could tell, but there was always a reason. Always.

Take a long step from trouble, take a long step from pain. Walk the streets forever lest it catch you up again.

Walker wasn't satisfied with the rhyme. The relationship between "pain" and "again" only worked when he twisted the accents in a way that sounded unnatural even to him. Too many things about the world were unnatural as it was, and that without considering sex at all. No reason for him to deal with that particular can of omelets and sperm before necessary. He just kept walking as long as he could. When he had to stop, he stopped, and waited until it was time to walk again. Not that he thought it mattered. Sooner or later divinity was bound to catch up with him.

I wish it was up to me...

Walker turned onto Liam Street. It was good street, narrow, but there were few homes and too much traffic. Large water oaks shaded the asphalt from the August sun; the air was cool and still and smelled faintly of earth. The hint of wildness in the overgrown lots alongside it made him almost want to stop, but he didn't dare. Not yet.

As he walked past Strangfellow's Funeral Home he stumbled, then felt a sudden cool breeze where there shouldn't have been one. He looked down, saw the tattered remnants of his right sneaker lying a good two feet behind him. The last scrap of cloth holding the laces together had finally given out. Walker looked at the ruins, sighed deeply, and started walking again. His pace was a little uneven now that his legs were no longer quite the same length, and he found himself watching the ground even closer than before, keeping an eye out for glass.

•

Her arms aching, Liddy Ashford loaded the last of the laundry into the camper on her husband's pickup, then slid behind the wheel. She reached for the keys, then looked at her husband's hunting boots sitting on the passenger floor of the pickup.

Oh, no, Mel. Not this time.

Mel always started this way, weeks before the season. First the boots casually left on floorboard. Later there would be a box of Remingtons in the glove compartment, followed in a few days by the camo vest draped over the seat. By the time deer season was officially open he would be all packed, then it was off to the deer camp for three days or more, using precious vacation time to drink beer in the woods with his buddies, away from her.

Does the silly bastard actually think I wouldn't notice?

She'd borrowed the pickup to go to the laundromat. Washed his dirty clothes, just as she cleaned his dirty house and had for twelve years now. If there was any free time to be had, she wanted her share. And this year, damn his hide, he was going to give it to her, and if he thought otherwise he was going to get that fight he was always trying to avoid by sneaking in his packing a little at a time. Unless...

It's not too bad a plan, to tell the truth. Let's see if I can use it too.

Liddy looked at the boots. If both disappeared, he'd accuse her of taking them. That was both. What about one? One was an accident. One boot left was unfortunate. One meant Mel shopping for a new pair with Liddy, because he was worse than useless when it came to buying clothes of any kind, including hunting attire. A pair of boots was trouble of the right sort. Liddy felt ready for a little trouble, but one boot was better. One boot was fraught with possibilities. One boot seemed there was no other word that fit right.

Liddy started the truck and pulled out of the laundromat. When she passed the corner of Liam and Lee, she reached down and tossed the right boot out the passenger side window. She was still grinning when she got home, but Mel didn't ask. He didn't want to know, which was really too bad; he was soon to discover that he didn't have much choice.

•

One boot.

Walker considered the piece of footwear lying beside the road with dread. Was it happening already? He didn't know. The boot could be just that a boot that someone lost. But...what if it hadn't been lost? What if it had been placed there, specifically placed there for him? Not so simple as a man without a shoe finding a shoe. Providence, or luck, was all that amounted to. What if this was a chain of effect that, unlike blind luck, specifically had him in mind? That would be something else. That would be something very serious. Still, there wasn't much he could do about it one way or another. And he did need a shoe of some kind.

Walker tried the boot on. It fit perfectly.

Of course.

•

Johnnie Ray was a walker too, but that's not all he was. There was no virtue in his variety so far as he could see, and there was a purity about Walker that Johnnie lacked. He wasn't jealous of Walker, exactly, but he felt a connection that he didn't like. A contrast, as if Walker were one thing and Johnnie was a mere shadow of it, no more. Or less. A shadow that was, however, growing stronger. He would go where Walker went, because, being a shadow, he really didn't have a choice.

Johnnie wasn't homeless. He got a small check every month from the government, though he didn't know why. Something to do with service in a war he did not remember. Perhaps it was a mistake, but Johnnie didn't question. It paid for a small place On the less posh side of town. He did not work because that was not possible. He walked because there was nothing else to do. He bummed cigarettes when he could; he wished for them when he couldn't. The wished cigarettes hadn't appeared yet. Soon, he thought. Very soon.

•

These damn things are killing me.

John E. Waller had said the same thing every day for the last ten years. At forty seven, he found himself involved in the common pursuit of men his age explaining his mortality. He didn't sleep well more and more often; morning brought aches and stiffness that used to need a hard day at the mill to explain. It was as if pain had just found and a home and settled there. He wasn't that old, he told himself. He exercised, he ate right. Mostly.

John stared at the cigarette pack when he stopped at the light on Northridge. Unfiltered, the same brand his grandfather had smoked. Matthew Waller was a great old guy and John had loved him more than any relative before or since. But maybe he'd taken the adulation too far.

His grandfateher died of a massive everything, according to Doc Patterson. "Couldn't have done a damn thing if I'd been right there," he said. Hell, he was only fifty three.

Once that had seemed ancient but now, as John came within spitting distance of that age himself, it didn't seem old at all. Certainly far too soon to be finished with a life. There was still so much to do. See his own grandchildren, for one. His son Estes had given them the news barely a week before, and John was still trying to get his head around it.

"I'm going to be a grandfather," he said softly.

If he lived long enough to see it. John took one last look at the pack, balancing the need for one thing with the need for something else and suddenly, for the first time, the balance turned. The light changed and John turned right on Broken Elm, watching the traffic. He was only vaguely aware that he'd thrown the nearly full pack out the window somewhere between Liam and Meadowview; he only knew that he didn't have it anymore.

Which was fine with him.

•

"Damn."

It didn't help. Johnnie Ray swore with more invective and color then, rising to a crescendo of profanity that was something close to art. Little changed. He felt a welling anger that he did not like but could not stop. He knew it did not come from himself and that made it worse.

The pack of cigarettes his favorite brand still lay on the grass beside Liam. Johnnie Ray didn't kid himself that the pack was empty, mere litter. He knew better. Johnnie Ray started to walk away, but there was no point. He could refuse them if he wanted to; that was a separate thing altogether. He couldn't change the fact that they were there.

Johnnie Ray picked up the cigarettes and noted with disgust that the pack was almost full. He pulled one out and lit it. He pulled in the aromatic smoke, sighed with a mixture of content and despair as the nicotine and all the little carcinogens danced in his lungs. He savored the taste and scent of it for a moment and then blew one perfect smoke ring.

Try as he might, he'd never been able to do that before.

"The Wheel is turning. Time to talk to the Walker, I do reckon," Johnnie said, and sighed again. It was inevitable now, but that didn't mean he was looking forward to it. Probably futile, too, but that didn't mean he was excused from trying. Regret was coming for him one way or another. No reason to add to the burden.

•

Walker noticed the man following him, mostly because the man was silent. Not that he didn't make the ordinary noises: he whistled a tune that Walker almost recognized; his shoes crunched on the rocks and dried leaves on the shoulder of the street. No, it was the vast and profound silence of him amidst the babble in Walker's head. From the man following him, Walker heard nothing. It was almost enough to make him stop. Instead, he started singing again. Aloud, this time.

"Take a long walk from trouble, take a long walk from pain, walk the streets forever lest it catch you up again."

"That's wrong, you know. Trouble will catch you no matter how fast you walk. I know, Walker. Better than you."

Walker went faster. His legs moved in impossibly long strides, as if he wore seven league boots from the fairy tale. Huge old trees loomed to left and right to disappear behind him in a blur of green and shadow, cars and people flashed by at random, oblivious. Walker walked faster than he ever had but the presence that followed kept right on his heels.

"We need to talk," his shadow said.

There could be no talk. Especially now. Walker stretched out. Cities flashed by, then rivers and oceans. Walker was afraid of how fast he traveled now, but he did not stop. He was afraid to stop.

"You're only making it worse; don't you know that?"

Walker had trouble with words that weren't a song. Songs were incantations of a sort, ritual and fixed; easier to deal with. As a human he needed it little, but now he was becoming something very different. He forced something like communication through his brain, arranged the neurons just so, watched the interesting patterns for a time that could not have been long, fractions of a second perhaps, then pushed the words out onto the crackling, howling wind that was the mark of their passage.

"Making...what, worse?"

"The mess we're in," Johnnie Ray said. "You know what's happening, don't you?" When Walker nodded, and Johnnie Ray went on. "Do you know who I am?"

"No."

"I'm your Shadow. That's why I'm here, why I'll be here, no matter where you go or how fast or how far. Hide in the light and I'll be there, hide in darkness and I'll be everywhere. Whenever your time comes, so does mine. I hate it."

Walker wasn't convinced. He walked faster. He wouldn't have thought it possible, but he did it. Continents flashed by, then, when the earth could no longer contain his speed, planets and stars. He saw the void and knew it, but felt neither hot nor cold. He walked on what he did not know, but it didn't matter. He bestrode galaxies and saw the place of his birth reduced to a pinkling of light on the arms of a vast pinwheel of stars, and still the man was there. His shadow.

Walker stopped.

He stood in darkness with the fires of stars all around, and arranged the part of himself that needed to be changed. Beyond simple speech. He needed to understand, and so he became a being capable of understanding. As a human he was almost feebleminded, or so his parents had said. Not good for anything. He still wasn't good for anything, to his way of thinking. But feebleminded he was not, then or now. Especially now.

"I know you. What do you want?" he asked.

The man moved closer. "I want to end this thing."

"It has barely begun."

The man nodded. "Even more reason to act now. What do you hear?"

"Voices," Walker said. "What do you hear?"

The shadow man laughed. "I hear nothing. I feel, and that's far worse."

Walker increased his understanding. It was a simple matter now, but no matter how much greater his intellect grew it didn't seem to help. Expand though he did, there seemed little sense in what the other man...Johnnie Ray? said. He admitted defeat. He wondered if he'd be able to do as much so easily later. He even wondered if this was a failing. "I don't understand."

"They will sing to you," Johnnie said. "Your former shell was somewhat limited; the memory may not still be in you, but that is what will happen: they will sing."

"That does not sound so terrible."

Johnnie Ray smiled. "It's not. But it doesn't end there. It never does. Next comes the prayers, and you're the focus of all hope. Next comes the disagreements, and all sides will call your name as they pull the trigger or swing the ax. You'll be responsible, and you will hear every last one."

"No," said Walker. It was a weak, pathetic sound.

"Yes," said Johnnie Ray. "But, bad as that is, let me tell you what's worse the anger. You start with songs. How does it begin for me? Rage. Envy. Jealousy. Everything they struggle against in the dark and fail to beat? That's me. They will blame you for letting them fail. They'll blame me for making them fail. I'll be the source of a million troubles and feel every one of them. Feel them. Make your brain as large as a galaxy and you still won't know what that means. I say no, Walker."

"It is inevitable," Walker said. There may have been a hint of despair in his voice as it drifted with the dust of countless years, but there was no uncertainty.

Johnnie Ray shrugged. "So? Does that mean it has to happen now?"

Walker shook his head. "Now, or then? All the same, sooner or later."

"Not to me," Johnnie Ray said, softly. "You just walk and wait, but me? I had a life. Oh, I'll grant you rightly it wasn't much of a life. I can't work and I'm barely tolerated but, every now and then, good things would come to me and I had the sense to enjoy them. When this thing happens all that will be gone, and it will be gone for a very long time. All time may be equal, perhaps. All time is not the same."

"Words," said Walker.

"Words," Johnnie Ray conceded. "How else to carry a truth past the moment of its birth? Let's have some time of our own first."

"I am nothing but what I will become," Walker said. "I can't stop it. If I'm ahead of you in this I have no choice. I can't stop it." It sounded like regret.

"Together, we could," Johnnie Ray said.

Walker looked at the Adversary, then, in that vast empty place between the stars, and he considered. "Eternally opposite. I do not know if it is the same for the other gods, but it is for us. What we become. What they make of us. How can we do anything together?"

"It hasn't happened yet. You're very close to apotheosis now, but you're not quite there. Me, I'm still Johnnie Ray...mostly. I can help you. You needn't mistrust me, since you know what I will do. You need do nothing but decide."

"It won't change anything."

"It will hold back the darkness, for a time. That's all you'd do anyway. I want my life; you want to thwart the dark. It will serve both of us. And it won't hurt a bit."

After a time that might have been short or long neither of them could really tell Walker put out his hand and Johnnie Ray led him back to earth like a lost child.

Later, when they met at the agreed place, Walker was moved to mention that it did hurt a bit, but he didn't really mind. He was still divine enough to forgive Johnnie Ray that one lie. Johnnie Ray was still human enough to be grateful. Later some people came and cut Walker down from the tree and took Johnnie Ray away. He was locked in a large house with doctors and such who wanted to find out why he had done such a terrible thing, and he would tell them, and then go back to his room, or to take a short, always very short walk on the grounds, for a few days until they got bored enough to ask the same questions again. It wasn't a great life but, as Johnnie Ray said often, it was his.

Sometimes, looking through the fence he would see shoes lying beside the road. Always odd ones, never pairs, and always replaced before they were very old. Sometimes, yes, even cigarettes. New offerings.

Too late.

That's what Johnnie Ray liked to think. The answer gave him comfort, even though he knew it was wrong. Or rather, incomplete. Sooner or later the answer would change. It always did. Though Johnnie Ray thought maybe next time he would go up on the Tree instead. He wasn't sure such would work, in the divine pattern of things, but he made a promise to himself to ask.

After so many turnings of the Wheel, it was the least he could do.

Judgment Day

"Few parents nowadays pay any regard to what their children say to them. The old-fashioned respect for the young is fast dying out."

—Oscar Wilde

I love that quote, even though I think it's nonsense. Wilde was an interesting man. He didn't know me, but then recognizing God doesn't seem to have much to do with personality. For proof, take the rather nervous fellow in front of me right now. He doesn't look too bright, as men go. Yet he is the one, the only one this generation, who knows God when he sees Him.

Others say my name several times a day, but that's not the same thing. Others follow older or newer rituals, and that's not the same thing, either. This one just knows. Frankly, I don't understand how that works. Sure, I understand a great deal and said so in the appropriate places but then it got exaggerated, as it always does. I don't know everything. Wish I did.

I'm still waiting. Odd. We're on top of a cold bleak mountain, somewhere in the middle of the world. He knew I'd be here, and so I was. He gets to ask me one question. He came all this way, icicles hanging off his beard, and he's still thinking about it.

As I said, not too bright. Not for me to question that part, really. I only get one or two true worshipers, as a rule, per generation. There was that one time, near the turn of the 20th Century, when there were five. Hasn't happened before or since. I wait patiently, because that's what I do, but a mind as vast and restless as mine can't help but wander.

"*In the Beginning God created the Heavens and the Earth. The Earth was without form and void, and darkness moved upon the face of the waters. . ..*"

Not bad. Oh, a little ponderous, perhaps, but not without style even after so many translations. I race back along the Temporal River, take a look at myself then, at the beginning of it all. I was young in those days, and the whole project was just getting started. My very own cosmos. I was a little full of myself, to state a self evident fact. Ask Job. Or those two confused kids, Adam and Eve. "Because I'm the Father"? I may have said it differently, but that's what it meant. Was that really the best I could do? Oh, well. My fault entirely, what happened, but I wouldn't admit that at the time. Or now, unless someone asks. And they won't. They never have.

It's been a long time, and time is the problem. It's running out for this place; I can feel it. I don't know how much longer I've got to make it work, but at least I had the sense to get the stories in place as quickly as I could. Wasn't there something George Bernard Shaw said about how religion needs storytellers? That was one of the few things I got right from the Beginning. Pity Shaw didn't know me. He would have asked a good question; I know it. Perhaps another one I couldn't answer.

"You're God, aren't you?"

I don't reply. The silly thing only gets one question and I'm not going to let the fact that he's an idiot ruin it for both of us. I wait. The glowing orb of light that is me is blinding. I tone it down a bit.

He shields his eyes, despite the heavy goggles. Beyond him I can see the mountain guides making camp. They won't see what he sees, or hear. They think he's talking to himself, nuts. Maybe he is. I look in on Adam and Eve again, even though it's water down the Temporal River. I can see it, but I can't change it. There are limits.

Eve has a puppy. I didn't remember the puppy. It's licking her face and she's rolling on the grass, laughing. Such joy. How could I forget that?

"Umm. . .the thing I really want to know. . ."

Back to the here and now, as if there were anything at all real except for the moment that rests on the fulcrum between past and future. The future shrinks and the past grows until there's no more future and the balance fails. Judgment Day. Then what? Wish I knew. Let someone ask me that one.

"Why is there suffering?" he asked, and then stood very proud and still.

I don't smile at him. He doesn't expect it. I want to kick his ass but he wouldn't expect that, either. Not proper behavior for a deity. A lightning bolt would be more proper, but the sad truth is you don't spank a child for being a child, no matter what some people think. And we both have so little time.

BECAUSE CREATION MUST BE IN BALANCE. UP AND DOWN, TRUE AND FALSE, SUFFERING AND JOY. WITHOUT ONE, THERE CANNOT BE THE OTHER.

"Well, couldn't we. . . you know, vote on which we'd like?"

Silence from then on, and the golden ball of light winked out. He should consider himself lucky he got his answer and nothing else. It's not the right answer, but it was one he could understand and, perhaps, profit by. He won't, more than likely. It's a stupid question. More so because I don't really know the answer. I will one day, perhaps; I have reason to hope. He wants to understand the purpose and meaning of suffering? Try having children like him.

Like all of them.

•

I've been a bad parent. Sooner or later the Shining Ones will come to tell me. I remember when they came to me that first time, but not much before that. Where I was, who I was, all gone. I can't ride the Temporal River back that far, though I've tried. All I've got is memory, clear and strong even now, but not real. Maybe I don't remember it the way it happened. The advantage of the time stream is that you always know what happened. You don't always know why, but that's a different question.

They pointed to this Earth. *This is Yours to shepherd,* they said, *until the end of time. There are many souls adrift in the void, crying out. Bring them here, clothe your children in flesh, and care for them until that time.*

What then, I asked?

Judgment Day.

The words frighten me, because I know what the Shining Ones will do if I've failed. Not to me. My children. The seeds I grew and have tended.

I make mistakes. God should not make mistakes, but I do no matter how hard I try. I'm not perfect, though the children say I am. They don't know. I do. Just look around. Wars over what food to eat, whose father killed whose uncle a thousand years before? Lives like mayflies, and they can remember a thousand years' old wrong as if it happened to them. Vicious little bastards.

Only they aren't, and I know it. Their lineage is plain enough. I can rebuke them and have. I can try, often futilely, to guide them. The one thing I can never do is deny them, or stop loving them. Sometimes I think gods as a group are the most limited beings in the universe. That Free Will thing, for instance. I don't have it. I do what my nature requires me to do.

I still get it wrong.

It isn't fair. Is that what I should have told that silly twit? Life isn't Fair? It's true but it's not enough, and it wouldn't have helped him. Or me, come to that.

There's a war. A big one this time. It turns on the fulcrum and there's nothing I can do. Free Will binds me as it frees them. Time to sail upstream. I can't be here now. I used to stay, but I can't do that anymore. It hurts too much.

•

I'm walking with Adam in the garden. He looks so somber in the presence of his God. It's not just respect. It's also that sense of duty that kept him in line before a line even existed. He should have taken a cue from Eve sooner. That girl had her priorities right, whatever faults she had. We're being serious in the garden and she's off swimming, or playing chase with the lions for the joy of it, or lying naked under the sun. Adam's walking and having conversation with *me*.

Dear boy that he was, he could be such a yutz.

"Lord, why is there suffering?"

It's the oldest question, after all. Even before they knew suffering. Adam at least had the distinction of being first. So I told him the truth as I understood it then. He always asks, and I always tell it the same way. The answer has changed time and again, but not this one. Nothing can change here, where it all started to go wrong.

I don't know why I come here now, except that it feels good to walk in the garden in the pleasant cool of evening, good to see them both again and say the words and make the same mistakes, all the ones I made for love of them, my first born of the souls who called to me out of the darkness. I can't stay. Soon it's time to go. Then it's past time.

When I return to the Here and Now it's a different Here and Now. I tarried too long. The river raced ahead of me for a bit, and I have no choice but to catch it.

The world still turns, blue and green and white, and that's a relief. How long? I seek the answer and find it quickly enough: three hundred years and change. There were people born knowing me who never saw me. That's not fair either, but it can't be helped now. I have to act on the fulcrum of past and present just as they do, for only there is new action allowed. I can't make it up to them. I can't fix it. Once a tree falls its always fallen, forever and ever. I can't put it back any more than they can.

There's one still alive who knows me. A very old woman, very soon to die. She knows, as she must, and she comes to find me. I go to where I must be found, for that is the Law, and I wait for her.

She seeks me in a synagogue, and I am there when she hobbles in on her cane, alone and lonely. No burning bush or orb of light this time. Haven't the stomach for it now. I sit, just one more old man on a bench. I feel ashamed. Someone get your mind around that one and then tell me how you'd fix the world. Go ahead; I'll wait.

The old woman sits down next to me. "So," she says. "Where have you been?"

It's not an accusation, though perhaps it should be. It is simply her question, so I answer it. She digests this in silence. I could leave now. I usually do. Not this time.

"It must be difficult," she said. "For you."

It's not a question, and what I offer her is not an answer, yet it's all I have left to give.

I'M SO SORRY.

She reaches up, touches my cheek. I didn't know if that was allowed or possible; funny that I never tried to find out.

"It's all right," she says. She doesn't say anything else. Soon I know why; she's died there on the bench beside me. She just put her head down on her chest and left the world behind. Well, she was tired. She waited a long time, in human terms. I hope it was worth it.

•

Another century. Those who taught in my name still do. Those who recite the words still recite the words, and talk to something that is their idea of me. I listen anyway, but they have no questions, just demands. I cannot answer those. I still do what I can. That's all I've ever done. You can teach your children; you can't do their living for them.

Judgment Day is coming. Soon now. Very soon.

I can't stop it, and I'm afraid. I know what it means. They do not. The right hand and the left will be gathered, but John got the rest of it wrong. There will be no separating them; if one fails they all fail. That was the deal, the way the Shining

Ones explained all those years ago. "We cannot leave one. We will take all, or all will remain."

The world will be destroyed utterly, but that's not the worst part— I'll have to be the one to do it. The Flood was nothing compared to this. No Noah this time, and no hope for a second chance. None will be spared. I will scatter their souls into the void where I found them.

All my children, by my own hand.

I don't know what happens then. Maybe I'll start over, but I don't think so. I think it will destroy me, too. I'm not sure I'll care if it does. I have the past, and the Here and Now, but the future is as closed to me as to anyone. I wonder, now and again, but the Temporal River does not flow so far. At least not when it's carrying me.

Another hundred years. The world still exists. No nuclear exchanges. I'm surprised, but not relieved. There's so much that could still happen. Much of it does: war, famine, fear. Small stuff mostly. Are they getting wiser, finally? I can't be sure. I wish I had more time, but I know there is no more time. I've slammed up against the future, stepped on the fulcrum moment, and this time the balance does not turn. I'm hanging there when the summons comes.

It's the last, I think. Someone's coming with a question. I meet him in a city slum. His home, if a street can be a home. We're there alone. There's no one in the city, no gravcars moving on the streets, no streaks of atmospheric craft above, no points of light in the cold dark except the stars and planets. A yellowed piece of paper travels down the street, blown on the wind, but no people. I know that's wrong, and I know why it is this way.

We're all out of time.

His eyes are clouded. "Why am I alone?" he asks, in the shadow of a burned out building.

BECAUSE IT'S JUDGMENT DAY.

It's done. It's said. No taking it back now, no changing a moment that has passed. He's vanished, like the others. Now I am the one who is alone. Time to sit down in the big white chair and do what I have to do.

Not yet.

I know it's wrong, but I don't care. I sail back to the garden one last time. Eden is there, as I remember. The children are not. I visit all my favorite places but they are empty. I don't understand how this can be. I sail back down the time stream with the current until it reaches the future, and there it stops.

The angels are there. I haven't had much for them to do lately, but they don't mind. Aspects of my Will, they await that will with a patience even I admire. They stand behind my Seat as they must, majestic wings folded. I ascend the throne, as I must, and I sit.

Oh. So that's where you all got off to.

The children are here waiting for me. Every one of them. Row on row of vast multitudes, spread so far even I have trouble seeing all of them. All standing perfectly still, looking at me. I want to tell them how sorry I am, that I did my best, that I did love them all, but now the words won't come. It's too late.

I recognize every one of them. There's the silly man who asked about suffering. There's the wise woman who asked about me. There's the homeless man in the slum, who looks different to me now though I can't say how. It takes a moment; sometimes I'm a little slow.

Ah, now I see it: he's glowing. The woman is glowing too, as is the yutz. He doesn't look much like a yutz now, but I guess he never really did. He's beautiful. They all are. Those three separate from the rest and stand before me like three small people-shaped stars.

I KNOW YOU, I say.

They smile at me. YES. BUT DO YOU KNOW THE QUESTION?

I damn well should. Maybe it's right, maybe it's wrong. Maybe it's as stupid as I think it is, but I don't care. I ask, because it's the one thing I really do want to know.

WHY WAS THERE SUFFERING?

It's the old woman who answers, in her human voice. "How else could you learn?"

Of course. All this time I thought Judgment Day was about the children. Silly me.

Now the children are all removing their tattered clothing of flesh and putting on shining raiment, every one. . . no, not the clothes. It's the children who shine. I didn't understand. It's them. It's always been them. The Shining Ones.

ALL THIS BOTHER. . . FOR ME?

No answer. One question only; that's the Law. It's all right. The time for questions is past. They are not children, and now neither am I. They said they could not leave anyone behind. Now I understand what that meant. Now it's time to change, time to grow. Time to go. I take their hands in mine, all my brothers and sisters.

I shine.

Borrowed Lives

Joshua Cullen held up a black and white photograph of a very young woman in a very old-fashioned taffeta dress. "I wonder who she was?"

His daughter Mattie barely glanced at the picture, one of hundreds in a box on a table at the Canemill Flea Market. Mattie had taken one look at the revamped freight barn that housed the market and commented that surely they had a good supply of fleas. Joshua smiled more at Mattie for telling the old joke than any humor in it. It was good to see Mattie smile. She did it so seldom in the past few years, with her problems with Trish. She wasn't smiling now.

"Someone no one cares about now," Mattie said, shrugging at the picture. "What's that she's standing beside? A Packard?"

Joshua leaned on his cane, held up the photograph to a better light. "Studebaker . . . And how can you say that? It was her prom night, from the look of it. I bet her date took the picture. You know," he added, "Jake was conceived on your mother's prom night."

"I know, Dad. I think that was the first thing Mom was mad at you for. As for the rest," Mattie indicated the bustling market with a wave of her arm. The ceiling was a vault of tin braced with steel; it turned even the slightest whisper into an echo, and no one in the building was whispering. The concrete floor was covered by long rows of tables holding at least one of everything a regular person had ever used in a lifetime, and people sat behind those tables on folding chairs or benches, chatting with neighbors or potential customers, eating lunch, watching football, drowsing. It was nearly June and a few of the merchants had turned on old oscillating fans to keep the air moving in the barn, and the broad doors were open to catch the breeze. A slight wind disturbed Joshua's thin grey hair.

"Look around, Dad," Mattie said. "The only things that turn up here are things no one wants anymore. It's as true for this picture as a rusty colander or a Pee Wee Herman doll."

Joshua shrugged and turned to the merchant, a younger woman in a flowing skirt with bright, gypsy colors. She smiled at him.

"How much?" he asked.

"Quarter apiece. Three for fifty cents." She leaned closer, glanced at the picture he held, and smiled approval. "That's a nice one."

"I'll take it," he said, and the woman nodded as if the sale had been inevitable. He paid her and carefully placed the photograph in his shirt pocket as he walked away. After a moment Mattie followed him.

"You're missing the point," he said when Mattie caught up with him. "If no one wanted them, then they would not be here, for sale. Most things here do sell, eventually. Sometimes it takes years, they tell me. But it happens. This photograph was waiting for me."

Mattie shook her head. "She's no one you or I know. She's probably been dead for years, and everyone else that knew her is either dead or has forgotten, otherwise she wouldn't be in the 'quarter apiece' box."

Joshua took out the photograph and paused to look at it, leaning on his cane as the browsers parted and walked around them like a stream flowing around a rock. "She had a nice smile," he said. He put the picture back in his pocket and moved on. Mattie followed.

"You've thought about what we talked about with Jake and Connie, haven't you? Is that why you're acting so weird?"

"You think I'm just trying to annoy you?"

Mattie reddened just a bit. "The thought occurred, Dad."

Joshua smiled. "No. It's just my nature. For what it's worth, your mother didn't find it endearing either."

That was an understatement. Dolores stayed with Joshua until their children were grown and gone, then filed for divorce the day Mattie moved in with Trish. She died seven years later, twice remarried and kicking the tires on potential husband number four when a drunk driver intervened.

"I have thought about it, Mattie. And I appreciate you and the other kids bringing the idea to me personally. The answer is 'no.'"

"Dad, you're not exactly young. You know this is for the best."

"Yes, but whose? If I go into the rest home, that's one less thing for Jake and Connie to worry about. And don't tell me it hasn't crossed your mind, girl."

Mattie shrugged and matched her father truth for truth. "Of course it has. None of us can take you in, Dad, even if you would leave that old house. We don't have the room. And yes, we worry... I worry. What if you were to fall?"

"I'd probably die and solve the whole problem," Joshua said, pausing to look at some dusty books.

"You're a pig headed So-and-so, Dad. No wonder Mom divorced you."

•

Mattie had called it a big old house and that's what it was now. When he and Dolores had first bought it, the house hadn't been so big, not with Jake and Constance a constant handfull and house full and Dolores six months along with Mattie. Now it seemed very empty, despite the accumulations of thirty plus years. Joshua dropped the old photograph on the TV stand went to the fridge for a beer. He took one sip and made a face.

Ain't been the same since they stopped brewing Magnolia Brand.

Joshua sat down, sipping the beer slowly, adjusting, as he always had, to the things he could not change. He picked up the photograph from the flea market. The woman had been young when the picture was taken, about the same age as Dolores when they'd married. Joshua looked at the family pictures on the TV stand, a collection of several photographs matted into a single frame: there was himself and Dolores in a photo taken on their prom night, in front his father's brand-new Edsel. Then there was one of Dolores in the picture taken on their honeymoon at the Gulf of Mexico, and then there was Jake and Constance, aged twelve and eleven, playing croquet on the front lawn of that very house. Here was six year old Mattie, by herself as usual, dressed in Easter finery and glaring into the camera with all the holiday spirit she could manage.

It wasn't such a bad life.

Not bad at all, parts of it. There had even been some good times with Dolores, and he couldn't really call their marriage a mistake, since Mattie had come out of it. As for Jake and Connie...well, they were healthy. All parents want healthy, happy children, and Joshua had no reason to complain about those two in that respect. In most other areas they could stand improvement, but it was out of his hands now.

Joshua looked back at the old orphan photograph again. What was it that kept drawing him back? The woman was pretty but without the exotic beauty of Dolores. Her gaze was open and honest; her smile was friendly but no more than that. Whatever history she had carried with her was lost when she went into the box at the Canemill Flea Market. All who had known or cared about her were gone, just as, Joshua knew, the same would be true of him one day and probably sooner than was comfortable to think about.

You deserved better, whoever you are. I know that much.

The thought was barely that, barely even a notion, at first. Not so precise or coherent as that. Joshua glanced at his own collection of family pictures in their fine frame, and compared it with the old picture he held, with its crease on the left corner and wrinkled edges. He looked back at the framed photographs. You definitely deserved better. But then, so did all of us.

The notion had become an image, a mental picture of his family portraits, only there was one very noticeable difference. Joshua felt at once wicked, guilty, and elated as the impulse turned into a very solid idea. He could just imagine the look on Dolores' face, if she'd been there to see. Joshua grinned. What the hell.

He very carefully bent back the staples holding the cardboard backing to the matte and slowly teased it free. He took out Dolores' picture and dropped it into the drawer on the TV stand. He took the stranger's portrait and slipped it into Dolores' place. In a moment he had the frame standing properly again, with the woman in his ex wife's place as if she had always been there. You wanted out of my life for a long time, Dolores. Now you have your wish, he thought, firmly closing the TV stand drawer. He glanced at the woman in Dolores' place, the wrinkles in the old print ironed out by the glass almost as if they had never existed at all. "I wonder..."

•

"Who are you?"

"What a stupid thing to say, Josh. Where are the children?"

The woman lay in a hospital bed, eyeing him drowsily. She was right. It was a stupid thing to say. He knew her. Time and the chemo had taken their toll, but she hadn't really changed. Her name was Ruth. Middle name Marian. Maiden name Pugh. Born in Chatah, Mississippi, some sixty three years before. His wife for the last thirty five of those years. Ruth. He knew her better than he knew himself. Which was making it really difficult to say good bye.

"Jake and Connie are coming," he said. "Mattie's here." Joshua knew that what he said was true, though he wasn't sure how he knew. He looked at his dying wife. "It wasn't supposed to be like this," he said.

"How was it supposed to be, Josh? Did you know the day you met me?"

Which was....

Two memories came at his call then. A July 4th picnic on the Pearl River. Fireworks. And Ruth with a group of friends who knew some of his friends and introduced them. Fireworks again, at their senior prom and for many years after. He remembered it all. The long slow drive to the gym, the dancing among the red and white balloons and crepe paper, the anticipation for what they both knew would be the finest night of their lives. The long slow drive back and that wonderful stop along the way. The other memory was that faded photograph in its new place in his life, the place that once belonged to Dolores.

He remembered it all.

Ruth was dying, and it was worse than anything he had felt when Dolores had been killed. It wasn't that they'd been divorced; it wasn't about losing a possession or anything to do with pride or jealously. The trouble was that he and Dolores had divorced their souls long before they parted flesh, and when she died it was a sad thing but no more so than hearing about the loss of any other person who had crossed the path of his life at some point, somewhere, only to move on again when their paths diverged. It was different with Ruth. They had never diverged. Best friends and lovers they had remained from the day they met until now, and whether their true time had been just this instant or all the years he now remembered, it didn't make any difference. It hurt like all the pain in the world.

"Not..."

"Josh?"

"Like..."

"What are you "

●

"This!"

Joshua was back in his old chair in his old house. The frame was open again. He felt Ruth's picture in his hand, though he had no memory of reaching for it. He wanted to destroy it, tear it apart, burn it to ashes, anything. He couldn't. He settled for putting it down.

The memories were receding; Ruth seemed like a story he'd been told once, and he couldn't quite remember when. The life the story told was not his. The joy of it was not his. Neither was the pain.

The price of losing the pain is losing everything else.

A simple transaction and nothing, in any life Joshua had ever known, was free. He looked at the frame. There was his own picture, then a gaping whole where Dolores and then Ruth had been. Below that the windows cut into the matte, holding his three children, were slowing closing. After a few more moments there was nothing but a blank surface, no places in the matte for Jake and Connie and Mattie. Nothing.

Without a mother, there are no children.

He thought of calling Mattie but, oddly enough, he didn't remember her number. He thought of putting Dolores back into her original place in the frame, putting everything and everyone back where they had been, but he couldn't do that either. In the end he'd called a cab. Twenty minutes later he stood in the middle of the flea market, before the woman at the table.

"I'd like to return this," he said. He held up Ruth's picture.

Her smile didn't change. "I don't really think you do," she said, "but of course I'll take it back if you insist." She reached into her coin box and brought out a quarter. There was a nick on one edge; Joshua knew beyond question that it was the same quarter he'd used to buy Ruth in the first place. He hesitated.

"Where do these pictures comes from?" he asked.

She looked at him almost pityingly. "From cameras. From time passing. From lives that go one way and not another. From mistakes and misunderstandings and missed opportunities. From closets and estate sales too. They're just pictures."

"No," he said. "They are not."

"If that's so, why bother to bring back a photograph of someone you don't know to retrieve a quarter you don't need? The trip here cost you more than that."

"Why would anybody buy a picture of someone they didn't know in the first place?" he asked, as if Mattie hadn't asked the same thing the day before. Which, perhaps, she had not, in this particular version of the world.

The woman shrugged. "All you gave me was this." She held up the quarter. "And that's all I can give to you. Do you want it or not?"

Joshua thought about it. "No. I think I really wanted an answer."

She smiled. "Sorry. All I have are photographs. Answers you have to find on your own."

•

"Josh..?"

"I'm here, Ruth."

She smiled, and yawned again. "You didn't answer for so long, I thought you'd left."

"Sorry, I haven't slept much this last week," Joshua said, knowing it true though he didn't really remember much of the time. "Don't worry; Jake and Connie will be here soon. Mattie's asleep in the waiting room; she was here all night."

The words came easily, the certainty of understanding that backed them up was clear. Still, part of Joshua was still back in that other place, with the picture of a woman he remembered and yet did not, would not, shut away in a drawer.

"I haven't done much else, tell the truth," she said. "We always seem to be in a place the other is not, lately."

Joshua looked into that dear face, so new and so familiar. He took her hand. "I'm here now. Nowhere else."

She squeezed his hand. "Sorry it's taking so long. I remember reading about a king saying that, long ago. Dying by inches and apologizing for being a bother. It seemed rather classy . . . for royalty."

"You've got nothing to be sorry for."

"Oh, yes, I do. We all do. We're all scarred, busted knees and chipped teeth and blackened eyes to a man, woman, and child. Broken hearts, too. Regrets. I've got a few, here and there. How about you, Josh? Do you regret marrying me? Knowing how the story ends?"

Joshua looked into the woman's eyes, into Ruth's eyes, his lover and best friend and best enemy all in one, all the things that he and Dolores had never been for each other, and he understood.

She knows!

The words couldn't be said here. The fabric of this world couldn't bear it. Joshua knew that, for all that he remembered his first night with Ruth and then being married to Ruth and the birth of their children, and the accident that left him limping still and all the debris of thirty five years, he also knew that it had only lasted a moment. Dolores was still in the drawer, and that first, flawed life was still around, somewhere in a pocket of the universe that time and causality had overlooked. He knew that, even as he sat by a bed in hospital watching his one and only love die. Ruth knew it, too.

"I love you," he said. "I regret nothing."

Ruth nodded, yawning. "It was good that you married me, Josh. And the box you'll put me in is a darn sight better than the one I left."

"You're not making sense, Ruth," he lied. "The pills are taking effect."

"No they're not," she said, and that was all.

•

A week after the funeral, Mattie parked her Blazer by the curb in front of her father's house. She found him rocking quietly on the porch.

"You're late," he said.

"Trish is still getting over the flu, Dad. I don't want to leave her alone for long."

"Then we'd best get moving. It won't take a minute."

Mattie pushed the passenger door open, and Joshua crawled inside, pausing to get his weak leg straightened comfortably. He held the cane with both hands, waiting.

"Dad, Connie and Jake and I have been talking..."

"Good. Communication is important in a family, they tell me."

Mattie glanced toward heaven, then sighed. "Shut up and listen, will you? We don't want you living alone in that old house."

"So come live with me. All of you. It'll be fun. Bring Trish if you want. I like her. How is it with you two, anyway?"

Mattie reddened. "It's great, Dad, and she likes you too, but that ain't the point. I'd keep expecting to see Mom around every corner. Maybe it would get better with time...."

"Oh, I hope not," he said, but she ignored him.

"...but that ain't the point either. I want my own life. So do Jake and Connie and, as much as we owe you, we're still entitled."

"You are. And heaven knows I've already had mine and then some. So. Is it the Home for your old Dad?"

She ignored that too. "What we've decided, you miserable old coot, is that we're going to hire an LPN to check on you three times a week. You'll also be set up with one of those pager do flicketys. Anything happens, we'll be notified. This way you can stay on your own for as long as that's physically possible. And we'll visit often and unexpectedly to make sure you're co-operating. Count on it."

"And if I don't agree?"

She looked grim. "Then I'll haul your ass to the nursing home myself, you pig headed So-and-so. What's your answer?"

"I love you. All of you. And I think it's a fine idea."

Mattie let out a deep breath, almost as if she'd been holding it all this time. "Thanks. We love you too."

They drove across the unused railroad siding and parked near the entrance to the barn. Mattie waited patiently while her father extracted himself from the Blazer by himself; then she took his free arm as they walked into the Canemill Flea Market.

159

"What junk you got your eye on today?" she asked.

"Not getting anything today. Giving." Joshua paused by that one table, by the box of old photographs. The woman behind the table smiled at him. She seemed to be waiting. Joshua winked at his daughter, then pulled a photograph out of his pocket and dropped it into the box. Mattie glanced at it, frowning, then followed her father away from the table. He walked down the long aisle whistling.

"I don't recognize the woman in the picture," Mattie said.

"No reason you should. I found it while cleaning out some of Ruth's things. I think it got mixed into our stuff by mistake. I'm correcting that mistake."

"Why not just throw it out?"

"Because the picture doesn't belong to me. And it just might be exactly who someone else needs one day. We all deserve that kind of chance. I think your mother would have agreed with that."

"You're a weird old guy," Mattie said.

He nodded. "It runs in the family. Eventually."

Golden Bell, Seven, and the Marquis of Zeng

In the province of Zeng, in the time before the First Emperor QinShiHuang, there lived a bright young lad of a large family. By the time the boy was born his parents had run out of both patience and imagination, so the child was simply called "Seven." He was actually the tenth child, but that didn't seem to matter.

In those days Zeng was ruled by the Marquis Yi, but Zeng itself was under the protection of the more powerful state of Chu and at peace for the first time in many years. As a further blessing, the Marquis' love of music and wine and concubines kept him in his palace most of the time and not out and about causing mischief for his subjects. It was a good time.

Still, if people can sometimes be content, time and the fates never are. In the forty-fifth year of the Marquis Yi's time under Heaven, Seven came into the city of Leigudun on an errand for his father and there, to his everlasting delight and sorrow, he fell in love.

Seven had just counted out three bronze coins to the potter's wife for the new jar his father needed when there arose a commotion on the main street. Gongs, bells, and whistles collided in a divine racket; reed flutes and stone chimes added a softer counterpoint. Seven carried his jar from the side street where the potter had his shop to the main avenue of the city.

People lined the way like a living hedge, eyes turned toward the south entrance to the city gates. The street itself was clear, and two of Yi's mounted guards walked their horses up and down the cobbled road to make sure it remained that way. It was hard to see with all the people in his way, but Seven finally found a spot closer to the street. He turned and saw the vanguard of a procession, and now the shouts and cheers of the people added to the din.

The Marquis' personal bodyguard led the way walking four abreast, resplendent in their bronze and leather brigandines and red sashes, carrying shining spears. Next came two court officials wearing silk and high headpieces. Each carried a jade tablet with the letters of greeting and wishes for happiness to the Marquis from the King. Next came servants, and more guards, and dancers, and more guards, and musicians, and more guards, and then a wagon containing the most beautiful girl Seven had ever seen or even imagined.

"By the Circle of Heaven..." was all Seven could say, for several long moments.

She sat on a red cushion placed in a gilt chair. Her hair was long and fell down her back like a flow of black jade, shining with an inner light that had nothing to do with the glaring sun. She was dressed in a robe of red silk with Bat and Dragon motifs appliqued in yellow and black, and she wore red silk slippers on her dainty feet. She looked at the people thronged around her with a mixture of bewilderment and fear; she did not look happy, and it hurt Seven with a pain of fire that such a girl could be so sad when there might be something, anything, he could do for her.

Seven tugged on the sleeve of a well dressed man of the shih class standing near to him. "Your pardon, High One, but is this girl a princess? I'm sure she must be."

The man managed to look down his nose at Seven, a remarkable skill considering that he was a good three finger-width's shorter than Seven himself. "You're a foolish, ignorant boy to even ask such a question," he said.

"Certainly what you say is true, for I have asked," Seven said agreeably.

The man sighed. "Of course she is not a princess! She is a gift from Marqui Yi's overlord; do you think the great Hui, King of Chu, would give a princess away for a mere concubine? There are royal marriages and alliances going wanting! No. Her family were artisans at best or perhaps even of the peasant *nung*; she is barely adequate as a gift even under the circumstances." The man shook his head in disgust.

Seven merely shrugged. "She is very beautiful," he said.

"In a rough sort of way," the man conceded. "And the Marquis must surely accept her with appearance of gladness or admit the insult and lose face. He must have offended our overlord in some small regard."

"Insult?" Seven said wistfully, "My fondest hope would be to have someone insult me so agreeably."

"You are a foolish boy, as I said, and can not hope to understand these things. In any other circumstances the Marquis would be compelled to send her back and pretend it no more than a jest on the part of his lord, and diplomacy would flourish for months. But there's no time for such courtly games now."

"No time? You are certainly correct that I do not understand. It would honor me past expression if you would agree to enlighten me."

For a moment the man's haughty demeanor faded. "You have truly not heard?" When Seven assured the man that he had not, the man became somber. "It is sad to relate, but here it is—the Marquis Yi is very ill. His physicians do not expect him to live to see the new year. This is King Hui's parting gift to his royal servant."

"This is most distressing," Seven said, "but a concubine is certainly an odd gift under the circumstances."

"Not at all. She'll at least serve to increase the Marquis' entourage in the underworld. The larger the better, as befits his exalted station."

"The underworld?" Seven suddenly felt very ill himself.

"Of course. She and those who came before her are for the Marquis Yi's perpetual service. Their places in his tomb are already prepared."

•

"It's a great honor," Seven's father said, shaving a lintel post with his chisel. Though they lived in the country, Seven's family were not farmers. They grew flowers and vegetables for their own use, but Seven's father was a skilled carver and woodworker, a very worthy position. More worthy, perhaps, than Seven had realized. "I've been summoned to help finish the funerary buildings."

"Upon the Marquis' death, she's to be strangled!" Seven said.

Seven's father looked up. "Along with the rest of his concubines and servants, that they continue to serve their master in the Court of Heaven. That, too, is a great honor."

Seven shook his head. "I don't think she sees it that way."

If Seven's father's patience was exhausted, at least it allowed him to speak frankly above all. "You speak of things you do not understand. Seek wisdom or be silent. Better yet, do both."

Seven bowed and took his leave. His older brothers were his father's main helpers; Seven had neither his father's talent nor any interest in woodworking. He did have some skill at singing and metalworking, but there was no one to teach him the finer points of either. In truth, much of Seven's time lately had been occupied in consideration of what course his life should take, or had been until he saw King Chu's gift. Now all his time was spent in consideration of how he might spare the King of Chu's gift the great honor she was to receive.

He sought the answer at shrines and temples. It was not there. He sought it in the teachings of the ancients, available in some small measure in the city, and it was not there. Seven spent as much time as he could in the city, near to the palace and the treasure of beauty he knew to be within, waiting in vain for a glimpse of his love, listening to the daily rumors of the Marquis Yi's health. They were not good. The one thing Seven did manage to learn was the name of the King of Chu's "poor" gift: Jia Jin.

As the day of Marquis Yi's departure from the earth drew ever closer, Seven was overtaken with despair. He wandered the streets of Leigudun until he could wander no more, and finally sat down to rest on the side of a broad road on the outskirts of the city.

"Forgive me, Jia Jin, but what I want is not possible..."

WHAT IS IT YOU WANT?

Seven looked around him. "Who said that?"

I DID.

Seven looked around again, and again he saw no one. He finally noticed something a bit strange about the road he was on except for himself, it was deserted, and it was lined with immense creatures of stone. They were placed in pairs at wide intervals along the road, each creature staring at its counterpart across the broad flat avenue. There were dragons and serpents and strange animals that Seven could not identify at all.

This is a spirit road!

PRECISELY SO.

There was still no sound to the voice, but now Seven had a hint of its direction. He looked up into the face of a stone creature of immense size. Its body was like an elephant's, its head like a crocodile, though the jaws were shorter, the teeth larger. It had not moved, it could not speak, its visage was turned toward an identical creature across the way. And yet Seven was as sure that the creature had spoken to him as he was of his own, albeit unusual, name.

"Did you speak to me?" he asked, looking up into the cool stone features.

I DID. AND YOU HEARD ME, WHICH IS WORTH REMARKING. MOST PEOPLE DO NOT, EVEN WHEN THE VEILS BETWEEN EARTH AND THE SPIRIT REALM ARE THIN, AS THEY ARE NOW.

"My name is Seven. Who are you, Master?"

I AM NO ONE'S MASTER. I AM ONE OF THE SPIRIT GUARDIANS OF THE TOMB OF MARQUIS YI'S RENOWNED ANCESTOR, YUAN FEN. I WATCH FOR EVIL SPIRITS.

"Are there many such?"

SO FEW THAT EVEN A STONE CAN BE MOVED TO BOREDOM. SO I SPOKE. WILL YOU BE KIND ENOUGH TO ANSWER MY QUESTION? I HAVE SO FEW CHANCES TO CONVERSE.

"I-I wish to marry the girl called Jia Jin. But she belongs to the Marquis Yi, who will soon pass from my domain to yours, taking Jia Jin with him."

AH. THAT IS WHY THE VEILS BETWEEN MY WORLD AND YOURS ARE SO THIN; MARQUIS YI IS ABOUT TO CROSS. THAT IS UNFORTUNATE FOR YOUR LADY.

"Everyone says it's a great honor for her," Seven said. "I suppose I must content myself with that, for her sake."

I SUPPOSE YOU MUST, said the bixie. The silence that followed seemed an empty one, empty in that it wished to be filled. But the creature remained silent.

"I feel there is something else you wish to say," observed Seven. "I would be grateful to hear it."

YOU HAVE BEEN KIND TO ME. I WOULD NOT DO YOU EVIL AND ROB YOU OF YOUR COMFORT.

Seven shrugged. "It was a poor sort of comfort," he said. "Perhaps the truth would be better."

The creature's sigh was like a breeze. LOOK TO YOUR LEFT, DOWN THE SPIRIT ROAD. WHAT DO YOU SEE?

Seven peered down the *shendao* as the creature asked, past the paired bixies. "I see a wall of stone," he said.

BEYOND THAT WALL IS THE TOMB OF YUAN FEN. INSIDE THAT TOMB WAIL

THE SPIRITS OF THE SEVENTEEN UNFORTUNATE LADIES HONORED BY YUAN FEN. THEY HAVE NO PEACE AND, THANKS TO THEM, NEITHER HAS HE. I'VE ALWAYS THOUGHT IT SERVED HIM RIGHT, BUT IN TRUTH THE REASON MY BROTHERS AND I HAVE SO LITTLE TO OCCUPY US IS THAT EVIL SPIRITS WON'T GO NEAR THE PLACE. THEY'RE MORE AFRAID OF YUAN FEN'S CONCUBINES THAN ANY OF MY FOLK, AND IN THE SPIRIT REALM WE ARE QUITE FIERCE.

Seven looked at the creature's great teeth. "I can well imagine..." The bixie's words and meaning took a moment to settle in to Seven's brain, but settle they did. "Oh, poor Jia Jin! But this is so far beyond my skill or understanding." Seven sat back down on the ground, nestled beneath the spirit guardian's massive paws. "What shall I do?"

I AM ONLY A GUARDIAN AND NOT FULLY OF THIS WORLD; THE STONE YOU SEE IS BUT A MARKER OF MY PRESENCE. I CAN NOT HELP YOU. BUT I KNOW OF SOMEONE WHO MIGHT. HER PRICE, I FEAR, IS VERY HIGH.

"I don't care. Please tell me who she is, if there is any sense of kindness about you in my regard!"

VERY WELL. IN THE MOUNTAINS TO THE NORTH THERE IS A LADY NAMED GOLDEN BELL. SHE IS OF THE HEAVENLY COURT, A MISTRESS OF POETRY, AND HAS GREAT WISDOM AND POWER IN YOUR WORLD. IF SHE GRANTS YOU COUNSEL THERE MAY BE A WAY. BUT YOU MUST HURRY. FOR THE BARRIERS TO BE SO LOW BETWEEN OUR WORLDS THE MARQUIS YI'S TIME MUST BE VERY SHORT INDEED.

Seven thanked the spirit guardian profusely and went home to make provision for the trip. His mother wept bitterly and tried to dissuade him; his father merely shrugged. "He will return to his senses or he will die in the mountains; in either case I fear it is out of our hands."

So it was decided. Seven took food and blankets and a stout walking stick and headed for the mountains, visible only as a gray line to the north. He walked until his first pair of shoes fell to scraps and he was forced to put on another. By the time these were almost worn out, Seven passed into the foothills. He kept a wary eye out for bandits, but the years of the Marquis Yi's rule had reduced their number greatly and Seven reached the first plateau unhindered.

He saw his first ghost on the second night. It was a poor thing, little more than a few wisps of mist spiralling slowly among the stones, silent and lost. The next evening Seven saw two others, more substantial. They sought through the mountain passes with blind eyes, and Seven counted himself fortunate that they did not find him. It was as if, where living bandits had been driven out, ghosts had sought a refuge. Seven passed an abandoned bandit village, saw the white, vaporous forms gathered in shadowed corners and empty windows. After that, he was careful to leave a little food and beer some distance from his campfire, to distract them. On the morning of the fourth day, he found something besides ghosts and ruins.

A small stone house nestled into the base of a cliff in a narrow valley, one so insignificant seeming that Seven had almost passed it by, but the sound of a waterfall had drawn him in. He had taken ease of his thirst at the spring near the entrance before he saw the house. Seven thought it strange that such a perfectly fine, ordinary looking little house should be in that place. It was clearly no bandit hovel, but the weeds and vines seemed near to choking it, for all that it appeared to be intact. There was even a wisp of smoke from its chimney.

"Perhaps whoever lives here knows of Golden Bell. I shall ask."

As Seven approached the house, his eyes tricked him, or so it seemed. First he saw a perfectly ordinary little cottage, then it wasn't a cottage at all the windows were dark niches in the rocks of the cliff, the doorway merely a pattern of shadow where the massive roots of an ancient tree were exposed near the cliff face. Each image seemed to blend, one into the other until it was impossible for Seven to guess which he would see after the next blink.

This is very strange, Seven thought, but until I find Golden Bell, I can't ignore any possibility.

"Hello?" Seven said aloud when the house as indeed it did presently resemble a house was about forty paces distant. "I'm searching for Golden Bell."

An old woman sat on a stone bench in small patch of garden just in front of the dwelling, under the shade of a crab apple tree. Seven would have sworn, had there been anyone else about to inquire, that neither woman nor bench nor tree had been there just moments before.

"Who seeks Golden Bell?" the old woman demanded. Her tone was imperious, her manner impatient. She was, Seven decided then and there, the ugliest person he had ever seen. Her face was wrinkled, blackened, and shrunken in, like an apple gone rotten. Her teeth were yellowed and sparse, her eyes were like two black stones.

"I am Seven, son of a humble craftsman of Zeng province. A spirit guardian told me to seek Golden Bell's assistance."

"I am Golden Bell," the old woman said. "And I have no assistance to give."

Seven was stunned into honesty. "Such a beautiful name, I expected..." He managed to stop himself.

The old woman cackled, her eyes shining like dark fire. "Did you think I was born like this? I was more beautiful than my name, Seven, but that was long ago."

"I meant no insult, Lady. Forgive me for slandering the burden of your years."

"Surprisingly well spoken, but my years have little to do with the sorry state you find me in. I have a fever of poetry that consumes me, a malady of song that wears me down, and, sadder still, I have had nothing to eat or drink to sustain me for the past eight hundred years. I am famished."

A woman aged over eight hundred did not seem so impossible to Seven now, after talking with a spirit masked in stone. In truth, looking at Golden Bell, Seven could well accept that she was far older. "I have some food in my pack, Lady. I will gladly share."

She smiled at him. "It is kind of you, but I need a special sort of food that only my servants know how to prepare, and the wretched girls are hiding from me. They forget their duties."

"Then I will find them and remind them."

"You are welcome to try. They are hiding in my garden."

Seven's spirits sank. He feared that his easy acceptance of the unusual had misled him, and that Golden Bell was simply a crazy old woman. He looked about the small patch of ground. It was barely fifteen paces square, with small beds of pink and white peonies joined by paths formed of red paving stones. "Lady, there is no one here besides myself and you."

"Have you looked?" she asked mildly.

There seemed nothing for it but to humor her. Seven sighed, got down on his knees, and started poking about the flower beds and walkways. "I can't seem to " Seven stopped, his eyes growing wide in wonder. "Oh, my."

Nestled among the peonies was a perfectly formed little cottage of twigs, roofed with broad leaves. Golden Bell nodded. "So that's where they'd gotten off to. Pick it up."

Seven carefully picked up the little hut, and underneath it he found a miniature bed, and hearth, and two small snails in delicate spiral shells.

"What have you to say for yourselves?" Golden Bell asked. The snails, being snails, did not answer. She nodded. "Stubborn things. Even now they will hide from me."

Seven felt obliged to point out the obvious. "These are snails, Lady," he said.

"Or such they would choose, rather than take their rightful places in my service. But as long as they remain in their shells I suppose it matters little. You might as well return them."

Seven thought about it. "Suppose they could be coaxed from their shells?"

Golden Bell looked at them. "And how would you persuade them?"

"My father is a craftsman, but my mother is a gardener, and I learned a thing or two from her. Let me try."

Seven reached into his pack and pulled out a small bottle of the rice beer his mother had given him. He removed the cork and held the bottle over the snails. Seven fancied he could hear them protesting in high, piping voices. He poured several drops on each and they merely closed themselves tighter within their shells, hiding behind their iridescent doors. Seven poured more beer until the snails were nearly afloat. He heard a faint sound that might have been cursing or laughter, he wasn't sure. Then one after the other the snails opened their doors and crawled out, and kept crawling until they were clear. In a moment where there had been two garden snails there now stood two young women in brown robes with dark hair falling in braids down their backs. They glared at Seven fiercely and after a moment began to shrink and change, turning back toward their shells as the last of the beer soaked into the earth. Seven stepped in front of them and crushed the two empty shells to powder.

"Fool of an ill born goat! How dare you " wailed the first.

Golden Bell interrupted. "Wretched, wicked girls! To let your Mistress starve for so long! Get to your duties at once!"

As one, the two forgot their quarrel with Seven and bowed deeply to Golden Bell. "It was her fault," each began, pointing at the other. "A lark, a jape, that was all. An outing! I wanted to return, but she—" So intent were they on their explanations that it was a few moments before they noticed the gathering storm on Golden Bell's wrinkled brow. "We go at once, Mistress!" they said in unison, and scrambled off toward the cottage.

Seven watched them go. "They were very close, though transformed. Surely you could have found them before now."

"And scrabble about in the dirt like a peasant, to my humiliation and their laughter? I could no more do what you've done than you could call down the moon. I am grateful. Perhaps, after I've eaten, I will consider your problem."

"It would be my fondest wish," Seven said, bowing.

Presently one of the servant girls returned, looking very uncomfortable. "We've searched high and low, Mistress. There is no food in the house."

Golden Bell nodded, resigned. "I suspected as much. Shrink to the sum of your wretched worth and grow new shells, for all the good in you. Tell your sister."

The girl looked more than ready to obey—indeed, eager—but Seven spoke up. "Perhaps I can find you some food."

"Finding it is easy enough, but will you give it to me? That's the decision before you." Golden Bell said.

Seven frowned. "I don't understand."

"It's simple enough," said the servant girl. "The food our mistress requires is the human heart." The smile she turned on Seven then was not pleasant.

"Ah, then you are a demon after all, Golden Bell. Well, if it is to be that way, then alas for Jia Jin." Seven closed his eyes.

Golden Bell laughed, and the sound was much more melodious and delicate than Seven would have fancied coming from a demon. "Silly boy. You confuse a blood bellows with the heart? You speak of meat, Seven. I speak of sustenance. Men give their hearts away every day and live to see their grandchildren play. The especially wise or the especially foolish give them to me."

"But...how can I give my heart to you when it is already promised to Jia Jin?" Seven asked.

"You do not know Jia Jin. You have not spoken to her, touched her, tasted her wit or known her heart. You are in love with the idea of Jia Jin, and it is your mind that fills you with longing, not your heart. Perhaps that will come later, and your heart will grow again to encompass us both. Even I do not know that for certain. I only know that it is your decision to make."

"If I fail, Jia Jin is lost for certain. Whatever needs to be done, I will do it."

"So be it." Golden Bell reached out and took Seven's heart from him. He got a glimpse of it and she held it like some caged bird; it glowed as if with fire, and was many faceted like a gem. Golden Bell handed the prize to the servants who scurried away into the house.

Seven rubbed his chest, looking thoughtful. "In truth, I feel no different than before."

"Men don't always notice when their heart is given. You will in time, but how it will feel to you then is something I won't presume to tell you."

In a moment the servant girl returned, or perhaps, since Seven could not tell one from the other, it was her sister. "We have searched high and low, Mistress. There is no drink in your house."

"Well, then there's nothing for it. Food without drink sticks in the throat and inflames the belly." Golden Bell turned to the girl, "You and your sister may as well be snails, for all your worth to me."

Seven shook his head. "You know I will not allow that. Tell me what you need to drink."

"A human soul," said the girl, with a look of vengeful satisfaction on her face. "Only this can cool the throat and soothe the belly of our mistress."

"If I lose my soul, then the afterlife is denied me," Seven said, aghast. "I will be as nothing!"

Golden Bell smiled her yellow and black smile. "The soul is a shadow, an echo of the noise of life within. It is no more the sum of all you are than your heart is the sum of all you feel. Life always casts a shadow. Lose one, and there will be another in time."

Seven sighed. "I'd listen to my heart in this matter if I still had one. All I know is that, if I fail, Jia Jin is doomed. Do as you will."

So Golden Bell took Seven's soul from him, pouring it into her cupped hands, then letting it trickle into a crystal goblet the servant girl provided. There it pooled and sparkled like smoky wine.

The other servant emerged from the house carrying a steaming bowl on a small tray. The bowl glittered in the sun, casting sparks of light like a fire. Inside the bowl were red oblong jewels no larger than grains of rice. They filled the bowl. Golden Bell fed herself from the bowl with ebony chopsticks and sipped the cloudy soul wine.

She is not so ugly as I thought at first, Seven thought, *Perhaps I'm getting used to her appearance.*

Golden Bell ate some more, and drank again. The bowl and the goblet were both half empty.

Her form is not so bent and misshapen as I'd thought before, Seven thought now, *Strange that my eyes were so deceived....*

When the food and the wine were gone, Seven came to understand just how completely his eyes had been deceived. That day in the marketplace in Leigudun, Seven would have sworn before any god who cared to witness that Jia Jin was the most beautiful girl on earth. Now he thought that, perhaps, he had been mistaken. Perhaps the most beautiful girl in the world was Golden Bell.

Seven tried to find the old hag in the vision that stood before him now and his imperfect memory was the only place in which he still found her. Golden Bell wore robes of yellow silk, and her long black hair was braided with golden chord. Her eyes were bright as a summer day, her form long and ethereally graceful.

Seven bowed low. "I was told you were of the Heavenly Court but it is only now that I come to believe it. Forgive my lack of vision."

"It's a common failing for which you bear no blame. For my recovery I thank you. Your soul was sweet and your heart brave and good. I will give you fair trade for them."

"You are most beautiful," Seven said plainly.

She smiled again, showing dimples. "You gave me your heart and soul, Seven. How could I be less in your eyes now? Is it still your wish to wed Jia Jin?" There was a hint of mischief in her eyes.

As Seven gazed at Golden Bell a shadow of doubt fell where there had not been before. Seven was ashamed. "I am not worthy of her, yet that is still my wish, Lady."

"Well then, Seven, I must tell you what to do. Sit beside me and listen."

Seven did as Golden Bell directed, and Golden Bell, in a voice sweeter than the singing of birds, told him a marvelous secret.

•

When Seven left Golden Bell's house, he went in the direction she specified, deeper into the valley until the ground turned stony again and grass withdrew. He walked as far as he could until the base of a massive cliff rose above him. There was no break in the stone, nothing to climb that he could see, no openings of any kind that he could touch.

Seven shrugged. "It is here, or it isn't. There is only one way to be certain." He sat down on a rock for a few minutes' rest and then sang a song to the stone wall, a short rhyme that Golden Bell taught him. "It's not a very good rhyme," she had said. "But it must suffice." Seven's voice rose high and clear on the still mountain air:

Golden Bell, Chime of Jade,

This narrow path is one I made.

Seventh Son, heart and soul,

Traded for a bandit's gold.

Seventh Son, soul and heart,

Sings a song that stone will part.

He thought a moment, then added. "Golden Bell requests it."

The stone cracked with a sound like thunder, splitting cleanly in front of Seven to a height of thirty feet, then on either side at about ten feet distant from the first crack. These twin fissures spread up the stone cliff until they turned together like travelers greeting one another and joined with the first split. Now what had been solid stone moved aside, two massive doors on hinges of stone. Inside all was dark, and a faint mist flowed from inside like the breath of some beast on a cold morning.

Seven sniffed the air and corrected himself. Not mist. Smoke. Golden Bell had told him what to expect, and that was enough to tell him he should be terrified, or at least very fearful as he followed her directions, but he felt neither terror nor even simple fear. In fact, Seven felt little of anything.

Giving up heart and soul is a great sacrifice, but I can see there are advantages.

He understood now that he followed his quest still as an act of will, and that, perhaps, Golden Bell was right when she said he was in love with the idea of Jia Jin rather than a flesh and blood woman. Still, if love was gone, the idea remained firmly rooted. Seven pressed forward into the cave. It took him only a moment to locate the source of the smoke.

Two strange creatures flanked the passageway about ten feet inside the cave, and for a moment Seven could do nothing but stare at them. They were about four feet tall, with heads that looked somewhat like the pictures of dragon's heads that Seven had seen from time to time. Their bodies were bird like, their necks long and feathered like a crane's. Their feet had claws like a turtle's, only much larger. The creatures were secured to the wall on either side by golden leashes fixed to massive rings of bronze. Their leashes were just long enough for the creatures to meet each other in the center of the passageway and block admittance. They hissed and strained at their leashes as Seven drew near. Smoke and jets of flames spewed from their nostrils and mouths, their tongues tasting the wind as if searching for him.

Seven tried to keep his voice steady, and mostly succeeded. "Golden Bell commands: Be you submissive."

They were. The hissing stopped. They still strained at their leashes, but now their attitude was that of faithful dogs eager to greet their master. Seven found himself scratching each on the head as it rolled its large eyes and whined gently. He left them there and ventured deeper into the cave. The way was lit with torches as if the bandits for this was their secret hideout had just departed a moment or two before, rather than the twenty or so years since the hills had been scoured clean.

Seven passed bags of gold and silver lining the way and, as Golden Bell had commanded, took only one handful of each and placed it in the pouch on his belt. It was still a considerable amount. He left the gold and silver behind and came to chests of rare jewels and stores of lapis, jade, and amber. These, too, he took for himself in carefully restrained amounts. There were side corridors containing beds, rooms of weapons and armor, and the remains of cooking fires, but Seven ignored these. He kept to the main way until it opened into a large chamber, and there Seven found another marvel.

At the far end of the chamber stood a rack holding robes of silk trimmed with gold thread, and belts and pendants of jade. In the center of the room was a table. At each of the four corners of the table stood a pottery statue of a soldier in full armor, holding a spear of bronze. Just before the table was a statue of a dwarf made of the same clay, painted with a three color glaze of green and yellow and blue. Around the statue was a belt of jade, and two long smooth sticks were hung from that belt on the right side. On the table was a cage of bronze, and in that cage were a multitude of songbirds with glistening feathers of various shades of green, like all the known shadings of green jade. At Seven's approach they began to sing at once and the cave was filled with a sound sweeter than any Seven had heard before.

Seven spoke to the statue of the dwarf first. "Live," he said. "Golden Bell requests it."

The statue changed color like oil floating on a puddle, and then the dwarf was a living man who bowed to Seven and then stood, waiting.

Seven spoke to the four soldiers. "Live. Golden Bell requests it." As one the four statues went through the same changes and stood in their positions, waiting.

Seven walked to the back of the cave, dropped his poor garments and donned silken robes. His belt and cloth pouch he replaced with one of jade and fine leather, transferring the wealth he had taken from the corridor. He now stood before the transformed statues like a prince before his retainers. He instructed the dwarf to carry the songbirds' cage and all to follow him, and they obeyed silently. They followed Seven back to where the two guardian animals waited. Seven unhooked their leashes from the rings, and the two creatures waddled along beside him like two hounds at heel.

As Seven marched out of the cave with his new retainers, the cliffs closed tight behind them. He passed the place where Golden Bell's home had been, but he saw nothing, no house and no sign that there had ever been such at that place. Seven bowed once toward the place where it had stood, as best he remembered, and, dressed as a prince and with retainers finer and a menagerie more wondrous than any in the province of Zeng—or any other, come to that—Seven returned to Leigudun.

•

The Marquis Yi passed his shortening days with music, wine, and women for comfort, and the contemplation of eternity for a mystery. He thought it good to consider the mysteries of Heaven and Earth now that he was soon to know the answers to a few of them. It seemed to him a shame and a waste if he didn't at least know some of the questions. On this particular day, after the music was played and the wine consumed and the women for this was the limit of his interest now openly admired, the Marquis Yi sought to turn his attention to contemplation of the Immortals. Under the circumstances it was easier thought than accomplished.

"What is that noise? Why am I disturbed thus in my shortening hours? Put a stop to it at once!"

The Marquis' minister hurried from his presence and out to a window that opened over the main gate to the palace. After a moment the minister returned, looking bewildered. He whispered to a servant and the man bowed low and sped away.

"Well?" the Marquis demanded. "What is it?"

"I think, Heavenly One, you should see this for yourself," said the minister. "It is quite beyond my power to describe."

The Marquis frowned in annoyance but allowed two of his concubines to help him rise. He walked with slow, brittle steps to the window.

"Minister, this is indeed a marvelous sight."

A man in princely robes led two fantastic animals on leashes of gold, followed by a dwarf carrying a cage full of birds singing sweetly. Behind them were four fierce spearmen in armor that glittered like gold. Following and flanking the entire procession were the people of Leigudun, murmuring in low voices and staring.

"Who is this man? What does he want?"

The minister could only spread his hands in defeat until the servant reappeared and whispered something to the minister. The minister nodded and bowed low to the Marquis. "Son of Heaven, the young man below calls himself 'Seven,' and he wishes an audience with you."

The Marquis considered this. "I should refuse," the Marquis said. "I do not know his lineage, and he may be a sorcerer bent on doing me harm. Still, I see no reason to miss seeing what is plainly a Wonder of the Earth so soon before I must leave it. Bring him to me."

The young man called "Seven" came into the Marquis Yi's presence leading the two strange animals. He was followed by the dwarf carrying the cage of marvelous birds, and the four splendid guards. All bowed low. Even the birds bobbed their heads in unison at the Marquis. As amazing as this was, the Marquis Yi found all his attention drawn to Seven.

He has the calmest demeanor I ever seen.

Even long time retainers at his court always showed a bit of uneasiness in his presence, perhaps understandable since he had undisputed power of life and death over all in Zeng and had been known to exercise that power from time to time. If there was a trace of worry or fear in that young man's smooth features, the Marquis could not detect it.

"Young man," said the Marquis, "I think there is something missing in you."

"My heart and my soul," Seven answered frankly. "These I have traded for these things I bring before you. You have something I desire, Highness, and I seek a trade. Or, if it please you more, call it an exchange of gifts."

There was much murmuring and whispering in the court. The Marquis raised a hand for silence and then smiled grimly. "If you lack heart and soul, you certainly have no shortage of confidence to be so bold before me. I should be offended by your impudence."

"Forgive my coarseness, for such is my nature," Seven said. "I state clearly for all to hear that I mean no insult to your greatness and, indeed, wish to add to it. It may please you to see what I have to offer."

The Marquis was intrigued despite himself. "Show me."

Seven indicated the guards first. "When you pass from this earth, these men will go with you to guard your peace in the next."

"They are very passable," the Marquis agreed, "but I have enough guards of my own."

Seven shrugged. "Then these are not needed." He turned to the soldiers. "Return to what you were."

In an instant there were not four living men standing there but four pottery statues. In another moment they began to crack as if the weight of many centuries had suddenly descended upon them. Another moment and there was nothing left of them but four piles of dust.

The Marquis and all his court stared in open astonishment. Now the Marquis regretted his words, not out of fear of Seven but because the four soldiers had been the most splendid he had ever seen and his pride had led him to speak slightingly of them.

"This is indeed sorcery," the Marquis said, and that was all he said.

"It would be sorcery in your behalf, if it please you," Seven said. "I have one more gift to show you."

The Marquis nodded, not speaking, but his eyes missed nothing. Seven led the two dragon-headed beasts to a position about ten paces in front of the Marquis and had them stand about four feet apart. They kept those positions obediently, their long necks spiraling up like vines, their small leaf shaped tongues lolling like cheerful dogs.

Seven clapped his hands. "For the Perpetual Use of the Marquis Yi!"

At once the animals stood very, very still. Their color slowly changed, darkening until they were almost black. Seven approached them and rapped the rightmost on the neck like a man knocking at a door. The creature echoed with the faint ring of bronze.

The audience chamber was suddenly very quiet. Even the birds in the cage stopped singing. Seven went to the cage and opened the door. The jade colored birds flew out and immediately settled in the rafters. Seven lifted the cage and repeated the command: "For the Perpetual Use of the Marquis Yi!"

The bars of the cage changed in his hands like potter's clay, reshaping as if under his direction into a two tiered rack of bronze, with small hooks set at precise intervals along the upper and lower bars. Seven approached the two bronze animals and set either end of the rack down firmly on their heads so that the whole structure was now a very beautiful stand for a set of musical stone chimes. Only there were no chimes.

Seven looked to the birds in the rafters and repeated his command. The birds flew down in one great flock, and each one found its place on a hook on the rack and perched there. One by one they let themselves slip on their perches until they hung upside down and then began to grow and change. Each bird was now an exquisite curved chimestone of jade.

Seven turned to the dwarf. "Play for our Lord."

The dwarf took his sticks from his belt, bowed low again, and began to play the chimes. The Marquis Yi and everyone else present knew beyond question that it was the most beautiful music they had ever heard, or ever would hear again.

It was several minutes before the Marquis could bring himself to disturb the music with mere words. "Seven, what is it you wish of me?"

It was a simple question. Once the answer had been simple, too. Now Seven realized that, besides Jia Jin, he would spare all the Marqui Yi's concubines the 'honor' of that worthy's perpetual service if he could. But ask the Marquis of Zeng to forego his servants, and come to his ancestors alone and humbled? Seven almost wished he was as big a fool now as he had been, to believe in one more impossible thing, but that time had passed and taken his heart and soul with it.

Seven answered the Marquis and, if he did not speak the whole truth, what he spoke was true as far it went.

"I wish for the life and freedom of the girl called Jia Jin."

The Marquis Yi frowned. "Jia Jin...?" His minister appeared at the Marquis' elbow and whispered a reminder. "Oh, yes. The gift of my Lord of Chu. How can I agree without dishonoring his show of affection?"

"If she is truly a gift, you may do with her as you will," Seven said.

The Marquis considered this. "Jia Jin, please step forward."

There was a rustling and shuffling among the group of the Marquis concubines present, and then one girl robed in brocaded yellow silk emerged from the rear of the group and came forward, looking hesitant and frightened. She was exactly as Seven remembered, except, perhaps, even more lovely. She might still have been the most beautiful woman Seven had ever seen, if he had not met Golden Bell.

The more he remembered of Golden Bell the more that memory was of the beautiful woman she had become, and less of the crone he had first met. Yet both were the same, and it was still hard to separate them in his mind. Seven looked at Jia Jin, and for the first time he was able to see beyond the surface to what she might look like one day, and perhaps would if she ever had the chance to be free of youth. That was still to be decided, but Seven saw a woman now, and not an idea. He thought that would make a difference, but somehow it did not. He smiled at her and she returned the smile, hesitant but without guile.

"Jia Jin," Seven said. "If I were to rob you of the honor of the Marquis Yi's company for eternity, could you forgive me?"

The Marquis looked stern. "Young man, what are you doing?"

"I'm asking a question," he said. "Would you be kind enough to allow her to answer?"

The Marquis said nothing, and Jia Jin took a deep breath, then she fixed her gaze on Seven's face as if it were the one candle in an abyss. "How can I answer," she said, "without insulting either my Lord or you, noble sir?"

Seven smiled. "It's answer enough." He turned to the Marquis. "I await yours."

"Why would you trade such a treasure for this poor thing? She is nothing."

"Then you lose nothing, Lord. And gain very much indeed."

"Suppose my Lord of Chu hears of this and is not pleased?"

"At this point in your life's journey, is it really a concern?" Seven asked.

"True enough. Still, do you see this yue?" The Marquis pointed to a massive axe of bronze born by a guard. "This is the symbol of the power of life and death, entrusted to me by King Hui of Chu. It is within my rights to have you slain," the Marquis said musingly, "and keep all. Then I would have even less concern."

Seven shrugged. "If that is your wish, then of course it will be done. Forgive me for imposing on your notice, my Lord." He turned to Jia Jin. "And forgive me for offering you a choice you lacked the freedom to make." Seven spoke to the dwarf. "Return," he said, "to what you were."

There was another pile of dust. Seven opened his mouth to speak again, but the Marquis stood up so quickly he almost fell down again in his weakness. "Stop, I command you!" There was more desperation than anger in his voice.

Seven bowed. "You may kill me, Lord," he said. "It is your right. But not before I return this heavenly instrument to dust as well. In this one small matter I can not obey you."

The Marquis Yi considered, but not for long. "Take her," he said. "And leave Zeng if you value your life."

"As you command, I will do both," Seven said, and he bowed again. "May it please you to remember that I can speak the words wherever I am, and the effect is the same. I am honored by your gift, Marquis Yi. I know you have the wisdom to be honored by mine."

Seven took Jia Jin's hand and led her from the Marquis's palace. No one followed them. They were not even well away before they heard someone else playing the wondrous music on the jade chimes at the request of the Marquis Yi.

•

Seven bought a rich farm in the province of Chu with the treasure from the cave. The Marquis Yi died soon after and that chapter in Seven and Jia Jin's life was closed. Jia Jin remained with Seven, perhaps out of gratitude at first but love followed soon enough. Golden Bell had spoken truely and Seven's heart and soul, like pruned vines, did grow again and mostly restore themselves with Jia Jin's help. Seven knew fear again but he also knew love. Love for Jia Jin, and for the living woman instead of his perception of her, but the memory of Golden Bell remained too. No man can freely give both heart and soul to another and remain unchanged; Seven was never completely whole again.

Two years after the Marquis' death, Seven made a solo pilgrimage to the valley of the bandits. He did not find Golden Bell's house. He repeated the rhyme at the cave, but he could not bring himself to say that Golden Bell requested it, for he knew it was not true, and the cave did not open. He returned to Chu and Jia Jin and learned to write songs and poetry attempting to heal the parts of his heart and his soul that were still missing. He became quite well known for a time writing under the name Chu Yuen, but that time quickly passed as all time does and, after long and fairly happy lives, both Seven and Jia Jin followed the Marquis Yi from this world to the next.

The Marquis' tomb was soon forgotten and lost for many years, but eventually and quite by accident it was found again and his splendid treasures put in a museum. One especially is worth notice: a bronze rack of stone chimes, supported by two creatures with the heads of dragons, the bodies and necks of birds, and the feet of turtles. The one on the right lost his long, puckish tongue sometime in the past three millennia, but the one on the left still retains his. A visitor who looks closely at the tip will still find the following words written there in flowing white characters:

"For the Perpetual Use of the Marquis Yi of Zeng."

The End

About the Author

I'm a Mississippi native now living in the Mohawk Valley of central NY state. I play guitar and pennywhistle (badly) when I'm not thinking up stories...or discovering them, which is almost the same thing. The Ogre's Wife, my first story collection, was a finalist for the World Fantasy Award. If you want to know more, I hang out at "Den of Ego and Iniquity Annex #3," also known as:

www.richard-parks.com

Printed in Great Britain
by Amazon